# A Dance
## in
# Deep Water

## ALSO BY DOUG ALLYN

# A Dance
# in
# Deep Water

## Doug Allyn

ST. MARTIN'S PRESS
NEW YORK

A THOMAS DUNNE BOOK.
An imprint of St. Martin's Press.

Library of Congress Cataloging-in-Publication Data

Allyn, Douglas.
    A dance in deep water: a Mitch Mitchell mystery / Doug Allyn.
—1st. ed.
            p.      cm.
    "A Thomas Dunne book."
    ISBN 0-312-16807-1
    I. Title.
PS3551.L49D3    1997
813'.54—dc21                                            97-17822
                                                          CIP

First Edition: December 1997
10 9 8 7 6 5 4 3

A few years ago while rummaging through a box in the attic, I found a photograph of my son taken in 1882. It was actually a picture of his great-grandfather as a young man, yet the resemblance was so striking that for a moment I thought it was a trick photo.

Blood will out, they say, though sometimes that's hard to believe when your kids are going through an impossible phase. Or you are.

So, for my son, Doug, who was a perfect child for weeks at a time, and for every parent who's wondered if aliens could have beamed up their dream children and replaced them with contentious little clones . . .

# ONE

## THE CROSS-WOLF

ᏅᏋᏣᎵᎦ

"ARE YOU gay, Mom?" Corey asked.

I glanced at him. He was staring out the window at the passing pine trees, sitting in my Jeep Cherokee's passenger seat, stiff as a soldier, an eleven-year-old marine. His dark hair was slicked down and neatly parted. His blue school-uniform shirt was buttoned to the throat.

"Yes," I said. "I am. How long have you known?"

He turned to look at me. His little face looked pale to me. I know it's unfashionable to tan nowadays, but Corey looked wan. And I wondered how well they fed him at school, or if they made sure he ate.

"That's not true, is it?" he said at last. "You're not gay."

"Nope," I said. "Though if I get stuck on blind dates with any more losers I may consider it. Why did you ask?"

"Chad Holobeck's mother is gay. He met her lover last Easter break. He said it was mega-weird."

"And I'm weird, is that it?"

He shrugged. I couldn't read a thing in the gesture, not triumph or even satisfaction. I wondered if I'd lost a point in whatever game we were playing.

My son is a changeling. A stranger overnight. I was barely eighteen and on my own when he was born. I kept him with me my first few years of college, but when my work made me a nomad among offshore oil platforms, I thought a boarding school was our best option. It wasn't. I hated being apart from him. But I had no choice. Or so I thought.

But recently, when my father died and left me his cafe in northern Michigan, I jumped at the chance to make a new life with my son. And when Corey asked if he could spend his summer vacation touring Europe with a classmate's family I thought it was a godsend. I worked like a madwoman all summer getting the Crow's Nest on a solid footing.

But when I picked Corey up at the Huron Harbor airport last week, everything changed. He was different. Maybe seeing Paris with his wealthy friends did it. Or maybe aliens beamed him up and left a pod person in his place, one who couldn't quite conceal his disdain for my hometown and small business.

And possibly for me. Though to be fair, if he feels contempt for me, he's too well-mannered to show it. Or maybe I'm too dense to read it. But on his first night back, he asked if I'd mind if he returned to school next week rather than live with me. If I could afford it.

He said it so . . . rationally. And I was so stunned that I heard myself answering calmly that we could probably manage it. And now it hovered between us, unspoken and unsettled. Like an unfriendly ghost.

I was sure it would pass, this idea of our continuing to live apart. It was jet lag, culture lag, something. If we could just spend some time together, we could work through our differences. So I suggested we spend the last few days of summer rambling around the Upper Peninsula. I thought the beauty of the north country might change his mind.

Another mistake. The U.P. is stark, sparsely populated country. The locals call themselves "Yoopers" and occasionally threaten to secede from Michigan to form their own state. I've always loved the region but the lonely grandeur of Lake of the Clouds and the Porcupine Mountains didn't seem to touch Corey. And after two days in a Jeep with him I was beginning to wonder if school might not actually be the best option. God help me, I'm beginning to see his father in him, a man I once idolized, and now despise. Corey's my son. I love him with all my heart. But I'm not sure I like him all that much anymore.

"Can we stop someplace?" Corey asked. "I need to use a rest room."

We'd passed a roadsign a mile or so back, ANAHWEY 5 MILES, but when I saw a little roadside curio shop standing well off the road, I pulled in. The building was little more than a shack of rough, faded barnboard. The sign in front said INDIAN ARTIFACTS.

Inside, a lanky, wizened oldster in frayed coveralls and a red flannel shirt was sitting in a bentwood rocker behind the counter, carving a small totem out of pine. I asked about restrooms and he jerked a thumb toward the back.

"Have to take turns, I'm afraid," he said, smiling an apology. "It's only a one-holer."

Corey walked out the back door to the privy. Through the screen I saw him hesitate when he opened the door and I half-expected him to close it again, but he went inside.

I browsed. It was an intriguing little shop, antique bottles, carved wooden animals and toys, tribal shields and mandalas made of raccoon or rabbit fur. Everything seemed to be lovingly crafted by hand, none of the usual tourist crap from Taiwan or wherever. The air was richly scented, a heady mix of cedar and pine and woodsmoke.

The old man was watching me. A small bear caught my eye. It was hardwood, ash I think, beautifully carved and blackened by fire. I turned it over. There was no price tag. "How much is this?" I asked.

He was still staring at me. "I know you," he said at last. It wasn't a question.

"I don't think so," I said. "We're not from this area."

"No, I know that. But I know you. You got people around here?"

"No," I said. Or anywhere else, I thought. "How much is the bear?"

"Eight bucks," he said. He rose easily from his rocker and came around the counter, still eyeing me curiously. And still carrying his knife. He was almost a head taller than I am, and I'm tall for a woman. His hair was steel gray, and looked like it had been trimmed with garden shears. His eyes were black as obsidian. He smelled of pipe smoke and needed a shave. He took the bear from me.

"Never did get the forepaw quite right," he said, looking it over critically. "Make it six bucks. What was your maiden name?"

"Mitchell," I said, humoring him, wishing Corey would hurry the hell up.

"No," he said, frowning, "that's not it. Sorry to seem nosy. My name's Dolph Fereau. This is my place. Everything in here, I carved. From memory, no pictures, no models, nothing. I've got a pretty good eye for shapes and faces. And I'm sure I know you from somewhere."

"I really don't think so," I said. "I'll take the bear." The room shuddered with a deep bass rumble.

"Boy, you step away from there. Now!" Corey was standing near a pile of furs near the end of the counter. The pile raised its massive head. Corey backed away, his eyes the size of saucers.

"Jeez," he managed. "What is that, a wolf?"

"Nah," the old man said. "Keeping wolves is illegal. She's a cross."

"A cross?" Corey echoed.

"Cross-wolf. Half wolf, half somethin' else. Her mama was a cross too, so she's mostly wolf. Her pups are still nursin', so she's kinda surly. Not that she needs a reason." He said something in a language I didn't recognize. The cross-wolf sat up. Her coat was gunmetal gray mottled with black, the color of storm clouds. Her head was massive, roughly the size of a basketball. Her eyes were an intense, silver blue and glittered like moonlight on deep water.

"Coool," Corey said, with more animation than I'd heard from him in days. "What's her name?"

"Can't tell you that," the old man said, with a faint smile. "It's in Anishnabe. I never use it unless I want her to do something. In English it would be Bitch From Hell."

Corey looked at him doubtfully, his eyes cataloging the old man's clothing, grubby boots, calloused hands, the grime under his nails. "My friend at school has Rottweiler guard dogs at home. They're bigger than this one. How do you know she's part wolf?"

"I raised her myself. Her mother too."

"But how could you do that?" Corey said evenly, with smug, irrefutable logic. "You just said it's illegal to keep wolves."

"I don't keep them. To get a cross, you take a bitch in heat and stake her out near a trail wolves use. Sometimes a male scents her on the wind and mates with her. Or maybe the pack finds her and tears her apart and you lose your bitch. It's risky business. Wolves are like people. You're never sure what they're gonna do. That's why cross pups cost so much."

"How much?"

"A grand each for females, eight hundred for males."

"That is a lot," Corey said, frowning. "But if you're not sure who they mate with, how can they have a pedigree?"

"Pedigrees are for bookkeepers," the old man snorted.

"But with no pedigree, you can't prove what they are," Corey said patiently. "They could be anything."

"A pedigree doesn't prove what a dog is, only what its parents were. With a cross-wolf you don't even know that much. So you have to let it be itself." He reached down behind the counter and came up with a pup, a squirming ball of fur with slits for eyes and comically oversized paws. He handed it to Corey. Bitch From Hell watched with intense interest. "What do you think?" Fereau asked. "Does this little guy look like a wolf to you?"

"He smells pretty bad," Corey said, gingerly holding the pup.

"So did you at that age," Fereau said. "Me too. Maybe your mama will buy him for you." He glanced at me with a wry smile to show he was kidding. I think. The smile turned into curiosity. "Your mother," he said to me. "What was her family name?"

"Hubert," I said.

"Nope," he said, shaking his head with mock exasperation. "Don't know any Huberts either. I must be losin' it."

"Maybe I've got a twin somewhere," I said. "People say everyone has one."

"No," Fereau said positively. "No two things are ever alike. Not snowflakes or people or dogs. Not even dogs with pedigrees. You want me to wrap up the bear?"

"Please," I said.

He carried it to the counter, began rolling it up in a sheet of grubby newspaper, then hesitated. "Bear," he said, with a wry grin of satisfaction. "That's it. Not Hubert. Dubear."

"I beg your pardon?"

"Your mother's name, it had a small 'd' in front of it, right? d'Hubert? Up here we pronounce it Dubear."

All the air seemed to go out of the room. I nodded. It was all I could manage. Corey glanced up at me oddly.

"I knew you were familiar," Fereau said, twisting the ends of paper together. "All the d'Hubert girls look a little alike. Eyes like yours, thin jaw. Good looking women, no offense. Are you one of Corinne's daughters?"

"No," I said slowly. "My mother's name was Madeline."

"Madeline," the old man nodded. "Frank's youngest girl. I shoulda guessed right off. Except for bein' some taller, a little thinner maybe, you're her spittin' image."

"You knew her?" I said, stunned.

"Sure. I think our families are even shirttail relations or something. From Burt Lake."

"But . . . I thought she was an orphan."

"She tell you that? Well, maybe she's got her reasons, or thinks she does. She and ol' Frank had trouble when she ran off. But she ain't hardly no orphan. Tell you what, you see her, you tell her Dolph Fereau says hello. See what she says about that. How's she doin'?"

"She's ahm . . . she's dead," I said. "She died a few days after I was born."

Fereau blinked. "I'm sorry," he said slowly. "I didn't know."

"But you really did know her," I stammered. "Look, I was raised by my grandmother, my father's mom. She didn't know my mother, never met her at all. I was told she was an orphan. I've never even seen a picture of her!"

"Hey, look, I'm sorry," Fereau said uncomfortably. "Maybe I spoke out of turn. I could be wrong about this. Probably am."

"No. You knew about the 'd' in her name. I'd almost forgotten it myself. Please, what can you tell me about her?"

"Not much," he said reluctantly. "Look, it's been a lotta years—"

"Aaahh!" Corey shouted, dropping the puppy, flailing frantically at his arms. "It's got bugs!" The pup squalled as it hit the floor and the cross wolf bolted upright, snarling, her eyes ablaze, her bared fangs only inches from Corey's face.

Fereau shouted at her, grabbed Corey by the scruff of the neck and threw him in the general direction of the door. "You get outta here, now!" he snapped. "Christ, kid, are you outta your mind, fumblin' her pup like that? You're lucky she didn't take your head off. Ain't you never seen a flea?"

"No," Corey flared, "not on me anyway!"

"Lady, you'd best go. I'll hold Bitch here, but it ain't safe for you now."

"Wait, please, can we just talk a minute?"

"Dammit, it ain't safe! I can't tell you nothin' and it ain't my place to anyway. Check with the Indian Center in town, maybe they can help you out."

"Indian?" I echoed stupidly.

"Yeah. Jesus, you mean you didn't even know that? Your mother was Anishnabe, Ojibwa, or part anyway. Look, you gotta get outta here. If Bitch decides to take a chunk outta me I won't be able to hold her. Now move it!"

I stumbled out of the shop after Corey. He stalked angrily to the Jeep, got in and slammed the door. I climbed behind the wheel in a daze, trying to make sense of what Fereau said.

"Come on, let's go!" Corey snapped. He was flushed, and his nostrils were pinched with rage. "Did you see what he did? His john stinks and his dog's got bugs, and he put his dirty hands on me. Let's go find a town with a motel or something. I need a shower. You can catch things from fleas."

"Didn't you hear what he said?" I said, swallowing. "He knew my mother." I started the Jeep.

"He was just trying to con you into buying more tourist junk. French people did it to us all the time."

"No," I said numbly. "He knew her. My God, he probably knows more about her than I do."

"Yeah, well he claimed to be related to her, too. Is that what you want? Relatives like him? Jeez, mom, look at this dump. He's just trash."

I swiveled in the seat to face him. Except for a few spats on the behind when he was a toddler to keep him out of trouble,

I've never laid a hand on my son. Never had to. But at that moment I was only a word away from slapping him silly.

He must have read it in my eyes, because he went suddenly silent and edged away. I shifted the Jeep into drive, and eased it down the long, narrow driveway out to the blacktop.

# TWO
## STONEWALLED

"D'HUBERT?" THE woman said. "Doesn't ring a bell. Could I see your card, please?"

"My card?"

"Your tribal I.D."

"I don't have one," I said. "I'm not from here."

She didn't look particularly "indian" to me. I'd been half expecting someone in tribal dress. She was wearing a beige skirt, white blouse. Her face was squarish and large-boned, but her hair, worn short, was chestnut colored, and much lighter than mine.

The Indian Center was an ordinary office in a storefront building, a large, open bay partitioned into privacy cubicles. Only the wall mural, a village scene of tribal life, indicated it was anything but an upscale insurance agency.

"Do you mind if I ask why you want to find the d'Hubert family?" she asked.

"I—recently learned I may be related to them," I said. "I'd just like to talk to someone."

"I see," she nodded, tapping her front teeth with a yellow lead pencil while she thought. "Well, I'm sorry but we just aren't allowed to give out that information. But maybe it isn't necessary. If you're moving to the area, I can enroll you for medical care if you sign a declaration that you're at least one sixty-fourth native American."

"A sixty-fourth?" Corey echoed curiously. "How could anybody know that?"

"Basically, you just have to say so," the woman said dryly. "We'll take your word for it. The tribal council has to approve it, but they're fairly flexible. The declaration also qualifies you to work in a tribal casino or other industries. To share in any financial disbursement, though, you'd have to apply for—"

"Miss, I'm not interested in applying for benefits, I'm just trying to locate a relative."

"Sorry," she said. "No offense, but for a long time people didn't want to admit they were Ojibwa. Now that we have the casinos, folks are coming out of the woodwork claiming Pontiac was their great uncle. Unfortunately, he was Odawa. What's the name of the family you're looking for?"

"d'Hubert," I said, and spelled it for her. "I was told they were from . . . Burt Lake?"

"Lots of folks are from Burt Lake," she said curtly, moving behind a computer monitor at the end of the counter. "They're scattered from here to Canada now. Those that survived." She typed out the name on her keyboard.

"I don't understand," I said. "What was Burt Lake?"

"Burt Lake? It was an Anishabe town south of Cheboygan, quite prosperous at the time. The local *chemokman* sheriff showed up one day with a posse and a phoney-baloney writ that said the land was forfeit for back taxes. He turned the families out of their homes and burned the town to the ground. No notice, no hearings, no more town. The people lost everything. Some of them moved up here. Some went to Canada. Some starved that winter trying to live off the land. It was an ugly business. There are still plenty of families around whose parents were burned out at Burt Lake. But I'll bet a dollar to a donut that good-looking boy of yours never reads about it in his Michigan history books."

"I don't go to school here," Corey said.

"It wouldn't matter if you did," she shrugged. "d'Hubert. There are three families registered. Do you know which one?"

"Frank?" I said.

"I have a Francis d'Hubert registered. Wife's name Angeline?"

"I . . . don't know her name."

"I thought you said you were a relative of his?"

"His . . . granddaughter," I said. "I don't know much about him. My mother's name was Madeline."

"That checks," she said, nodding. "Daughters Corinne and Madeline. I'm sorry if I seem uncooperative, it's just policy to protect the privacy of our people. I can't give you any personal information, you understand, but Mr. d'Hubert has a local address. . . ." She frowned.

"Is something wrong?"

"Probably not. I just don't see any recent activity under this name, voting or anything. It's possible they've moved away without notifying us. The address is still shown as current, though. Do you want it?"

# THREE
## THE OLD FOLKS AT HOME

⊗⊌⊙

THE HOUSE had been handsome once, a turn-of-the-century two-story clapboard with a full-width front porch. The paint was flaking now, shingles were cracked or missing, and a patch of green moss was creeping up a corner of the building. The driveway was unpaved, but the garage was obviously in use. The door stood open and tools were scattered about on the dirt floor. No one seemed to be around.

I stepped up on the porch with Corey trailing reluctantly behind and rang the buzzer. No answer. I could hear sounds from within, though. A burst of canned laughter from a television set. I tried again.

"There's somebody inside," Corey said, peering through the front window. "A lady watching TV."

"Get away from there," I said. I rapped hard on the front door glass. Through the drapes I saw a shadowy figure of a woman move to the door. But she made no move to open it. She just stood there. "Hello?" I said, rapping again.

She opened the door. She was sixtyish, short, and stout. Her hair was tinted a reddish pink. She was wearing a teal-blue polyester bathrobe and slippers. And she looked nothing at all like me. "Yes?"

"Are you Mrs. d'Hubert? Angeline d'Hubert?"

"No, Angeline was Frank's first wife. She died . . . I don't know, back in the fifties, I guess. A long time ago. I'm Emma d'Hubert. What is it you want?"

"My name's Michelle Mitchell. This is my son Corey. I think we might be related to you. Can we talk a minute?"

"What do you mean, related?" she said warily. "I don't know you."

"My mother's name was Madeline d'Hubert. Does that name mean anything to you?"

"Madeline? Bull. You can't be Maddy's daughter. Maddy didn't have any kids. She was only a kid herself when . . ." She broke off, blinking as she peered at me more closely.

"She died having me, actually," I said. "Did you know her at all?"

"Yeah," she nodded grudgingly. "Sure I knew her. Look, what's this about?"

"I'm not sure myself," I said. "I only recently learned that . . . well, that my mother had any relatives. I'd really like to talk to someone about it. Is Mr. d'Hubert at home?"

"No, Frank's up north. I don't know when he'll be back. Maybe a couple weeks. Maybe a few months. He ain't much on clocks or calendars, Frank ain't. Comes and goes as he pleases."

"I see. Well, if you could tell me anything, I'd really appreciate it. Could we just talk a few minutes?"

"I don't know," she said doubtfully. "I'm not supposed to let strangers in, you know? There's a lot of nosy people around. Boone, my nephew, he gets awful hot about strangers bein' here."

"Please, it would mean a lot to me."

"Well," she grumbled, "I guess a few minutes won't hurt."

I followed her into the living room. The wallpaper pattern had been flowered once. The carpet was threadbare. A dime-store print of a forest in autumn hung above the sagging couch. The air was hazy with cigarette smoke, and the whole place needed serious vacuuming. Mrs. d'Hubert switched the TV to mute, settled into the rocker facing it, and lit another cigarette. There was a mixed drink on the tray beside her chair, Southern Comfort, unless I missed my guess. The coffee table ashtray was overflowing.

I sat on the edge of the couch across from her. Corey stood

by the door like a sentry on duty, unwilling to advance another step into the room.

"I can see it now," she nodded, eyeing me over the rim of her glass. "You favor Maddy some. I heard she died, of course, long since, but I didn't know about . . . you. What happened to her?"

"She died in childbirth. I never knew her at all."

"You said your name was Mitchell, right? That was the fella Maddy got mixed up with. He had an odd name. Irish, I think."

"Shannon," I prompted.

"Yeah, that's it. Shannon Mitchell. Kind of a wild character, as I recall."

"That's my dad," I nodded. "Or it was. He was killed in an auto accident a year or so ago. The thing is, he wouldn't talk about my mother. Ever. I only learned she had relatives here by chance."

"Frank and your father didn't get on. Frank's folks were burned out by whites and he never had much use for 'em. Except maybe for their women. Angeline, his first wife, was white. Like me. Look, what is it you want from me?"

"Anything you can tell me at all. About my mother, or . . . anything at all. What she was like?"

"She was a handful," she said sourly. "She was a teenager when Frank and I . . . got married. Frank's older daughter, Corinne, married a black guy, a flyboy from the airbase at Sawyer. It damn near killed Frank. It wasn't so much the guy was a nigger, though that probably didn't help much, but he damn sure wasn't Ojibwa. You gotta understand, things were different back then. There was a lot of pressure to keep the people together. So many Anishnabe people were driftin' off to find work or whatever. For awhile it looked like the People might just disappear, you know? Like what happened at Burt Lake. Frank married white himself, but he felt real strong about his family bein' Anishnabe. Especially later on, when all the unrest started buildin' up about Wounded Knee and all. He never would speak to Corinne again after she got married. Wouldn't even answer her letters. And after Corinne left, he tried to keep Madeline on a tight leash. Didn't work though."

"What happened?"

"Some guy hired Frank as a guide to work on a mining job

out in the boondocks east of Grand Portal. Your dad was
workin' the same job. He was some kinda diver, right?"

I nodded.

"Yeah, that was the crazy part. They were workin' in an old
flooded copper mine, whole thing was under water. And this
guy. I can't remember his name. Van somethin' maybe. He didn't
know the area at all, so he hired Frank as a guide and general
bull worker. And your dad, Mitchell, he was fresh back from
Vietnam, and more'n a little crazy himself. Maddy took supplies back to the mine site a few times, musta met your dad
then. The job was a big washout; Frank barely got paid. But
when Mitchell left, Maddy thought she was in love and took off
with him. And ahm . . ." Her voice faded away and she sipped
her drink.

"And what?" I prompted. She glanced at me, and I read
something unpleasant in her eyes. Satisfaction?

"She came back that fall, knocked up," Emma said. "Wanted
to stay a few days till she could find a place of her own. She and
Frank had a helluva row. He was drinking then, got mean when
he drank. He called her a whore, slapped her around some, ran
her off. I snuck out after, gave her money for bus fare. She was
in rough shape."

"What do you mean, rough?"

"He gave her a black eye, and she was . . . bleeding a little.
You know, from down here," she said, gesturing at her lap. "She
said Mitchell didn't know she was pregnant. She kept it from
him, didn't want to push him into anything. I told her she'd best
tell him, 'cause no way Frank would take her back. I guess she
must've."

"They were married in the hospital," I said numbly. "That's all
my dad would ever say about it. He told me she was an orphan."

"Maybe she was, as far as he was concerned. Might as well
have been. So if you've come here expectin' to get anything from
Frank, you'd best forget it. He won't want to see you."

"Perhaps that's just as well," I said, rising stiffly from the
sofa, a century older than when I came. "I don't think I care to
see him either. Do you have any idea where Corinne is now?"

"No, she wrote a few times, but Frank, he just threw her letters away. She could be on the Moon for all I know."

"I see. Well, thanks very much for seeing me. There is one favor I'd like to ask, though."

"Like what?"

"Would you have any old photographs of my mother? A snapshot, anything? I've never seen a picture of her."

"Pictures? No, I don't think so. Look, you'd best go. You don't wanna be here when my nephew gets back. He'll hit the roof if he finds out I let strangers in."

"I don't understand."

"No reason you should, it's none of your business. Look, there's only one place any pictures might be, and I can't reach it. I'll have Boone check it later. If there's anything there I'll send it along."

"I'll be glad to get it for you," I offered. "It'll save you the trouble of mailing it. Or I can come back tomorrow if you like."

"I guess we can look now," she grumbled. "No need for you to come back. It's in Frank's room."

I followed her down a narrow hallway toward the rear of the house. I glanced through an open bedroom door as we passed. It looked like a tornado had hit the room, unmade bed, girlie magazines and fast food wrappers scattered around.

"Boone's," she said, pointedly closing the door. "Him and his buddy live like pigs and their manners aren't much better. I never shoulda taken him in. This is Frank's room here," she said, opening the last door off the hallway.

I stepped into the spartan bedroom. An old-fashioned wrought-iron bedstead with a flannel coverlet filled one corner. A gilded crucifix hung near it beside a gun rack holding a few weapons. A fireplace filled the opposite wall, with a pair of framed photographs on its mantel.

Two of the photos were of the same person, a young man in an army uniform, WWII vintage I guessed. In the other shot he was older, standing with two other men in hunting clothes beside a Chevy pickup truck. Francis d'Hubert. My grandfather.

I knew him without being told. Perhaps Fereau was right, there was a family resemblance. Or perhaps we simply know our blood kin by some atavistic sixth sense, the way wolves know members of their clan. There was something eerily familiar about the look of him. I decided it was his eyes, a bit wider apart than normal, with a flat, impassive gaze very much like Corey's. I wondered how deep the resemblance ran. There were no women in the pictures. I wondered if that was significant. Probably.

"The box is on the top closet shelf there," Emma said, sitting on the edge of the bed, sipping her drink. "Don't mind the dust, I don't get around so good anymore."

I retrieved the cardboard box she pointed out, carried it to the bed and opened it. There wasn't much in it: Some out-of-date insurance papers, a title to a truck, 1964. A brown envelope contained some snapshots, but they'd been there so long they were stuck together. I swallowed my disappointment without much trouble. I was getting used to it.

"Is this all there is?" I asked.

"Afraid so," she said. "Frank went on a tear after Maddy left, threw everything of hers away, pictures, everything. If he missed anything it'd be in that box."

Corey had followed us into the room, and wandered over to the gun rack. He reached up and touched one. "Let those be," I said, picking up the box.

"Look, you can have it," Mrs. d'Hubert said. "It's just a bunch of old junk anyway, but please, you've gotta . . ." Her voice was drowned by the thrum of a motorcycle rumbling up the driveway to the garage.

"Oh Jesus, now we're in for it," she said. "You'd best get out of here now."

"No problem," I said. "Come on, Corey."

We didn't make it. When I stepped out, the hallway was blocked by a hulk in a grubby denim jacket. His shoulder length hair was the color of mouldy hay, and he was wearing Terminator-style mirrored shades.

"What the hell's goin' on here?" he snarled. "Who are you?"

"A distant relative who's just leaving," I said. "Nice to meet you."

"You stay right where you are, lady, until I get some straight answers. What's going on here, Emma?"

"She's one of Frank's granddaughters, Boone," Mrs. d'Hubert quavered. "It's nothing to do with you."

"No? So what's she got in the box?"

"Junk," I said. "My junk. Look for yourself."

He snatched the box out of my hands, pawed through it hastily, then tossed it aside. I knelt and retrieved it, struggling to keep my temper. I was losing the fight.

"She show you any I.D., Emma?"

"No, but I *know* her, Boone. I knew her mother."

"Yeah, well I don't know her or her mother, either. Come on, lady, cough up some I.D."

"In your dreams," I snapped. "Look, sport, I don't know what your problem is. I came to look up my grandfather, it didn't work out, we're outta here. If that's not good enough for you, there's a phone in the living room, why don't you call the police, have them straighten it out?"

"Boone, it's okay, really," Mrs. d'Hubert said, pushing past me. "They're going, they won't be back."

Anger and something else were battling in his eyes. Fear?

"Well?" I said.

"Okay, get the hell out," he said abruptly. "But I catch you sniffin' around here again, you're the one's gonna be leavin' in a box."

I almost lost it. The anger and disappointment I'd been holding in check all day, first with Corey, then with Frank, nearly exploded. I found myself unconsciously casting about for some sort of a weapon, a ball bat, a golf club, some way to forcibly move this Neanderthal out of my way when Corey firmly took my wrist and simply led me past him. Boone stepped grudgingly aside, then started in on Emma about letting strangers in. We could hear them shouting all the way to the Jeep.

# FOUR
## THICKER THAN WATER?

―――――――――――

✿✿✿✿

"WHAT WAS the matter with that guy?" Corey asked as he snapped on his safety belt.

"He's just a jerk," I said. My hand was trembling so fiercely I could barely fit the key in the ignition.

"He was also really big," Corey said, looking at me oddly. "I was afraid you were gonna do something crazy. You scare me sometimes, you know that?"

"I'm your mother. It's my job."

"But why were you so angry? I mean, so he was a jerk. When I got in that fight with Bobby Yaeger, you said if I punched out every jerk I met my hands would swell up like catcher's mitts and I'd never play Nintendo again."

"Did I say that? Well, I was right. And please note that I didn't punch him out or whatever."

"But you were thinking about it. I could tell. Why?"

I turned onto Anahwey's main drag, using the interval to think. How much truth do you tell a child? I've tried not to lie to my son, but I don't always tell him the whole truth. About his father, for example. I've told him our relationship didn't work out, which is the truth, and as much as he needs to know, for now. But Corey's growing and changing too fast for me. I'm not sure how much longer I can shield him from unpleasant truths. Or even if I should.

"I don't know much about my mother," I said, keeping my tone neutral. "I do know I was born prematurely, about a month. And that my mother died a few days later."

"But I don't . . . oh," he said, his eyes widening. "That lady said Frank and your mother . . . had a fight."

"Right," I nodded. "That's what she said."

"God, some family tree," he said after a bit. "Crazy grandfather, crazy mom. I may be the sanest one of the bunch."

"That's a scary thought," I said.

"It sure is," he agreed, for the first time in days. "So, are we about through with our trip down memory lane?"

"I guess so. Sorry the old family tree turned out to be more of a weed."

"You should've known it would. Look at us."

"What's that supposed to mean?"

"You know what I mean." He glanced out the window, avoiding my eyes. "We're a . . . dysfunctional family. Like Richard the Third. Or Lizzie Borden."

"I can't speak for Richard, but I think I know how Lizzie felt. If I ever meet my grandfather Frank face to face and there's an axe nearby, we may both be in a lot of trouble."

"No," Corey said slowly, "I don't think you should meet him. Let's just forget we ever came here."

"Why? Because of Boone? Maybe you're right. It's probably more trouble than it's worth."

"No, not just that. I'm pretty sure that lady was lying to you."

"What do you mean? Lying about what?"

"I'm not sure, but I think she was. I was watching her face when she talked. She was afraid of you. Or afraid of something. Besides, some of the things she said didn't make sense."

"What things?"

"What she told you about your grandfather Frank," he said, exasperated. "She said he'd be back in a couple of weeks, right?"

"That's right."

"His guns, the ones in the rack? They were rusty."

"Maybe he's a lousy housekeeper. She certainly is."

"No, I don't mean dusty, mom, they were rusted, bad. And

he's some kind of a guide or something, right? But nobody who's serious about guns would let them get rusty like that. I don't think they've been touched in a long time. Years maybe."

I stared at him, my ultra-logical son. "Since when did you become a firearms expert?"

"We had a gun-safety course at school. And Mr. Whitmore, Ricky's dad, has some. He keeps 'em in a glass case."

"I see. Okay, so maybe the guns are in lousy shape. So what?"

"I don't know, I'm just saying they didn't get that way in a couple of weeks. Another thing, she said Frank hates white people because of what happened to his family at that place?"

"Burt Lake?"

"Right. And he ahm, he roughed your mom up and kicked her out because she was . . . pregnant by a white guy, right?"

"Something like that. So?"

"So what about that goon who gave us all the static? He lives there, and he's white. Does that make sense to you?"

"Not goon," I said automatically. "His name was Boone."

"I know what his name was," he said, annoyed. "I'm not dense, you know."

"I know," I sighed. "Believe me, I do know that."

Neither of us spoke for awhile. The afternoon shadows were lengthening into dusk as we drove out of Anahwey on M-95 toward Witch Lake, twenty-six miles to the south. I was so lost in thought, replaying conversations in my mind, that I scarcely noticed the headlights coming rapidly up behind me. Until suddenly they divided, and became two motorcycles. A Harley-Davidson roared up alongside us. Boone.

His scruffy mane was streaming in the wind and his eyes were alien behind the mirrored sunglasses. He shouted something at me over the thrum of the bike, then jabbed his finger at the shoulder of the road. Pull over.

"Mom," Corey said matter-of-factly, "there's another motorcycle behind us, and we're in the middle of noplace out here."

"I know. Are you buckled up?"

He nodded. "What are you gonna do?"

"I don't know."

Boone had to drop back momentarily as an eighteen-wheeler howled past on the narrow two-lane blacktop. Then he gunned his cycle alongside us again and jabbed his finger at the shoulder. When I didn't respond, he reached behind his seat and unhooked a length of chain with a padlock attached. Dangling it from his wrist a moment, he let the windblast swing it like a pendulum, then without warning he swung it savagely at the Jeep.

I flinched, instinctively cramming the wheel to the right to avoid the chain. It thumped on the hardtop as my right front tire hit the shoulder, and then we were skidding and fishtailing as I fought the wheel trying to get the Jeep under control.

Boone was ahead of us now, half-twisted in the saddle, grinning back at me. His partner was somewhere behind us. I wrestled the Jeep back on the road and floored it. The little Cherokee surged ahead, whining like a vacuum cleaner and with only slightly more horsepower. It was a light duty recreational vehicle for carrying groceries or banging around the boondocks. It was never meant for anything like this. Neither was I.

As the Jeep got up to speed again I kept it straddled on the centerline, trying to keep Boone off. It was hopeless. The biker behind us roared up on the other side and swung a tire iron at our rear window, exploding a hailstorm of glass into the car. I swerved right, forcing him to veer off, but only for a moment.

"Mom!" Corey wailed. "He's coming again!"

And so was Boone. He'd braked momentarily in the other lane to let me by, but now he and the other biker were both coming on fast.

I swerved wildly back and forth over the centerline, trying to keep them behind us, but I knew I couldn't keep it up. The Jeep felt like it could flip over at any second. It was none too stable even on dry pavement and the cycles were too fast and maneuverable for me. It was like trying to outrun horsemen on foot. In the gathering dusk, the highway and countryside were as empty as the back of the moon, no traffic, no houses. No help.

Dammit! I continued to veer, but narrowed the swing a little, giving Boone's buddy room to come up on my right. He took the opening, gunning up alongside the rear fender, swinging his weapon. I jammed the wheel hard right, and touched the brakes. He did the same, easily avoiding the Jeep, but he dropped the tire iron as he hit the shoulder and fought to control the bike. I cramped the wheel sharply right again, but this time I stomped the brakes to the floor, throwing us into a broadside skid!

No choice, he had to swerve hard right, but he ran out of road. The bike lurched as it hit the grass beyond the shoulder then tilted into a skid, tearing up the turf until it hooked on something and went airborne. I glimpsed the rider tumbling along the shoulder like a rag doll. Then I lost sight of him in the dust and was too busy wrestling the Jeep back on the highway to worry about him.

Boone was well ahead of us now; he jammed his brakes, wheeled his machine around in a U-turn, and gunned straight at us, wielding his chain like a flail.

Now I was the one with no options. I was moving too slowly to try to avoid him or even to hit him, and if he swung at the windshield as he passed on either side . . . "Hang on," I yelled. I dropped the Jeep into four-wheel drive and cranked the wheel hard to the left.

# Five

# The Trap

I swerved off the road into a field, bumping and bucking over the turf, fighting to keep the Jeep from going over. And to keep it moving. I was still in the transmission's high range and if I stopped to shift down he'd have us. But I'd glimpsed a building up ahead: a curio stand in the middle of nowhere.

We didn't make it. The left front wheel dropped into a hole and we lurched to a dead stop. I sat there a moment, my head ringing, stunned by the impact. The roar of the motorcycle snapped me out of it. Boone had howled past when I veered off, but he was U-turning to come back again.

"Are you okay?" I shouted at Corey, unsnapping his seatbelt. He was too dazed to answer. I grabbed him by the shirt and dragged him out, carrying him bodily as I stumbled through the underbrush toward Fereau's shack.

Boone had an easier run. He raced along the road, then turned off and roared up the long driveway, skidding to a halt just as Dolph Fereau stepped out of his shop. Boone vaulted off the bike and stalked toward us, carrying his chain. And then he stopped, abruptly. Bitch From Hell moved between us, eyeing everyone but Fereau with equal distaste.

"Now everybody just cool off a minute," Dolph said. "What the hell's going on here?"

"This crazy broad ran down my friend!" Boone shouted, starting to circle around the cross-wolf toward us.

"Which friend?" Dolph asked. "That Vasco guy you run with? The biker from Pontiac?"

Boone stopped, startled.

"Yeah, I know who he is," Dolph continued reasonably. "Know who you are too. What'd you figure, couple of knot-heads like you move up to the sticks to lay low and the locals wouldn't notice? Hell, sonny, we got nothin' else to talk about. Now I don't know what happened to your buddy, but if he's really hurt like you say, maybe you'd best go back and check on him. It may take a few minutes for the law to get here."

"The law?" Boone echoed, swallowing. "What law?"

"I dialed 911 when I seen the lady run off the road," Dolph said. "Sheriff's on his way."

"You stupid old fart," Boone said, turning on him. "You just made the biggest mistake of your life."

"Not as big as the one you're makin'," Dolph said, as Bitch From Hell moved stiffly toward Boone, fangs bared, growling deep in her throat. Boone froze. Fereau reached through the door of his shack and came out with a double-barreled shotgun. "You got no manners, Mr. Boone," he said, holding the gun casually in the crook of his arm, the barrels aimed at the ground. "Now you get your bike off my place in the next five seconds or I'm gonna blow it to hell and you can walk back to town. And if you mouth off to me one more time, sonny, you'll be walkin' with a limp. You hear what I'm sayin'?"

Boone's glasses flicked from the shotgun to the dog, and back to Fereau. He swallowed, then backed off and swung aboard his cycle. "I'll be back," he shouted over the roar of the bike.

Fereau didn't answer. Boone roared out the long driveway, and headed away from town. And his fallen friend.

"A real sweetheart," Fereau said, shaking his head. "You two all right?"

I nodded mutely, too shaken to speak.

"What happened in town? You find Frank's place, and maybe rattled Boone's cage?"

"Something like that." I knelt feeling Corey all over to make sure he was in one piece. He squirmed away from me. "What was all that about, anyway?" I asked.

"With Boone?" Fereau said. "Ah, hell, him and his brain dead buddy came up here last spring, moved in with Emma. He's some kinda kin to her, I guess. Anyway, the two cityboys have been dealin' dope, crank, pills, whatever. Big secret. In small towns, everybody knows everybody's business. Word was out on those two from day one. I imagine Boone's got some dope stashed at the house. I'm sorry I let you walk into that. I was just so surprised, when you showed up. I didn't think about them bein' there until after you left. I woulda called to warn ya, but I got no phone."

"No phone?" I said. "But you said you called the police. Aren't they coming?"

"Nah, I lied about that. Local law's spread kinda thin up here. People are used to handlin' things their ownselves."

"I see," I said. "In that case I appreciate what you did for us just now even more."

"No charge. It was probably my fault you got into trouble."

"Why? Because you didn't warn me about Boone? Or because you didn't tell me the truth about my grandfather?"

He eyed me a moment without speaking. His face was a mask, as lifeless as one of his carvings, ridged and shadowed in the fading light.

"Mr. Fereau, I think Emma lied to me about my grandfather. And I think you did too. But I don't know why. Why would either of you lie to me about Frank?"

"Boy," he said quietly to Corey, "why don't you wait out here, keep an eye peeled, case Mr. Boone comes back. I got something for your mama."

I followed Fereau into his shop. There was no light but the last golden glow of dusk through the window. He laid the shotgun on the counter and picked up a paper-wrapped parcel.

"Your bear," he said, tossing it to me. "You forgot it when you left this morning."

"Thank you," I said. "That's not what I came for."

"I know," he said quietly. "Look, I want you to understand

something. Frank d'Hubert and I grew up together, boy and man, friends our whole lives. So when I realized who you were this morning, and you said Madeline died havin' you, I thought Frank might be in serious trouble over it. I knew about the argument him and Maddy had, but I didn't know what happened . . . afterwards."

"It was a lot more than an argument," I said flatly. "She was pregnant and he roughed her up. He may even have caused her death."

"You don't know that for certain, lady, not after all this time. Let it be. Whatever happened, it was over a long time ago."

"Not for me. It didn't even begin for me until today. If she was your mother, could you let it go?"

"I don't know," he shrugged. "Maybe not."

"Then tell me what's going on. Where is Frank now?"

"I don't know for sure. Canada, maybe. He's got Anishnabe relatives in Ontario, near Nipigon, or maybe Lac Seul. Might be he's up there."

"His wife said he'd be back in a few weeks or a month."

"I don't think so. For one thing, Emma ain't his wife, not legally, anyway. She was livin' with him common law before he went off. I expect she lies about him coming back so she can keep the house, maybe cash his Social Security checks. But after what happened to your mother, I don't think he'll come back here."

"Then maybe I should go to Canada."

"Why? You'd never find him up there. There's a dozen different Ojibwa towns and half those people don't even speak English, just French or Anishnabe."

"I speak a little French," I said, "and you speak whatever it is. Maybe you could help me. I'd pay you."

"No," he said. "What's the point?"

"To face him, to tell him what I think of him. Or maybe just to ask him the truth about what happened. I don't know much about my family. I'd like the little I do know to be true."

"Truth," he snorted. "Now there's a word. When I carve an animal I try to make it as true as I can, but I don't show the fleas, or the mange, or old scars. Maybe that means my carvin' ain't absolutely true, but I don't think it's the worse for it. Truth doesn't always make things better. A lotta times, things that are true, you kinda wish they weren't."

"Like what?" I said. "What are you trying to tell me?"

He looked away a moment, and in the shadowed room, his face was a mystery. Unreadable. "Your father was Shannon Mitchell, wasn't he?"

I nodded.

"Thought so. I met him that time Frank worked with him. Ex-soldier, just back from Vietnam. Nice young fella, but kind of wild. Had some hard bark on him, from the war I guess. I didn't know him well, though. Was he a pretty good hunter?"

"Hunter?" I said, puzzled. "No, he never hunted. I mean, he did as a boy, but never after the war. He said he lost his taste for it. Why?"

"Then I must be wrong," Fereau said. "I thought I saw him in Anahwey later on that year. Guess it must been sometime after your mother died. I barely recognized him. He looked different. Had a beard, and his eyes were . . . dead. Empty. He was in hunting clothes, you know, camouflage? He was at a sporting goods shop buyin' ammunition. I spoke to him but he walked by me like I wasn't there. I never saw him again."

I stared up at him, trying to read his eyes.

"I never saw Frank again either," he continued. "Never once. I thought then, that after his trouble with Maddy, he'd maybe gone north for awhile. But now I'm not so sure. You see, we were friends, Frank and me. But I've never heard from him again since that time. Not once. Not in all these years."

I tried to speak, but nothing came.

"Let it go, lady," he said softly. "Don't go up to that north country. You won't find any answers there."

And suddenly my eyes were stinging. I turned and walked blindly toward the door. And blundered into Corey. He was standing in the shadow of the doorway, listening. And from the dazed look of him, I knew he'd been there all along.

# Six
# A New Game

~~~

"Mr. Fereau could be wrong you know," I said. We were headed south in my battered Jeep. I'd used low range 4WD to buck it out of the hole I'd hit at Fereau's. Then we'd driven into Anahwey and given the local sheriff our statements about Boone. Sheriff Feige was honest about it. With six deputies to cover three counties, he didn't expect to run Boone to ground anytime soon. He wasn't worried about Fereau, the old man could handle Boone and five more like him. He suggested we spend the night in Anahwey and have the Jeep repaired in the morning, but I didn't want to wait. I wanted to be gone. So I taped a plastic bag over the shattered rear window and hit the road.

"Wrong about what?" Corey said at last. It was the first thing he'd said since we'd left.

"Fereau could be wrong about seeing my father that fall. It was a long time ago. Maybe he saw someone else."

"I don't think he was wrong," he said in that cooly rational tone of his. "He seems to be pretty good at faces."

"Yes," I admitted. "I guess he is. And he was right about truth, too. Sometimes it's better not to know."

"No," Corey said positively. "I think he was wrong about that part. It's always better to know."

"Why?"

"Because if we don't know about things, then we're stuck with our programs. Like geese."

"What?"

"Geese," he repeated, annoyed. "They know where to fly in the winter when they're born. It's not something they learn in school, you know."

"You've lost me," I said.

"Animals are already programmed to do certain things when they're born, mom, like computers. Geese know where to fly south, salmon can find the streams they were born in, and wolves are always afraid of fire even if they've never seen it before."

"I see," I nodded. "And what are we supposed to be programmed for?"

"Trouble, I guess," he said glumly. "Your mother had trouble with her father. You didn't get along with yours. And here we are again."

"Right," I said. "Here we are." I glanced at him, but he was looking out into the darkness beyond his window. Miles away.

"We're not them, you know," he said at last. "We're smarter."

"Speak for yourself."

"No, we really are," he insisted. "We know what happened to them. That makes a difference."

"Different how?"

"We're not like geese. We can learn."

"Learn what?"

"To coexist, maybe," he said. "Like the Russians and Armenians."

"Armenians? Corey, what—?"

"Suppose I don't go back to boarding school," he said abruptly, swiveling to face me. "If I stay with you, can I have a dog?"

"No," I said.

"I can't have a dog?"

"No. Look, you're my son, and I love you. But we don't seem to get along very well, and after what we've learned today, I'm not even sure we can. Maybe our programs don't match or something. So I want you to stay with me, more than anything. But I won't bribe you to do it. You'll have to make up your own mind. Besides, if you change your mind later, I don't want to be stuck with a dog."

He nodded, digesting that. With icy logic, no doubt. I wondered if I'd ever understand him.

"Okay," he said. "I don't want to go back to boarding school. I want to stay with you. I'll go to school here. If that's all right with you."

"Good," I said. I blinked and the road ahead blurred for a moment. "I'd like that."

"So since I can't have a dog, how about a computer? I'll be able to keep in touch with my friends at school, and if things don't work out, I promise to take it with me if I leave."

I turned to stare at him. If he was kidding, I couldn't read a hint of it on his face. "You're incredible," I said.

"Yeah, I guess I am, sometimes. I wonder where I get that from?"

# SEVEN
# BODYWORK

I WAS in the parking lot of the Crow's Nest the next afternoon, looking over the damage to my Jeep, when a black and white patrol car pulled up and Sheriff Charlie Bauer climbed out. He was in his summer uniform, tan short sleeved shirt and slacks. He's bear-sized, tall with square shoulders, a square face and a viewpoint to match. He sauntered casually around my vehicle, pausing at the smashed rear window, then moved up beside me and touched the dents on the hard top with his fingertips.

"Chain?" he asked. The question seemed matter of fact, but the darkness in his eyes wasn't. Charlie's a friend, one of the first I made when I moved back to my hometown. He was a linebacker in his college days at Michigan State, and he still has a take-no-prisoners attitude when it comes to the safety of his town and his friends.

"A chain with a padlock on it, actually," I said. "The rear window was smashed in with a tire iron."

"Nice fellas," he said. "I got a call from Ernie Feige, the sheriff up at Anahwey. He said that the biker that took the spill . . . Vasco? Is that his name?"

I nodded, swallowing.

"Feige says he's gonna live. He'll be in intensive care for a few more days to be on the safe side, but he's gonna make it. Be awhile before he tries to stomp anybody again, though. They

pinned his left leg together with enough iron to ballast a small
boat."

"Good," I said.

"On which count?" Charlie asked. "That he's gonna live or
that he'll be laid up for awhile?"

"Both. I'm glad he didn't die, but I doubt I'll send him a get-
well card. What about the other one?"

"Your friend Mr. Boone's dropped out of sight. He'd already
cleared out of Mrs. d'Hubert's place when Feige's men got there.
They found a small amphetamine stash in his room, and enough
crank dust scattered around to be fairly sure he took a lot more
with him."

"To where? Do they have any idea?"

"Not yet. Mrs. d'Hubert wasn't much help. Boone apparently slapped her around before he left. Feige said she's terrified
of him and rightly so."

"And what about Corey and me?" I said, facing him directly.
"Should we be terrified?"

"You should be cautious," Charlie nodded. "Boone's got a
record for drugs and violence. He did hard time at Milan for assault. Plus, the methamphetamines he's dealing, crank, the bikers
call it, has some nasty side effects. Paranoia, agitation. Guys who
are relatively level-headed turn violent when they're on it, so God
only knows what it'll do to a scumbag like Boone who's violent to
begin with. How much does this Boone know about you?"

"Nothing. He's been crashing with my grandfather's . . . God,
what do I call her? Common-law wife?"

"That's as good a term as any," Charlie said. "Kind of an odd
situation there. Ernie said your grandfather's apparently been
gone quite a while. It seems the Ojibwa council's been paying
the property taxes on his home for years, and Emma's been signing his social security checks herself. Ernie did a thorough
records check, but came up with zip. Frank d'Hubert's last driver's license lapsed nearly thirty years ago, and he's never renewed a vehicle registration, voted, or done anything Ernie
could find a record of. Emma said he left Anahwey about that
time and she hasn't heard from him since. There's no death notice or anything, but Ernie thinks there's a good chance that
d'Hubert died somewhere up north, maybe in Canada, and sim-

ply wasn't properly identified. John Doe'd as we say in the trade. I'm sorry."

"No need to be. I never met the man and from what I've heard about him he was no great loss."

"Still, he was blood."

"You can't choose your ancestors," I said coolly. "I'm more worried about Boone. The guy's definitely a couple of bricks shy of a load, Charlie. I met him at Frank's place, we had a few words, and the next thing I knew they were trying to run us down on the highway."

"Does he know where you live, or work, anything like that?"

"I don't see how. We didn't spend much time on the social amenities."

"Then you're probably all right. Boone's on the run and doesn't know where you are. It's unlikely he'll cause you any more trouble. He's got a plateful of his own. The only flaw in that theory is, I'm assuming he's operating with a functional brain, and with crankheads that's not a safe bet. You'd best keep an eye out for him, and if you don't mind, you'll be seeing me and my people around a bit more often."

"Why would I mind? I'd appreciate it."

"Good," he said. "I'll keep you posted if I hear any more from Ernie Feige. Let me know if you spot anything odd, anything at all, okay? I'll see you, Mitch."

"Right," I said. He climbed back into his cruiser, fired it up and eased out of the parking lot. I was sorry to see him go. I've often wondered if Charlie might become more than a friend if conditions were right. He's older than I am by a decade plus, but that matters much more to him than to me. Still, there is a tide that carries such things along, and perhaps it had already passed us by. A pity, that. Nice guys are such a rarity in this world. Especially nice guys I like. And vice versa. Just once, I wish something in life could be simple.

# Eight
## School Daze

❧

COREY STARTED school the following Tuesday, a perfect autumn morning, crisp and bright. My heart was brimming as I walked him through the tiled halls of the old middle school I'd attended as a girl. It seemed smaller than I remembered, and a bit run-down, but Corey didn't seem to mind. After I'd gotten him registered, I offered to stay and share lunch with him in the school cafeteria. No chance.

"I'd rather meet people on my own," he said. "It's uncool to have your mom around like you're a little kid. I'll be okay. It's not like I haven't done this before, you know."

I did know. And I was beginning to realize something else as well. That I was going to have to deal with Corey very straightforwardly. Because when it came to gamesmanship, either he had me totally outclassed or he truly didn't care much about my feelings or anyone else's, a thought I found utterly chilling.

As much as I hated the idea, he was beginning to remind me of his father. And I wasn't sure how to deal with that.

Over the years, Corey's asked me about his father, of course. I've always told him the truth, (or as much of it as I thought prudent), in digestible bits and pieces. I've told him that our relationship didn't last long, which is true. I've said that his father knew I was pregnant, but took no responsibility; also true. But

Corey's never heard the term "date rape" from me. Nor did I tell him about the bribe his father offered me to have an abortion. He's too young to deal with those particular truths. Or perhaps I'm too young to tell him. If I make it to ninety, I'll still be too young.

Fortunately, Corey's accepted the orts and torts I've offered him at face value. He's never pressed me for details. At his boarding school, absent fathers were common enough, and in our own case, it was just as well. Personally, I didn't care if I ever saw Jason Devereaux, Corey's father, again. I'd worshipped him when I was a girl. I despise him now, and not just for what he did to me. He's a charming, selfish, soulless sonofabitch.

And Corey? Could I keep him from turning out the same way? Or was it already too late? Had I made some irreversible mistake by being away from him for so long? There was no consolation in telling myself I'd done my best. One of the first lessons you learn in diving deep water is that your best may not be good enough. Anything less can be fatal.

Over the following few weeks Corey seemed to settle in at school, and we adjusted to our new arrangement without any major gripes, though to be fair, Corey isn't much in the complaint department. Silence is his forte.

He's no slouch at electronics, either. We spent several afternoons wading through the options at a local computer mart. Or rather Corey did. I was simply a chaperone, tagging along to make sure he didn't buy every option available. He was remarkably knowledgeable about computers. Even the salesmen were impressed, and not just because he was a kid. He clearly knew what he was talking about and his questions often sent them scurrying to their manuals for answers.

In the end, we bought a 486 unit with a modem and . . . hell, I have no idea what we actually bought, only what it cost. But both Corey and the store's top salesman were satisfied that it was a terrific deal.

We installed it in the sewing room at the cottage, again with Corey in charge. It went together without a hitch and he had it up and running and linked to the Web in a single Saturday afternoon. Which had a dual result of bringing my home into the present century, and making it, in a small way, Corey's home as well.

I'd worried that he might not like my father's old cottage, but he seemed entranced by the place, as I had been when I first came here to live with my father all those years ago. The house doesn't look like much, it's a quaint fieldstone and clapboard cottage built by a smalltime lumber baron in the 1880s. He must have been a solitary soul, because he built the place out on the tip of Ponemah Point, a narrow peninsula that juts out into the vastness of Lake Huron from the southern shore of Thunder Bay.

The cottage is a bit primitive, a two bedroom sprawling misfit of a place. Its walls are lacquered knotty pine and the floors are tongue in groove hardwood. The furniture is oaken, all handcrafted and probably as old as the house. The electricity's supplied by a gas-powered generator in a shed beside the boathouse. The place has fewer amenities than your average army barracks, yet it's oddly comfortable, a snug blend of form and function, a home happy to be what it is, where it is.

It nestles on the shore facing the solitary grandeur of Lake Huron. Some people would find it lonely. It never felt that way to me. Nor to Corey, apparently. He seemed to thrive on the isolation, wandering down to the beach at all hours, to some of the same spots I'd haunted as a girl. The only drawback was that he preferred to visit them on his own; to dream, to brood, or whatever it was he did, alone. I was a little concerned about that. Perhaps I shouldn't have been. I was the same way at his age. Some wolves aren't born to run with a pack, as my father used to say. And he could have written the book on being a wolf.

Another positive indication, I think, was Corey's friendship with Red. When I inherited the Crow's Nest, my father's bar/restaurant/tackle shop on the beach in Huron Harbor, Red was working there. The place was a dive then, but Red pitched in to help me clean it up that first day, and in the year since, we've made it into something quite special, a lakeside bistro with an interesting menu and new deck overlooking the harbor.

Red was my first friend in Huron Harbor, and has grown to be my closest friend in this world. But she's not everyone's cup of tea.

I'm five-nine in stockings, and Red tops me by a full two

inches. She's a big-boned woman with hard eyes, a salty mouth, a mane the color of flame with a temper to match. If Jack Palance had a tough sister, she'd probably look a lot like Red.

She's also a gifted amateur painter, an empathetic bartender, and a lesbian who's not shy about her lifestyle. Why she and my introverted, surly son should have developed such an instant rapport was beyond me but they did. Not just pals, cronies. Go figure.

Corey came to the Nest each day after school. If he had homework, he'd do it in my office. If not, he'd hang around the kitchen chatting with Red. If I asked him to do some little chore, he always complied, though without noticeable enthusiasm. Let Red ask him to do the same thing and he'd hop to it like Billy Budd.

I asked him about it once over dinner at the cottage. He simply shook his head. "Are you kidding, mom? Red's crazy. If I don't do what she says, she'll kill me."

"And that's why you hang around the kitchen? Because you're terrified of her?"

"No, she's interesting. She has some unusual ideas. I didn't meet many people like her at school, you know."

"You won't meet anyone quite like Red anywhere," I said. "She's special. Do you miss being at school?"

"Not so much anymore," he said. "Did you ever read *Coming of Age in Samoa* by Margaret Mead?"

"Um, I think so. In college. Aren't you a little young for that one?"

"Chronologically, maybe. One of the upper classmen had a copy back at boarding school. He only read the funky parts, but I liked the idea of being in a strange culture trying to figure out how everything works. Like an alien or something."

"And that's what you're doing now? Studying a strange culture?"

"You have to admit some of the people in Huron Harbor are a little strange."

"People everywhere seem strange when you're from somewhere else. They'll seem more normal after you get used to them."

"There's a scary thought," he said.

Whether he was joking or not, we really were beginning to adapt to our new situation. I could see it happening. We were slowly working out a *modus vivendi*, and our guards were even coming down a bit.

Or at least mine was. And maybe that was a mistake. I was trying so hard to adjust to the present that it never occurred to me trouble might sneak up on us from the past. From long, long ago.

# NINE
## WILLIAM THE CONQUEROR

❧

IN MID-OCTOBER, a month or so after our return from the
Upper Peninsula, I found a box with UPS markings on the desk
in my office at the Nest. Phoenix Photographic Laboratories? It
took a moment for the return address to register. Photographs.
The snapshots in the box Emma gave me were so badly
gummed together that the local photography shop suggested
sending them to a photo restoration lab in Detroit.

And now they were back. With shaking hands, I lifted the
box as carefully as an unexploded bomb. My first thought was
to rip it open to see if any pictures of my mother were inside.

But I didn't. I'd waited a long time for this. A lifetime, really.
Long enough to know that anticipation might turn out to be the
best part.

Besides, the box wasn't only mine. Any heritage it contained
was Corey's as well. Still, my heart was dancing like a child's the
night before Christmas. I just couldn't help it.

That evening at the cottage, Corey and I carefully peeled the
brown packing tape off the ends of the box. It held a plastic
packet, an invoice and a letter. I hastily scanned the note.

"It says they couldn't save some of the shots, but they were
able to recover eight of the sixteen photographs," I said. "Whoa,
seventy-four bucks?"

"If you don't open those packets right now—"

"Okay, okay," I said. I lifted the cover of the plastic envelope . . . and there she was. A girl of seventeen or so stared at me from a black and white snapshot. Her face was more square than mine, and her eyes were darker and more serious. My mother. Madeline d'Hubert Mitchell.

"Mom? Are you okay?" Corey's voice seemed to come from a great distance. A generation away. I tried to give him a reassuring smile but his face seemed blurred and I realized my eyes were streaming. I eased carefully down into one of the oaken captain's chairs.

"Is this her? Your mother?" Corey asked, gazing intently at the photo. I nodded.

"But there's no name on it and there were two daughters, your mother and another one. Corinne. How do you know this is the one?"

"It's her," I said. "Trust me. This is Madeline. Your grandmother."

"She looks like you," he conceded, still staring into the photograph. "Or you look like her, I guess. But gol, she doesn't look old enough to be anybody's grandmother."

"She's a teenager in this shot. Sixteen or seventeen maybe. She um, she didn't make it to twenty-one, so this picture must have been taken a year or two before . . . everything happened."

"She's pretty," he said, almost to himself. He sounded surprised. He carefully placed the photograph aside. The next few were nondescript shots of a motorboat moored at a dock and a '64 Ford Fairlane apparently taken when it was new. The fourth snap was of the sisters, Madeline and Corrinne, standing arm in arm on the lawn of the house in Anahwey, wearing similar white blouses, dark skirts and matching flowered scarves. Corrinne was an inch or two shorter than Madeline, with a fuller face and riper figure. She was wearing horn-rimmed glasses and a mischievous smile, as though she'd been needling Madeline only a moment before. Thirty years before.

And suddenly I'd had enough. I rose unsteadily and wandered out to the living room. Corey watched me go, but made no comment. Perhaps he had emotions of his own to deal with. I stood at the broad picture window that dominated the room and stared out over the lake, as the dying light turned the swells to copper and then to bronze. But there was no peace for me in the lakescape on this evening.

My breast was a cauldron of emotions: loss and longing and a dozen more I couldn't even put a name to. I'm not sure how long I stood there. Half an hour. Maybe more. When I finally collected myself and glanced around, Corey was missing.

I wandered back to the sewing/computer room and looked in. Corey had the computer on, but he wasn't looking at the screen. He was staring off into space, his brow furrowed in thought.

"Are you okay?" he asked, glancing up at me.

"I guess so. How about you?"

"I'm fine," he said with a small shrug. "It doesn't mean the same thing to me. She wasn't my mother."

"It's not just that," I said. "They were so young. It just seems so . . . sad."

"I guess it does," he said. "Look at this picture." He handed me a snapshot. It was a photo of my father and grandfather, Shan Mitchell and Frank d'Hubert, arm in arm with a third man I didn't recognize. The picture was taken out of doors, the three of them grinning at the camera, dressed in rough work clothing, boots, jeans, and flannel shirts.

"What about it?" I asked.

"They look like they're all best friends, don't they," Corey said. "But it wasn't true. Look how things turned out."

"We don't actually know what happened. And even if things ended badly for them, that doesn't mean they will for us."

"Maybe not," he said, staring somberly at the photograph. "But . . ."

"But what?"

"Let me show you something," he said carefully. "Check this out." He tapped a few keys and the screen filled with a display of multi-colored triangular shields. "Do you know what those are?"

"They're heraldic shields, right?"

"Right. In olden days, knights could tell where a guy was from and who his family was by the marks on his shield. That one in the top row with the X on it is Scottish, it's called a saltire.

This one with the wavy line . . . I forget what it's called but it means something. All these insignias mean something."

"So they could identify each other in battle," I said.

"Or any other time," Corey nodded. "Look at this one, with the black diagonal bar. Know what it means?"

I shook my head.

"Bastard," he said calmly. "If I had a shield, it would have that bar on it."

I didn't say anything. Couldn't. I was stunned, as though he'd slapped me. "These aren't the Middle Ages," I said, trying to keep my tone level. "That word isn't commonly used in polite society anymore. And I would prefer that you not use it with me."

"I didn't mean to offend you—"

"Didn't you?"

"No, really I didn't. I read about this stuff back at school, you know, the Norman invasion? And I decided that being a— that being like William the Conqueror wasn't so bad. He was one, you know. A b-word. It didn't slow him down much. He conquered England. In a way, it makes life simpler."

"Simpler?"

"Sure. I'm not real good with people anyway. Coping with you is tough enough sometimes. I don't know how anybody handles having two parents."

"Some of them muddle through. And you still haven't told me what's bugging you."

"It's a little complicated," he said slowly. "It's . . . what happened up north mixed up with all this." He gestured toward the screen.

"What about it?"

"That old Indian guy, Fereau? He said he thought your father killed your grandfather Frank, right?"

"That's not exactly what he said," I objected.

"C'mon, Mom, he hinted at it real strong. That's what he thinks happened, isn't it?"

"Yes," I admitted. "I guess that's what he thinks."

"What do you think?"

"I honestly don't know. My father had a spectacular temper,

especially when he was drinking and sometimes when he wasn't."

"And he was just back from a war then," Corey prompted.

"True. And he never talked about my mother. I thought it was because her memory was painful, but maybe there was more to it. But what Fereau was talking about, hunting someone down in cold blood to kill them, I don't believe my father was capable of something like that."

"Murder, you mean. Or can't I use that word either?"

"You can use it, but that doesn't make it true. And Fereau doesn't actually know what happened."

"But neither do we," Corey pressed. "And we should, you know? A thing like that, a murder in our own family, wouldn't you like to know if it's true?"

"Why? What difference does it make now?"

"Because it would be a place to start from," Corey said simply. "Those old knights, you could tell everything about them just by looking at their shields, where they were from, what church they belonged to, even whether their parents were married or not. But us? We don't even know a basic thing like whether your dad killed somebody or not."

"*If* anything actually happened, it was over long ago. They're both dead."

"But that's just it, we don't even know that. If Fereau is wrong, your grandfather could still be alive."

"From what Charlie tells me, that's unlikely. Why is this so important to you?"

"I don't know. It just is. It's like . . . we make an awfully short family tree, you and I. And that's okay," he added hastily, "it's not like I'm hoping you'll get married or anything. But since we have such a small family, I'd like to know as much about it as I can. Maybe so I'll understand myself a little better. Does that make any sense to you? Or am I just being weird, as usual?"

"Yes and no. Yes it makes sense and no, you're not weird. You'd have to be an eggplant not to be curious about it. I've wondered too. But I'm not sure how much we can find out now."

"Maybe more than you think," he said cautiously. "If you look at this picture, there's a sign in the background. Kewadin d-r-i-. The last few letters are blocked out by the blonde guy's head. Drive, maybe?"

"Drift, more likely. That's what they called the ore."

"Okay, Kewadin Drift then. Do you think we could find it?"

"Possibly," I said. "But why would it matter? It was just a job they worked on together. Nothing ever came of it, or at least that's what Emma said."

"That's right. And that's kind of the point if you think about it. Because if your father really did . . . do Frank in, then that's probably where he put him."

"In the mine?" I said, surprised. "Why would you think that? The Upper Peninsula's a big place. He could be anywhere."

"No, Emma said Frank was hired as a guide," Corey said patiently. "The mine was in the boondocks and your dad and the other guy didn't know the area. And Shan was a diver, like you. So, let's say he was angry enough after what happened to your mom to go up there to get even. It wouldn't have been logical for him to bury a body in the ground where animals could dig it up or people could stumble over it. Not when he could hide it down an old, flooded mine so deep that nobody would ever find it. Except maybe you."

"Maybe not even me," I said. "Besides, all this is just guesswork. Don't get me wrong, I'm not faulting your logic. What you've said makes sense as far as it goes, but we don't actually know that there's anything down that mine."

"No, we don't. That's my point, Mom. We don't know. And there's no one we can ask. If we want to find out, we'll have to do it ourselves."

"You mean by checking out the mine? It might not be that simple, sport. For openers, we'd have to find it, and. . . ."

I let my objections die a natural death. Corey's eyes were getting that guarded look, the one he'd worn home from Europe. I sensed I was dealing with more than I was aware of. I often have that feeling with Corey. Maybe I always will.

"On the other hand, we're reasonably clever folks," I continued. "There must be records of old mines somewhere. If your grandfather found the place, I don't see why we can't."

"Do you mean it?"

"We can try, sure. And if we find it, we'll check it out. With luck, it'll be empty as a pol's promise. Either way, we'll know more than we do now, and if this is important to you, then it's important to me. We'll have to get cracking, though, if we want to do it this year. Snow comes early in the U.P."

He hesitated, as though he was marshaling another argument. It took a moment for him to realize that he'd won. "*Tres cool*," was all he said, and his tone was doubtful, as though he expected me to change my mind. I wish to God I had.

# TEN

## NORTH TO THE DRIFT

❧

IT TOOK Corey all of three days to track down the Kewadin Drift. "I copied this in the main library downtown," he explained, spreading a sheaf of papers out on my desk at the Nest after school. "This is a plat map of Copper County, 1891. The mine's located in the northeast corner a mile inland from the Lake Superior shore."

"We've been through that area," I said. "Or near it, anyway. On our way to the Shipwreck Museum at Whitefish Point, remember? There wasn't much out there."

"Does that matter?"

"It might even be better," I said. "Maybe we can sneak in and look things over without bothering anybody."

"Sneak?" he echoed.

"Corey, for openers, the mine may not be there anymore. For all we know it's caved in or someone could have built a ski resort on top of it. We'll have to find it first, then, if I think the dive is possible, we'll try to get permission from the owners."

"But . . . you're still willing to try?"

"Wild horses couldn't stop us now," I said, tousling his hair. "This is gonna be fun."

We planned the trip as a camping weekend. October's a slow season at the Nest. The cook and waitresses could cope for a day or two without me. I hoped. Red volunteered her pickup truck to haul the lot of us and agreed to come along to help with the gear, for which I was doubly grateful. A dual set of diving tanks weighs over a hundred pounds, plus we had a tent, Coleman stove, sleeping bags, and munchies.

We left after school on Friday afternoon, headed north on U.S. 23 along the Huron lakeshore. I'd helped Corey pick out some new clothes for the trip, but somehow his rough country ensemble seemed out of sync. He was decked out in brand new Red Wing hiking boots, tan chinos, and a loden-green chamois shirt. He'd carefully hung the chinos to retain their knife-edge crease and he kept his shirt buttoned to the throat. With his wire-rimmed glasses and his hair neatly combed, he looked like a poster child for nerds, an owl in wolf's clothing. And he looked so young and vulnerable that he melted my heart. And I wondered how well he was really doing at school socially, whether he was making any friends.

I tried to probe a little on the drive north, but Red and Corey were more interested in the scenery than in talking about school. I didn't blame them. U.S. 23 is a gorgeous stretch of highway, especially in the fall, with the silver and gray waters of Lake Huron glittering in the afternoon sun and the gentle, forested hills of the mitten top dozing in their autumn shawls of red and gold and ochre.

I first came to this part of the state when I was thirteen. I was brought up in Detroit by my grandmother Mitchell, my dad's mom, a terrific lady who gradually drifted away from me into the shadows of Alzheimer's disease. In the end, my father brought me north to Huron Harbor to live with him. Or work for him, to be more accurate. He'd been living alone before I came, though he hadn't been lonely. A series of interchangeable women drifted in and out of his life like clouds, with roughly the same degree of emotional attachment for him.

I suppose he wasn't much of a father by modern standards. He was a hard man whose life hadn't prepared him for parenting. He took care of me, though, and took the time to teach me his trade, diving.

If he loved me, he never actually said so, but perhaps he just wasn't good at showing affection. Most men aren't. Nor most women, for that matter.

It's fashionable nowadays to blame your parents' flaws for all of the problems in your life. I could never afford that luxury. I was too busy scrambling to support my son and myself. And since my father gave me the means to do so, I could hardly resent him for coming up a tad short in the emotional support department.

I've decided he did the best he could, given the times and the man he was. So maybe he wasn't a world-class parent. Most days, I'm not sure my personal best is so much better.

We drove over the Mackinac Bridge just as the sun was beginning to melt into Lake Michigan, turning the dark water to brass. The glow flickered through the cables and struts like a deranged strobe light. Quite an achievement, the Big Mac: a four lane highway suspended more than five hundred feet above the Mackinac Straits; an engineer's fantasy realized in steel and concrete and blood.

Suicides rarely jump from the Big Mac. Maybe the drop is just too intimidating, but more likely they simply change their minds. You'd have to be in the grip of one helluva dark muse to gaze across the miles of tousled whitecaps and taste the tang of a Canadian breeze and still want to toss your life away like a gum wrapper.

We stopped for a quick dinner in St. Ignace on the north side of the Straits, settling for soup and a sandwich at a Hardee's. When I was a kid, there were all sorts of neat mom-and-pop diners in the U.P. but they're mostly chained out now, by the likes of McDonald's and Burger Doodle. And by people like me who claim to like the ambience of small places but opt for fast food convenience. If we aren't careful, we're going to get the kind of world we deserve.

We stepped out of the restaurant into the teeth of a sudden gusty rain squall that had blown in off Lake Michigan all the way from Chicago from the feel of it. We sprinted for the pickup and scrambled inside, grinning.

"So whaddya think, gang," I said. "Do we find a nice isolated campground and pitch our tent in the eye of the hurricane like voyageurs?"

"I vote for a Holiday Inn with cable TV," Corey said. "The voyageurs would've gone for that if they'd had them in those days."

"Let's split the difference," Red said, firing up the truck. "We'll push on for awhile, camp if it quits raining and take pot luck on the road if it doesn't. That'll give us more time for the hunt tomorrow."

She goosed the pickup out of the Hardee's parking lot and headed west on U.S. 2. It wasn't the most direct route, but the lakeshore highway is one of the loveliest drives on the planet. Even Corey couldn't watch the last of the light winking at us through the storm clouds over Beaver Island without commenting.

"Cool sunset," was all he said, but considering his mood on our first foray here, I took it as a good sign.

We swung north on 117. The route took us well to the west of Anahwey, which was fine by me. I had no desire to run into Boone or his friends again, accidentally or otherwise.

We wound up crashing at a small motel on the outskirts of Newberry. It was a motley collection of tiny concrete-block cottages, but we were groggy, and in the Upper Peninsula you take what you can get. The population's so sparse that there's no guarantee you'll find basic amenities like motels or even gas stations on any given road. Assuming there is a road headed in the direction you want to go.

We were up at sunrise, scarfed a quick breakfast, then pushed on to the northwest, toward the Two Hearted River country. The driving gradually got rougher as the roads changed from narrow, two lane blacktops to gravel roads with no shoulders and then to dirt roads that were barely more than trails.

As we meandered through the outback, there were no road signs or any other indications that human beings had more than a passing acquaintance with the area.

Still, Corey kept us on track, reading the county map like a pro. And in the end a track is all it was, a narrow red dirt road that looked like it was designed for covered wagons. Or maybe chariots. There was an unmarked fork ahead, and I pulled over and stopped.

"Break time," I said. "Are we lost?"

"I don't think so," Corey said, scowling at the map. "If I'm reading this right, the road back to the mine is four or five miles ahead if we take the west fork. We can get there by taking the other fork, the one to the north, but I'm not sure we can get back to the mine that way. What's this line stand for?"

"Some kind of a trail," I said, scanning the map. "It's probably an old railroad grade. The miners built narrow-gauge railroads to haul the ore down to the lakeshore and then freighted it out by boat from there. I doubt there are any rails left on it, they usually ripped them up when they pulled out."

"So maybe we can drive on it? It looks shorter."

"Not in my truck, buster," Red put in. "The roads up here are bad enough without giving 'em up altogether. Let's try the other way first."

I revved the truck back on the road, keeping the speed low. This was rough country, low hills covered with scrub brush, tag alders, and stunted jack pines. It would be easy to miss the trail we were seeking, assuming it was still visible at all. But finding the trail proved to be the least of our problems. After a mile or so we began to see warning signs, foot-long pieces of yellow aluminum siding nailed to trees or stumps at regular intervals along the road, with "private keep out" hand-painted on them in crude black letters. I hoped they'd peter out before we got to the mine area, but when we finally found the trail, a steel cable was stretched across it, padlocked to a tree on either side, with one of the warning signs wired to it.

"Terrific," Red said, as I eased the truck to a halt.

"You could drive around it," Corey said. "There's plenty of room."

"We could also get arrested for trespassing," I said. "We'll just have to drive to the county seat, check the record books and find out who owns the mine now. Maybe we can get permission to explore it," I said, climbing out of the truck and stretching. Red and Corey followed suit, but instead of limbering up, Corey trotted over to the warning sign for a closer look.

"What does this 3CM painted in the lower corner of the signs stand for?" Corey asked.

"I don't know," I said, joining him. "Maybe they're the owner's initials."

"A guy named Three?" Red said. "Not likely."

"Hey, we're in the U.P. now, remember?" I said. "Not everybody up here's named Sven or Stosh."

A shot cracked in the distance and we both jumped. Three more shots followed, much closer.

"What was that?" Corey asked, his eyes wide.

"Gunfire," I said, scanning the forest. "It's small game season up here."

"What are they hunting? Us?"

"No," I said. "Those shots sounded a lot closer than they were. Sound carries a long way in the woods."

"So do bullets," Red said. "Let's move on."

We walked back to the pickup and climbed in. "What's the nearest town of any size?" I asked, dropping the truck into reverse and backing out.

"The only town is Grand Portal," Corey said, checking the map. "It's about ten miles up this road to a state road, then turn left."

"I hope it's big enough to have a restaurant," I said. "I'm hungry enough to eat a bear."

"From the looks of this neighborhood, I'll bet bear's on the menu," Red said. "Probably with a choice of Kodiak, black, or grizzly."

# ELEVEN
# GRAND PORTAL

AFTER A half-hour drive through the backwoods, we came to a state road along the lake shore. We turned west and followed the coastline for several miles through rolling, forested hills. The trees, mostly jack pine and ash, were stunted, with skeletal branches and gnarled trunks, sculpted by fierce Canadian gales off the lake and by the winter ice.

Grand Portal took me by surprise. We crested a hill, and there it was, laid out below us in a cove on the Lake Superior shore, sleeping in the sunlight like Brigadoon. It was larger than I'd expected, population two thousand one hundred and twelve, or so the village limit sign claimed, a metropolis by Upper Peninsula standards.

The business district was only a couple of blocks long, mostly mom-and-pop shops, a drugstore, a couple of antique shops. The only municipal building was a turn-of-the-century brick courthouse and town hall, which I noted for future reference. Our search for information could wait. Lunch had priority.

Some of the homes near the town center were surprisingly sumptuous, legacies of the lumber baron days. One of them, a white clapboard three story palace complete with turrets and gables, had been converted to an inn/restaurant, which unfortunately wouldn't open until four-thirty. We had better luck on the outskirts of town. A roadside diner called Fat Annie's was not only open, it looked like half the folks in town were crammed inside.

The ambience was basic roadhouse, a long dining counter of turquoise Formica from the days when cars had fins. The booths along the windows were rough pine, occupied by men in various combinations of hunting clothing, though there were quite a few women as well, similarly dressed.

Our little trio took the last empty stools at the end of the counter near the door. A harried waitress in a pink gingham uniform parked water glasses in front of us before we'd even found the menus.

"Hi," she said brightly, "are you ready to order?"

"Do you have pasties?" Red asked.

"Does the pope wear red shoes?" she said. "Five flavors, beef, pork, venison, chicken, and vegetarian. Personally, I'd rather eat roadkill, but some folks like 'em. Which'll it be?"

"I'll have the vegetarian," I said. "Corey?"

"Beef, please," he said. "Do you have chocolate milk?"

"Not ready made, but I can whip you up some in two shakes of a lamb's tail," the girl answered. "Anything else?"

"We saw some signs that said 3CM on them," Corey said. "Do you know what that stands for?"

The girl eyed him oddly for a moment, then shrugged. "The Third Coasters," she said. "They've got a chapter here in town."

"A chapter?" I echoed.

"Chapter, unit, whatever they call it. They're a militia group, you know? Weekend warriors? Guns and uniforms and stuff? What'll you have, ma'am?"

"Just coffee and a donut," Red said. "Do you know how we could get in touch with them?"

"The Thirds? Why? Are you guys reporters or something?" she said, glancing curiously at Corey.

"No, we saw some property I'm . . . interested in," I said. "It was posted with 3CM signs."

"Yeah, well, if the signs said keep out, you'd best believe 'em, honey. Them ol' boys do a lot of shootin', at targets and whatever else. If you wanna talk to somebody, go back through town, turn right at the light and drive till you see a blue house with a whole lot of flags in the yard. You can't miss it. That's Dan

Cezak's place. He's some kind of honcho with the Thirds. Be sure to call him major. He likes that. Be back with your eats in a jif."

"Thanks," I said as she bustled off. "For everything."

"Guns and uniforms and stuff?" Corey said.

# TWELVE
# THE THIRDS

ANYTIME SOMEONE tells me "you can't miss it," I cringe. I usually can, and do. Not this time. A myopic bat could have found the place by the sound of the flags flapping in the breeze. An American flag, a Michigan state flag, a rattlesnake "don't tread on me" flag, a black POW/MIA flag, and a red, white, and blue tricolor with 3cm sewn on it.

The house wasn't particularly imposing. It was set well off the road on a large, fenced lot, a split-level ranch-style home with a brick facade. Except for the flags and the barbed wire that topped the six-foot chain link fence around the grounds, the house looked typically suburban. Strawberry Fields Forever.

A pickup truck and a couple of Chevy Blazers were parked in front of the garage. All three vehicles were decked out in military camouflage paint, swirls of black and dun and olive drab. They looked official, but instead of having US Army stenciled on the doors they had the Third Coast Militia logo.

"What do you think?" I asked.

"Chic, if you're a Banana Republican," Red observed. "It doesn't look particularly threatening. This is a mom and pop neighborhood, not the *Riechstag*. Still, maybe Corey should wait here."

"Not a chance," Corey said, scrambling out. "What's more American than militias? Come on."

The front door opened as we followed Corey up the walk and a man stepped out. He was my height, five-nine or so, but he was carrying about forty more pounds of solid muscle from the look of him. He had a lean face with hawk's eyes and brows, not unfriendly, but wary. He was wearing loose-fitting, military surplus duds, an olive drab jacket and fatigue pants. Half the mail order catalogs I get carry pre-stressed clothing styles along these lines, but I had the feeling this guy's clothes were the real thing.

"Can I help you folks?" He had a faint accent, southern, maybe.

"I hope so," I said, trying my best disarming smile. "I'm Michelle Mitchell, this is Miss Clements and my son Corey. We'd like to see Major Cezak."

"Are you a reporter, ma'am?" he asked, his tone neutral. "If so, I can save you a trip. He's not talking to the press anymore. Period."

"I'm not a reporter, but you're the second person who's asked me that. What's the deal?"

"We attract a lot of press people," he said with a shrug. "Mostly dweebs with an attitude. Their stories are written before they get here, they only talk to us so they can say they did some research for the hatchet jobs they do on the unit, so we voted to quit talking to 'em."

"I'm not a reporter," I repeated. "I don't even know any reporters. I'm here on business, and I'd like to see Major Cezak. If that's okay with you, Mr . . . ?"

"Thorp, ma'am," he said, stepping aside. "Jack Thorp. Excuse my manners, come on in."

"Just Jack?" Red asked. "Not major or general or something?"

Corey gave Red an elbow in the hip but Thorp smiled.

"No, ma'am," he said easily. "I was a lieutenant once, but that was a while back."

We stepped in, and I stopped in surprise. It was all one gigantic room. Every wall in the house had been knocked out, leaving only steel jackposts to support the roof. The floors were hardwood, gleaming with wax. The place looked more like a union hall than a private home, except for the long gun rack on the opposite wall. It held at least twenty weapons, all military style. A dais dominated the far end of the room, facing rows of folding chairs, forty or so, at a quick guess. There was a plain metal desk in the corner, gun metal gray. A lanky older man was seated at it, fifty-ish, with a round face, a fringe of steel gray hair and a neatly trimmed gray beard, worn very short. He was wearing an Ike jacket with a major's brass insignia on it over a plaid flannel shirt.

He was talking with a second man, ferret gaunt, and dressed in an immaculate black battle fatigue uniform and gleaming, spit-shined combat boots. There were captain's bars on his collar and the metal tag over the front pocket said Pettiford. His dishwater blond hair was bootcamp short, but somehow his bearing wasn't military: too edgy, more a zealot than a soldier.

Pettiford eyed us suspiciously as we approached. And then Corey stepped past me, snapped to attention, and rendered a perfect salute. I was startled, but the major rose stiffly and returned it with a smile as though it was the most natural thing in the world.

"Ladies," he nodded to Red and me. "I'm Major Dan Cezak, Third Coast Militia. What can we do for you folks?"

"I'm Michelle Mitchell," I said, offering my hand. "This is my son Corey, and my friend, Miss Clements. Actually, we're looking for information, Major. I understand your organization owns a tract of land about fifteen miles east of town, near the lake?"

Cezak glanced a question at Thorp. "She's not a reporter," Thorp said. "Or at least, so she said."

"The Third Coast has some property there, yes," Cezak acknowledged. "What about it?"

"There's an abandoned copper mine on it," I said, "in the high country near the shore. It was called the Kewadin Drift. I'm hoping to get permission to explore it."

"There's nothing to explore, lady," Pettiford said. "The whole damned thing's under water."

"I'm aware of that," I said. "My father did some diving at the mine back in the sixties."

"Right after he came back from Vietnam," Corey put in.

"Your dad's a vet?" Cezak asked, raising an eyebrow.

"Was," I corrected. "He's gone now."

"I'm sorry," Cezak nodded. "Of natural causes?"

"No," I said surprised at the question. "He was killed in an auto accident. Why?"

"Nowadays when a vet dies of natural causes, it's news, or it oughta be," Cezak said. "We've got a higher death rate than any population bloc except ghetto punks. I'm sorry about your dad, but I'm not sure I can help you. Do you know anything about this mine, Jack?"

"Not much," Thorp said. "Harlan's right, there's nothing to see. Just a scummy pond that stinks to high hell at the far end of the firing range. We've been using the high ground there as a backstop."

"The stench would be from hydrogen sulfide," I said. "It leeches out of the rock formations when they're disturbed. It wouldn't affect the dive one way or the other."

Cezak eyed me for a moment, frankly appraising me. There was nothing prurient in the look. Strictly man to man. Or something like that. "Dive?" he echoed. "You're saying you want to scuba dive the mine?"

"That's right, I've—"

"You've got to be kidding," Pettiford snapped, cutting me off. "There's nothing to see, it's just a hole in the ground. If we wanted to look at it, we'd do it on our own. Diving an old mine like that's no job for a woman anyway."

"Really?" I said. "Are you a diver?"

"I've gotten wet a few times," he said smugly. "I had the basic military course."

"Then you'll know what this is," I said, fumbling in my shoulder bag. I came up with a small plastic packet and handed it to Cezak. "This is my diver's passport. My certification number is on the first page, the rest is a log of the work I've done in the past three years. As you can see, a year ago I logged nearly six hundred hours in deep water. I was working maintenance at the time, on an oil rig in the Texas Gulf."

"Maintenance?" Pettifod snorted. "They don't hire women for jobs like that."

"You're right, sport, they don't," I said, turning to face him. "They hire divers who can do the work. Some are men, some are women, but none of them are tadpoles who've 'gotten wet a few times.' Any more questions?"

"I have a few," Cezak said, smiling at Harlan's confusion. "You said you were diving a year ago. What do you do for a living now, Mrs. Mitchell?"

"I own a restaurant with a diving shop attached down in Huron Harbor. It's called the Crow's Nest."

"I see," he nodded. "So, you're kind of an amateur explorer, something like that?"

"I don't do it for money, if that's what you mean, but I'm no amateur. I worked as a professional diver for nearly ten years. I know my business, Major. I'll be happy to sign any liability releases you think necessary."

"I don't think we'll worry much about releases. If you're talkin' about diving down a hole in a mountain you either know what you're doing or you're a section eight, miss, and you don't strike me that way."

"You claim you're some kind of pro diver," Pettiford said. "Where'd you get your training? In the military? Or maybe some kind of government program? Or police work?"

"I was trained by my father," I said. "I was never in the navy and the only police work I've done was to dive for bodies once or twice."

"And where was that?"

"Once in Texas. A child drowned near the mouth of the Rio Grande and all the divers from the oil platforms volunteered to help search. I've gone down after bodies twice for the local sheriff's department since I moved back to Huron Harbor."

"So you and the local sheriff must have a solid working relationship," Pettiford pressed. "Pretty good friends, are you?"

"He'll vouch for my credentials if that's what you're asking," I acknowledged, wondering what the hell he was getting at. "Give him a call if you like. He's in the book."

"I'm sure he is, ma'am," Pettiford said. "And what do you expect to find in this mine?"

"I don't actually know," I said carefully. "Mostly I'd just like to explore it and take photographs."

"And perhaps recover some artifacts?" Pettiford said, glancing sharply at Cezak.

"I doubt that are many artifacts down there," I said. "The miners stripped the sites pretty thoroughly when they left."

"Of things that were of value to them," Pettiford said, confident again. "But that was a hundred years ago, right? Who knows what some bureaucrat might decide is valuable now? Major, there's no way we can let her do this."

"Why not?" I said. "What harm could there be?"

"Oh, I think you know very well what harm you could do, lady. Whatever you saw, or claimed that you saw, could be used by the feds to declare the area some kind of historic site. Which would give them a legal rationale for seizing the land and evicting us."

Pettiford's tone was so level, so rational, that for a moment, what he was saying almost made sense. Almost. "Let me get this straight," I said carefully. "You think we're . . . *agents provocateurs* or something who're plotting to steal your land?"

"No one's saying that," Major Cezak said, "but Harlan has a point. We can't give the federal government the smallest window of opportunity. I'm afraid our answer will have to be no."

"Look, Mister Cezak, I don't know anything about your politics. I never heard of your organization until about an hour ago and. . . ." I shook my head. I could see from his expression that I was talking to a wall. End of discussion. Damn. I took a deep breath, getting a handle on my anger. "But of course, that's what I would say, isn't it?" I continued, "If we really were . . . government spies sent to sabotage your little boys club."

"Nobody's said anything about spies but you," Harlan put in. "It's an idea, though, Major. Two women and a kid? It's the kind of cover the Feds might go for."

"Feds?" Red echoed, not bothering to conceal her disbelief. "Are you on furlough from a funny farm or something? Good grief, where do you people come from?"

"From America," Cezak said evenly. "The same country you do. We just see its problems differently. We try to live as far from the central government as we can, here and in Idaho, and Montana, but we know they'll come for us eventually. The way they did Randy Weaver and Koresh and the Freemen. I mean no offense, ladies, you're probably exactly what you claim to be, but

Captain Pettiford's right, we can't take the risk, you see. My decision stands, Miz Mitchell. I'm sorry."

"In fact, you'd better head back where you came from," Harlan added. "Winter's coming and the U.P.'s no place for tourists when the snow flies. You could get buried here."

"Put a cork in it, Harlan," Thorp said. "No need to get pushy."

"Maybe it's time we did get pushy," Pettiford said, wheeling on Thorpe. "If some of us had more fire in their bellies—"

"That's enough, gentlemen," Cezak snapped. "Ladies, if you'll excuse us, we have other business. Jack, see them out, please."

"Oh, we can probably manage to find the door, kind sir," Red said sweetly. "We're not nearly as helpless as we look."

"It was nice meeting you, sir," Corey said, snapping to and giving the Major another salute. Then he did a neat about face and walked out. Red and I exchanged a glance and followed. For a moment I considered goose-stepping, but decided against it. I was afraid they'd ask me to enlist.

# Thirteen
## The Mercenary

❧

"Nice job, guys," Corey said, when we were safely back in the pickup. "Are you planning to be politicians when you grow up?"

"I am grown up," I snapped, pulling out of the driveway. "Well, sort of, anyway." I shot him a death-ray glare, and realized he was grinning. As wide a smile as I've ever seen.

"Your little boys club," he said, mimicking me perfectly. "Jeez, Mom, way to go." And then he burst out laughing, and then we all were, whooping and guffawing until the tears came. I nearly had to pull over to the side of the road to keep from piling us into the ditch.

Fortunately, there wasn't much traffic; in fact, the streets of Grand Portal looked remarkably quiet considering that a junior-league Fourth Reich or something like it was cooking just down the block.

"By the way, where did you learn to salute like that?" I managed at last.

"Saturdays they had an ROTC prep class at school," Corey said, with a trace of his usual wariness returning. "I was a squad leader."

"A squad leader," I echoed, surprised. "I don't remember signing you up for anything like that."

"It was an optional class," Corey said. "It was part of the phys ed class, you know, marching and stuff."

"And you were . . . interested in all that?"

"Not so much," Corey said carefully. "I was good at it, though. I'm not big enough for football or basketball, but I can run a long time and stand up straight and salute. It's nice to be good at something, even if it's just marching around a dumb gym."

"But you must have been doing this for awhile, why didn't you tell me about it?"

"I wasn't sure how you'd feel about it. Your dad was a soldier, and I know he was in Vietnam. But you've never said anything about it."

"I don't know much," I said. "He never talked about it. Or at least, not to me. If it came up, he'd always change the subject."

"A rare thing," Red put in, "because your grandfather could shoot the breeze about any subject on the planet. A master storyteller."

"A liar, you mean?" Corey asked.

"That isn't what she meant, but he was no slouch in that department either," I admitted. "He could tell you a fib you'd swear was true, or tell you the truth so that you'd never believe it. A rare talent. One I didn't inherit, unfortunately."

"Maybe it skips a generation," Red said. "If Corey inherits it, God help us."

"We might need help sooner than you think," Corey said quietly. "You know those weird looking army trucks that were parked back at the Third's place? I think one of 'em is behind us."

"Where?" I said, checking my mirrors, but I spotted it even as I spoke. One of the camouflaged Blazers was trailing us, a few blocks back. "Maybe the Major takes this 'get out of Dodge' stuff seriously," I said.

"Or that other creep does," Red said. "What do we do?"

"Probably just a coincidence," I said, picking up speed. "Maybe he just happens to be going in the same direction." I made a quick right turn at the town's only stoplight.

"He's staying with us," Red observed, "and picking up speed to do it."

"Well, if we're going to have a problem, let's make it as public as possible," I said. "Anybody hungry but me?"

"We just had lunch," Corey said.

"That was days ago," Red said, as I pulled into Fat Annie's parking lot and screeched to a halt. "Personally, I could eat an iguana. C'mon, sport, it's feeding time."

We piled out and hurried inside. The diner had emptied a bit since we'd been there earlier, but it was still three quarters full. I left Corey with Red at the counter, then stalked back out to the parking lot as the camouflaged Blazer pulled in.

It parked near Red's pickup and the driver climbed out. Jack Thorpe. "Hi," he said raising both hands, palms up. "Peace, lady, okay? I'm not looking for any problems."

"Aren't you? Are you following us?"

"Yes, ma'am, I certainly am. I'd like to talk to you for a minute if I could. Suppose I buy you lunch? How does that sound?"

"We can buy our own lunch. Besides, aren't you guys supposed to chew C-rations or tree bark or something?"

"Touché. Look, I really don't mean any harm, scout's honor. In fact, I'm here to help if I can."

"Help how?"

"It's a little breezy out here and I've got thin blood," he said. "Why don't we find a nice booth inside? If you don't like what I've got to say, tell me to take a hike and I will. My word as a gentleman. Okay?"

I hesitated. If he wanted trouble, then we were better off inside the diner. And he didn't look all that dangerous. In fact, in the right light and minus the paramilitary duds, he'd be almost presentable.

"I suppose it can't hurt to listen," I said.

He followed me into the diner, then led the way to a booth toward the rear of the place, away from the front windows. Red and Corey slid in beside me a moment later.

"All right," I said. "We're listening, what's on your mind, Mr. Thorpe?"

"Actually, I'm more interested in what's on your mind, ma'am."

"What do you mean?"

"It's just that you didn't look particularly discouraged when you left headquarters. I thought you might still have some idea about snooping around that mine you asked about."

"And you're going to break my legs or something if I do?"

"No, ma'am, not at all. Tactical assistance is my business, and I thought maybe I could offer you some."

"What kind of assistance?" Red asked.

"Advice, for openers. Messing around on the Third's land on your own would be a mistake. Nobody'd harm you intentionally but there are war games and guns going off out there at all hours and some of those boys aren't real accurate. Plus we've got a few flakes like Harlan, you know?"

"What's his story?" Red asked.

"Ex-army, got booted for white supremacist activity. A real prize," Thorp said with a shrug. "Point is, being on the tract without permission isn't safe."

"Didn't your boss—excuse me—your commanding officer, just give us this speech," Red asked.

"Sure, but the key phrase is, without permission. There may be a way to get what you want. If what you want to see is the mine."

"We're not interested enough to get shot over it."

"There's no need to. You see, the Third Coasters don't actually own that tract. They lease it for chump change from the Outreach people."

"The what?"

"Amerasian Outreach. They sponsor immigrant kids from Southeast Asia, American fathers, Asian mothers, orphans, whatever. They run a kind of prep school west of town here."

"Sounds like a good cause. What's the connection between them and your amateur army?"

"None, except that they own the four hundred acre stretch you're interested in. Unimproved hunting land's a drug on the market up here and the tract the Third Coasters hold isn't even good for hunting. There's no game in the area because of the smell from the mine. What did you say it was?"

"Hydrogen sulfide," I said. "It's harmless, though the animals may not think so. So what are you saying? That if I talk to these . . . Outreach people, they might give me permission to look at the mine? Whether the Thirds approve or not?"

"It can't hurt to ask. The Thirds got a real sweetheart deal on their lease. If the Outreach people give you an okay, I doubt the Major will buck 'em over it. He can't afford to tick 'em off."

"I see," I said thoughtfully, reading his face. It wasn't a bad face, not conventionally handsome, but strong. A bit weather-beaten around the eyes, as though he'd spent a lot of time out-doors. There's no justice. Women and men seem to age at different rates. Maybe that's why some men never grow up. They have so much farther to go.

"What are you doing with an outfit like the Thirds?" Red asked. "You're not from around here."

"No, ma'am, southern Missouri, originally. Little town called Reynolds. I'm a soldier. Did a couple of hitches with the army, one of 'em in Panama. Operation Just Cause. Remember that one? Killed fifty Americans and a thousand Panamanians and everybody forgot about it before lunch. After that I got out, stayed on in Panama awhile, trying to help clean up some of the mess we made."

"As a mercenary, you mean?" Corey asked.

"More like a substitute teacher, son. I helped train the Panamanian police force. When that job ended I bounced around some. When I heard the Thirds were hiring training officers, well, there aren't many jobs in my line of work. So here I am."

"Isn't it a bit like a pro ball player being sent down to the minors?" I asked.

Surprisingly, he smiled. "Yeah," he said ruefully, "in some ways that's exactly what it's like. But all kidding aside, I've got no beef with the Thirds. They're good people for the most part, and they're sincere in what they believe."

"From what I've read, Hitler was sincere," I said.

"They're not that bad," he said. "Some of their ideas may sound a little off base to you, but I'm sure the local Tories thought the same thing about the farmers who fought their own government at Bunker Hill. You don't have to be political to realize the country we have today isn't anything like what those first rebels had in mind."

"And that makes your Major Cezak the next George Washington?" Red countered.

"That's a bit of a reach," Thorp admitted, unfazed. "On the other hand, who would've thought the FBI would use a tank against a church compound at Waco and burn American women and kids alive? The Third Coasters may be paranoid but that doesn't make 'em altogether wrong."

"I think we can agree to disagree on that," I said. "I'm not prepped to debate it. So whom should I contact at this Outreach outfit?"

"I'm not sure, but a local lawyer named Pete Hagstrom drew up the lease. If he isn't the guy to talk to, he'll know who is. His office is downtown over the Rite Aid, across from the bank."

"Pete Hagstrom," I repeated. "Thanks. I'll check it out."

"I'd better get back," he said, rising. "I'd like to ask one small favor, though. If you don't mind, we never had this conversation, okay? Some of the Third Coasters have no sense of humor."

"If helping us can get you into trouble, why are you doing it?"

"Maybe I like the way your boy salutes," he said, with a quirky grin. "He's got style. And I'd say it runs in the family. If things work out, y'all can buy me a cup of coffee sometime. Fair enough?"

"Fair enough," I nodded.

He turned and walked out. He didn't march, exactly, but from his stride, I think most people would have spotted him as a soldier from a mile off. I certainly could have.

"So what do you think?" Red asked. "Could they be setting us up?"

"By suggesting we see a lawyer?" I said. "I don't see how."

"You've got to be kidding," Red said. "Some of the sorriest times of my life have been spent with lawyers."

"It can't hurt to ask, right?" Corey offered. "I mean, we've come a long way and all."

"That we have," I acknowledged. "Okay, we'll ask. But if

they're not jerking us around, I wonder why our pal the mercenary decided to help us out?"

Corey and Red exchanged an "oh puh-leeze" look.

"What?" I said.

# Fourteen
## Let's Not Kill *All* the Lawyers. . . .

𝕾𝖇𝖉𝖕

Hagstrom's office was easy to find, he had an old-fashioned shingle over the door next to a drugstore that looked like something out of a black-and-white movie. In fact, the whole town had that kind of atmosphere, as though time had frozen for it during World War II. The cars were new, of course, and a few of the signs above the shops were state of the art computer generated, but the buildings all dated from an era that was fading long before my father was born.

"Why don't you guys go on without me," Red said. "I've never met a lawyer I liked, and some of these shops look interesting. You want to tag along, Junior?"

"And leave Mom to handle this on her own?" Corey said. "That was a joke, right?"

"Good point," Red said. "I'll meet you back here in half an hour. Good luck." She strode off, window shopping as she walked.

The drugstore's facade was faced with sand colored brick that gave it a Main Street 1950 look, but the dark, narrow stairwell that led up to Hagstrom's office was a generation older. As we made our way up, I half expected to hear Caruso crooning from a scratchy Victrola.

Instead I heard the whine of a vacuum. Hagstrom's office door was ajar. I rapped once and stepped in. A pudgy little doughboy of a guy in dark slacks, a white shirt, and red suspenders was busily vacuuming the waiting room. He glanced up, startled, and shut off the vacuum.

"Sorry, I didn't hear you knock," he said, straightening. "Can I help you?"

"I hope so. I'm looking for Mr. Hagstrom?"

"You've found him, hard at work clearing up a few cases," he said with a smile. "My cleaning lady heads south in the fall like a robin. An intelligent bird, the robin. What can I do for you?"

"I understand that you handle some of the business for an organization called . . . Outreach?"

"Amerasian Outreach?" he said, eyeing me quizzically. "Yep, I'm the attorney of record for the corporation and I'm on the board of trustees for the school as well."

"Then I guess you're the guy we need to talk to," I said. "I'm Michelle Mitchell and this is my son, Corey."

"Pete Hagstrom," he said, shaking our hands in turn. "Step into my office. It'll give me an excuse to put this drudgery on hold." He waved us into an inner office, a wonderful, antique room panelled in dark walnut with floor-to-ceiling bookcases, a twelve foot high embossed metal ceiling and an honest-to-God crystal chandelier. His massive desk was hand carved and the Victorian furniture was upholstered in burgundy leather.

"Have a seat. Can I offer you anything? Coffee? A Coke?"

"Nothing thanks," I said, easing into the comforting embrace of a well-worn chair. Corey took the seat next to mine, sitting ramrod straight, his hands folded in his lap. A little soldier again. All business.

"I understand that this . . . Outreach Corporation owns a tract of land southeast of town," I said. "Land that's being used by the Third Coast Militia."

"That's correct. Are you a reporter, Ms. Mitchell?"

"No, though I must look like one. People keep asking me that."

"We're a little wary," Hagstrom said, with a shrug. "Every time a bomb goes off somewhere, some editor sends a flack to do another Yooper Yahoos from Deliverance Country article. I don't mind, really, as long as they spell my name right. I just like to know whom I'm talking to."

"I'm not a reporter, I'm a restaurant owner from Huron Harbor. I'm also a professional diver. Here's my driver's license and my diver's passport," I said, fishing them out of my purse and passing them to him. "The numbers on the first page of the log are my personal certification numbers. The rest is a log of the work I've done in the past two years."

"A diver's passport?" he said, examining the log book. "I don't understand."

"There's an abandoned copper mine on the tract of land in question, Mr. Hagstrom. The Kewadin Drift?"

"It can hardly be called a mine anymore," he said warily. "If there are any problems, the present owners wouldn't be liable. Outreach has only owned the land for the past twenty years or so, but the mine's been abandoned for a century."

"Which is why I'm interested in it. I'd like to get permission to make an exploratory dive of the mine, to photograph it and catalogue any artifacts it may contain."

"What kind of artifacts?" he asked, puzzled.

"We really won't know until I get down there. The old miners didn't leave much behind, but there may be structures of historical interest or equipment that wasn't cost effective to remove a hundred years ago."

"I see," he nodded, guardedly. "That sounds logical. Tell me, would some of these items be hand made? Built by the miners or local merchants?"

"Probably. Any structures would have been, certainly."

"And could you recover some of them?"

"Not immediately," I said, choosing my words carefully. After blowing my chance with Cezak I'd tailored my pitch to appeal to Hagstrom's self interest, but I wasn't sure what had hooked him, if anything had. "These old mines are historic sites whether they're listed in a register or not. If there's anything worth recovering, you'd need a permit from the Department of Natural Resources and it might take a team to bring them up. I'm just talking about an exploratory dive."

"I understand. Forgive my bluntness, but what would all this exploration cost?"

"Professional divers usually charge somewhere between eighty and a hundred fifty dollars an hour for this kind of a job, but my fee to explore the site will be zero, zip, nada. My father dove the mine once, and I'd like to see it myself."

"I see," he said thoughtfully, thinking it over. "That's very generous. Too generous, in fact. I'd have to insist that you allow the school to reimburse you for your expenses. What kind of money would that be?"

"Not much," I said, surprised at his offer. "Not counting my time, probably less than a hundred dollars."

"That's more than fair, I'm sure," he said. "Of course, we'd need some paperwork absolving the school of any liability. Any problem with that?"

"None," I said. "You're interested, then?"

"Interested? To be honest, Ms. Mitchell, I'm hoping you're the answer to a prayer."

"I don't understand."

"Are you familiar with the Outreach Corporation's work?"

"Not really. I was told it has something to do with Amerasian children."

"Exactly. Over the past decade or so, the organization's been striving to aid the last victims of our involvement in Southeast Asia: the children we left behind. They were often abandoned by their mothers and despised in their own countries because of their heritage. They're a generation older now and having children of their own, but because of their supposedly tainted blood, they suffer the worst kind of racial discrimination. Their best hope is to come here, to the land of their fathers, or grandfathers. The land of the free. Unfortunately, it doesn't always work that way."

"Why not?"

"We bring Asian families here to escape racism, only to stir up a new batch. The local folks, the Yoopers, are an odd lot. Nobody moves to this part of the country to get their career on the fast track. We have no industry to speak of, and the climate's not exactly congenial. Still, the lakes and the land are beautiful, and most Yoopers like the life. A maverick bunch."

"Like the Third Coasters?"

"No," he said firmly. "Definitely not like the Thirds. Many of them aren't locals anyway. Have you met them?"

"I talked to Major Cezak before I came here."

"Dan's not so bad. If you read the national press you'd think they were all mad dogs or Nazis."

"Maybe some of them are. We also met Captain Pettiford. Don't you find the idea of a private army a little scary?"

"But they're not private," he said mildly. "They're local citizens who've formed a militia, a right guaranteed under the constitution."

He paused, but I didn't rise to the bait.

"Okay," he sighed, "maybe I don't believe it either. The truth is, for a time the Thirds were the only organized local support our school had. A lot of them were Vietnam vets and they accepted the students we brought here and helped us raise funds. But lately, all that's changed. We're running into a lot of resentment."

"But why should Amerasian children bother anyone?"

"Some of it's simple racism, but mostly it's more complex than that. There's a memorial pillar in front of city hall with the names of local boys who died in Vietnam. It's one helluva long list for such a small town, people up here take patriotism seriously. But Vietnam ended badly, and now the locals see these Asian young people leading the lives, in effect, that their own sons should have had. And they resent it. Or at least some do. That's why I think this project of yours might be just what the doctor ordered."

"You've lost me. What does diving a mine have to do with your school?"

"It could strengthen our links to the community," he said smoothly. "The school opened a museum last year, but our only exhibits have been general interest stuff, Ojibwa artifacts and lumber-era photographs that we borrowed from Michigan State. This mine business should generate some local interest. Some folks probably had relatives who were involved with it."

Corey glanced at me uneasily.

"Mr. Hagstrom, you understand I can't promise anything," I said. "The whole thing may have collapsed by now."

"Then why don't we find out? What time frame did you have in mind?"

"Actually, I'd hoped to be able to make an exploratory dive this weekend. I have my equipment with me and a quick look-see dive should only take an hour or so."

"Excellent," he said, rising. "Well then, why don't I see what I do about clearing away the red tape. I'll check with Mr. Van Amstel and some of the board members, but I'm sure they'll be as enthusiastic as I am."

"And Major Cezak? How enthusiastic will he be?"

"But dear lady, that's the beauty of it," he said with satisfaction. "If Cezak doesn't like it, we'll regretfully cancel their lease and refund their deposits. All in the interests of science, of course."

"I see," I said. And I really did. "The bottom line is, you want to break their lease and I'm giving you an excuse."

"You're very perceptive, Ms. Mitchell. Given the circumstances, if you'd like to withdraw your request . . . ?"

"No," I said. "We're still interested."

"Excellent," he said. "I'll get right on it. Are you staying somewhere in town where I can reach you?"

"Not yet," I said. "We'd planned to camp out at one of the parks."

"I've a better idea. As a gesture of goodwill, why don't you let the school put you up at the Grand Heritage House? It's an inn in a converted lumber baron's mansion. It's quite a place."

"Really, I wouldn't want to impose—"

"Nonsense," he said briskly. "The school keeps several suites of rooms for out-of-town guests. You're welcome to use them. Make yourselves comfortable, do a little sightseeing, and I should have news for you by late this afternoon. How does that sound?"

"It sounds like a gift horse we'd be crazy to turn down," I said. "We accept your offer. Thank you."

"My pleasure," Hagstrom said, rising. "I'll phone the inn and tell them you folks are coming."

He walked us to the door, but as I turned to usher Corey out ahead of me, I hesitated. The wall beside the door was decked with pictures and community service awards, but something was odd. . . .

There. The third picture down from the top was a group shot of Hagstrom accepting an award from a tall, balding Nordic type in a tuxedo. The tux wasn't what threw me, though, it was his hair. The last time I'd seen him he had a tousled blond mane. It was the man standing between my father and Frank d'Hubert in the picture of the Kewadin Drift mine taken thirty years earlier.

"Mr. Hagstrom, who's the gentleman who's giving you the award in this picture? The one in the tux."

"Tux?" he said, frowning. "Ah. That's the president of Outreach, Nick Van Amstel. Do you know him?"

"No. He looks familiar, though. I've probably just seen his picture somewhere."

# FIFTEEN
# A ROOM WITH A VIEWPOINT

❧

"IT WAS the same guy, wasn't it?" Corey asked, as we walked out to the truck. "The one in the picture with your dad."

"I think so," I said, climbing into the pickup. Red came trotting up, and slid in beside Corey. "It's hard to be sure after all this time," I continued. "Look, we'd better get something straight. I don't want you to get your hopes up that . . . well, that we're actually going to settle anything on this trip. Even if we can wangle permission to dive the mine, I may not find anything."

"Would there be anything to find after all this time?" Red asked.

"Things decompose very slowly in water polluted with hydrogen sulfide," I said. "If the body is deep enough and the water's cold enough, then, yes, there'll definitely be something to find."

"And if we find something?" Corey asked. "What will we do?"

"We'll worry about that when it happens," I said briskly. *"If* it happens."

"But you'll tell me about it, right?" Corey pressed.

"Absolutely," I said. "Why wouldn't I?"

"Because people don't always tell kids the truth, you know? For their own good, or at least that's what they say."

"I'm not promising to always tell you the truth, the whole truth and nothing but," I said. "Life's not that simple. I may decide to keep a hurtful truth to myself, occasionally. But not something as important as this. We've come too far for fibs, buster. Whatever I know, you'll know."

"Okay," he said, nodding. "I just wanted to be sure."

We pulled up in front of the Grand Heritage Inn. It was a spectacular old pile, a three-story Victorian mansion with cupolas, pergolas, and a lawn broad enough for polo. We collected our duffel bags out of the back of the truck, walked up the broad staircase, and stepped back in time nearly a hundred years. The interior contained immaculate hardwood floors with colorful islands of oriental carpeting. The furniture was mostly Queen Anne, but there were several massive handcarved captain's rockers as well, probably of local origin.

A small counter stood in front of a vestibule, manned by a slender reed of a young man wearing a red blazer, a bow tie, and a northwoods interpretation of a maitre d's ever-so-slightly-bored expression.

"Can I help you, ladies?"

"Hi, I'm Michelle Mitchell. I believe Mr. Hagstrom called ahead about our rooms?"

"Mr. Hagstrom?" he said, eyeing us curiously.

"That's right. Is there a problem?"

"Nope, not at all," he said bit sheepishly. "Sorry, I was expecting . . . well, someone else. Here, just fill out the registry card and you'll be all set."

"Should we have dressed for dinner to check in?" Red asked, as I took the card from him and jotted the required information in the blanks.

"No ma'am, it's not that, it's just that most people that use the Outreach suites aren't . . . like you."

"What does that mean?"

"You know, they're Chinamen, Asians, whatever you call them."

"I think the term is Americans, once they're here," I said, sliding the card back to him.

"Maybe you'd call them that," he said, glancing at the card and filing it. "A lot of people around here wouldn't."

"Why?" Red asked. "Because their last name isn't Swenson?"

"Not everybody up here's named Sven," he said dryly as he sauntered around the counter and picked up our bags. "We have a few Oles too. This way please, folks. Mind you, the Outreach people don't bother me. I'm used to 'em. But some of 'em do have an attitude, and that's a fact."

"What kind of an attitude?" I prompted as we followed him up the broad staircase.

"You know, snotty, kind of. Like they can buy and sell you. Which I guess most of 'em can."

"Students with money?" I said.

"Oh, we don't get students here. Our guests are mostly relatives or family of some kind, definitely grownups."

"And their kids are going to school free and you're toting their luggage," Red said.

"Something like that," he said cheerfully. "Actually, I wouldn't mind if some of the students did stay here once in awhile. Some of those Chinese girls are cute, you know? Here we are," he said, ushering us into a lovely, sunlit room on the second floor. "There's an adjoining bedroom through that door, if that'll be okay? Hope you enjoy your stay."

"Thank you," I said, offering him a folded fiver.

"Thank you, ma'am, but we aren't allowed to accept tips."

"Take it anyway," I said. "It'd be un-American not to."

"Yes ma'am," he said, brightening. "I guess it would at that."

# Sixteen
## Dinner and a Dance

❧

I was still unpacking when the bedside phone gurgled. I answered it.

"Ms. Mitchell? This is Pete Hagstrom. I've made a few calls about your project and everything looks good. Are you free this evening?"

I hesitated.

"Actually, I phrased that badly," he said. "Let me try again. There's a faculty mixer at the Outreach campus this evening and most of the people we need to talk to will be there. Can you make it?"

"I . . . have my son and a friend with me," I said.

"No problem, bring them along," Hagstrom said. "From what I saw of the young man this afternoon, he'll fit right in."

"What about clothes?" I said. "We don't have anything even semi-formal with us."

"This is the U.P., Ms. Mitchell," he said, chuckling. "We're not much on formality up here. It's strictly come as you are."

"In that case we'll be there," I said. "Where is it, exactly?"

"Just head west of town on highway fifty-eight for six or seven miles. It'll be on your left. You can't miss it."

"Famous last words," I said, but I was wrong again. We had no trouble finding the place.

The Outreach campus was nestled on a hilltop at the end of

a quarter mile entrance drive and looked less like a school than a very expensive and expansive private clinic. The five buildings were constructed largely of native stone topped with color-matched brick, and its Frank Lloyd Wright-ish architecture blended into the countryside so seamlessly that it could have sprouted from the earth.

A glass-walled kiosk stood beside the drive, and a uniformed security guard waved us down as we approached.

"Welcome to Amerasian Outreach," he said, leaning down to scan the interior of the pickup cab. "Your business, please?"

"I'm Michelle Mitchell, we've been invited to some kind of a mixer. . . ."

"Mitchell and friends, yes ma'am," he said. "You're on my list," he said, checking a clipboard. "Here's your pass, ma'am." He handed me a plastic rectangle the size of a charge card. "Please turn this in when you leave, ma'am. It identifies your vehicle electronically. Thank you, have a nice evening." He waved us on.

"Cool," Corey said, fingering the card. "I've heard about these, but I've never seen one."

"Electronic monitors for a school?" I said. "Isn't that a bit extreme?"

"Maybe not," Red said, "look at this place." The school buildings formed a rough semicircle around a central courtyard and were linked by glass-walled walkways, a concession to the winter storms that would be sweeping down from Canada all too soon.

The dean's residence was the only building separate from the others. It rose atop a small mount, and was more traditionally built in the north country/New England style, a two story salt box with a stone veranda. The last light of dusk was fading as we strolled up the stone stairway.

I didn't bother to knock; the door was ajar and the conversational din from within would have drowned cannon fire. The combination living/dining/sitting room occupied most of the ground floor. It was crowded with a colorful array of folks dressed in the standard north country mixture of suits or tweedy sportcoats over flannel shirts, some with ties, some without. The women were mostly in pantsuits or slacks and blouses with only an occasional skirt in sight.

Red and I had decided our camping duds were too tacky, so we'd made a lightning tour of Grand Portal's small shopping district and settled on blazers over bluejeans, blue for me, green for Red to set off her hair. I'd worried about making a good impression, but as I glanced around I decided we could have worn rodeo clown outfits without feeling out of place.

As we made our way in through the crush we earned a glance or two of curiosity, but beyond that no one paid much attention to us. Then Corey tugged on my sleeve. I followed his eyes and spotted Pete Hagstrom in the far corner of the room, talking with a tall, tanned gentleman with strikingly silvered hair and a matching gray suit. And in person, there was no doubt: He was the man from the photograph.

Hagstrom noticed us at the same time and waved us over.

"Ms. Mitchell, I'd like you to meet the president of Outreach School, Nick Van Amstel. Nick, these are the folks I told you about."

"I'm glad to meet you, Mr. Van Amstel." We shook hands and I introduced Red. Up close, Van Amstel had an interesting face, narrow, with a high forehead and deep seams along his mouth, a sensual ascetic.

"And you must be Corey," he said, stopping to shake Corey's hand. "Pete's been telling me about the project you have in mind, Miss Mitchell, but there's something I don't understand. The mine's been closed for a century but Pete says you had a— relative, who worked there?"

"Actually, I'm not sure what he did there, but I believe you knew my father, Shannon Mitchell?"

"Shannon . . . my God, you're kidding. You're Shan Mitchell's daughter? Pete, you didn't say anything about this."

"I—didn't know," Hagstrom said, confused.

"I didn't mention it to him," I put in. "If you knew my father, you'll understand why."

"I knew him only too well," Van Amstel nodded, with a broad grin. "So how is your dad? What's he up to these days?"

"He passed away a year or so ago. Traffic accident."

"I'm genuinely sorry to hear that," he said, his smile fading. "He was one of a kind. Look, I have a little trouble hearing in a crowded room like this. Could we step into my study and catch up a bit? Pete, why don't you check on Mei, see if she needs any-thing."

"Glad to," Hagstrom said, "I'll catch up with you later."

"I think I'll mingle," Red said. "I'm starving, and the hors d'oeuvres are calling my name." They pushed off through the crowd together. Corey and I followed Van Amstel to the end of the hall where he ushered us into a pleasant, book-filled room, done in Tudor style, all dark woods and stark, stylish furniture. The antiques looked authentic, immaculate, and devastatingly expensive.

"Please sit down, Ms. Mitchell," Van Amstel said, waving me toward a chair. "There's a computer at the corner desk, son," he said to Corey. "One of my daughters was running a game on it. You're welcome to—" Corey had the screen flickering to life before Van Amstel finished. He gave a shrug of amusement, then rested a hip on the corner of his desk and folded his arms, as relaxed as a crane at rest.

"For openers, please accept my sympathy on the death of your father. He was a true character, your dad. We served to-gether in the war, you know. Did he ever mention me to you?"

"No, but Shan never talked about the war. From the little he did say I guessed he had a bad time."

"There weren't many good times there, and that's a fact," Van Amstel nodded. "We were with the Brown Water Navy, Shan and I. He was a SEAL, a hardcore combat soldier, and I was a green ensign assigned to the quartermaster's office. I helped keep Shan's unit supplied with whatever they needed, a job not unlike what I do now, except that these days I scrounge for funds rather than food and ammunition."

"I found a picture recently, of you and my father and my grandfather together in front of an old mine, the Kewadin Drift?"

"I'm not likely to forget that," Nick said. "It was the summer we came home, an appropriately goofy chapter in a crazy period in my life. Did your dad tell you about it?"

"No. I came across it by accident."

"I see. Well, there isn't that much to tell. In Vietnam, we all had things we did to stay sane, to get us through. Some men smoked dope, some drank, some got religion. I read history books, obsessively. Looking back on it, I was probably hiding in the past to make the situation more bearable. Does that make any sense?"

"I think I understand. When I worked on oil rigs out on the Texas Gulf, I used to plan elaborate flower gardens, read seed catalogs, that sort of thing. I've never actually planted a garden or grown anything, but I spent a lot of happy hours planning them."

"You were wise not to plant one. Our realities rarely measure up to our dreams. That damned mine is a perfect example."

"How do you mean?"

"I grew up in the U.P., at Marquette, and the history of this place has always fascinated me, especially the mines. In the last century, there were copper and iron mines here, and even gold. They struggled with the land, the bad roads, the godawful winters. I expecially liked reading about the six-foot snowdrifts since I was sweltering in an Asian jungle at the time. In any case, I came across some figures on the mortality rates of the miners and their children. They were startlingly high, even by the standards of the day."

"Mortality rates?"

"Exactly. They used child labor in those days, you know. Boys no older than your son used to work twelve hour days in the pits, loading the ore by hand into sacks and dragging it out."

"I'm familiar with the mines," I said. "I've explored one or two and I've done a lot of reading."

"Then you know what a difficult life they had," he nodded. "But that's not what caught my attention. I was reading about a miner's hospital in Marquette, and it mentioned that the miners suffered from some unusual ailments, cuts that wouldn't heal, wounds that behaved more like burns. And their children seemed to have a high rate of birth defects. And it occurred to me that perhaps in their search for copper and iron, they'd dug right past something more valuable than gold. Pitchblende. Uranium ore."

"You thought the birth defects and injuries might have been caused by radiation?"

"Exactly," he said, nodding. "The miners wouldn't even have been aware of its existence at the time. And in the jungles of Southeast Asia, it seemed to make sense. In any case, the idea served as a kind of . . . grail, for me. Something to plan for, to look forward to. If I could just manage to get out of Vietnam alive, I could buy up the mineral rights to an abandoned mine for pocket change, find uranium, and we'd all get rich."

"And did you?" I asked. "Get rich, I mean?"

"Hardly. There's more radioactivity in the average watch dial than your dad and I found in that mine. We pooled our discharge money to buy the mineral rights to the Kewadin, and when it was over I had to sell my car to give him gas money to head south. I can't believe he never told you about all this. As I recall he was one helluva storyteller."

"He was, but not about this. I think it was because he met my mother here, and he'd never talk about her."

"Met her here? Then . . . your mother must have been our guide's daughter? Frank . . . ?"

"d'Hubert," I prompted. "Her name was Madeline. Did you know her?" Corey glanced toward us at the mention of the name, then returned to his game, his face aglow in the reflected screen light.

"Only in passing. She used to bring us supplies, and after she saw your father, I was lucky to rate a nod. It was one of those . . . chemistry things. Love at first sight, if you like. I take it they didn't part friends?"

"She died in childbirth. Having me, in fact. And my dad would never talk about her afterwards. Ever."

"I'm sorry," he said softly, shaking his head. "Truly I am. What a shame." He looked away from me a moment, into some hazy, imagined distance. I heard a fragment of music from the other room. Someone was murdering a Beatles song on the piano. Nick didn't seem to notice. He was somewhere else.

"The last time I saw your father," he said absently, "we were having breakfast at some roadside diner the day he left. I knew that Madeline was running away with him. And I remember saying something like, at least one of us is coming out of this a winner. And it was true. I envied him. I really did. They were very happy that day."

"You never heard from him again?"

"No, but it's not uncommon for old Navy buddies to lose track of each other. I went back to Southeast Asia afterwards, and met my wife and found my life's work. When I came home again, I had no idea where to contact him, or vice versa. It happens."

"And Frank?" I asked carefully. "Have you stayed in touch with him?"

"Frank? Hardly," he said wryly. "The last time I saw Frank, he threatened to beat me to death unless I told him where your dad had gone, and I think he meant it too. I would have told him if I'd known. He was a formidable man, your grandfather."

"So I understand."

"I could hardly blame him. I have daughters now myself, and, no offense, but I certainly wouldn't want one of them to get mixed up with guys like your dad and I were in those days, two wild-eyed Vietnam vets who'd just blown their last dime on a hare-brained scheme. Actually, I liked Frank as a person. He wasn't a bad fella, he was just concerned about his daughter."

"Have you seen him recently?"

"No, not since the old days."

"But he lives nearby, or used to, in Anahwey. Are you sure you haven't seen him?"

"Well, I suppose I can't be absolutely certain. It was a long time ago. Perhaps I did see him again after that, but if so, I don't recall it. It's not as though we were pals, we just worked together on the one project, and it was a failure. And I'm afraid it still is."

"How do you mean?"

"Pete tells me you're interested in exploring the mine. Do you mind if I ask why?"

"Diving is what I do," I said simply. "I did it professionally for a long time, and now I do it partly for pleasure. I'm interested in photographing what's left of the mine if it's still possible, mostly because of the family connection, following in my father's wake, so to speak. And maybe if we get lucky, perhaps I can recover an artifact or two for your museum."

"I see. I take it your father never told you the condition the mine was in."

"No, but I assume it must have been pretty good."

"Why do you say that?"

"Because you were on the site long enough to need supplies. If the mine had been in really dangerous shape, Shan would never have gone inside it. And he would have known that in the first hour or two."

"But that was nearly thirty years ago."

"The mine was abandoned for seventy years before that. I doubt that much has changed since my father was down there, but I only know one way to find out."

"I see," he nodded. "Unfortunately, I'm afraid exploring the Kewadin Drift's simply not possible at present. It's true the school owns the land it's on, but we've leased the tract to the Third Coast Militia, and it's my understanding that Dan Cezak already vetoed the project."

"Mr. Hagstrom seemed fairly sure you could change Cezak's mind."

"Changing Dan Cezak's mind about anything is no mean feat. What Pete really hoped was that we could use Dan's objection as a lever to pry the militia off our land. I can't blame him for trying. The Thirds are definitely an embarrassment. Do you know what we do here? What this school is all about?"

"I . . . was told that you're involved in bringing Amerasian children to the U.S."

"Right, and with all modesty, I think the work is important and we're on the side of the angels, so to speak. Unfortunately, that's not a universally held opinion. Some locals see Asians come here who can barely speak the language, and after a period of tutoring and hard work, they're able to enter the American mainstream. Instead of being inspired by their example, a few malcontents resent it. Many local people support our work, as you can see from the group gathered here tonight, but as an administrator, I do have to take the feelings of others into account."

"Like The Third Coasters, for instance?"

"Exactly," he nodded. "They're a potent political force locally, with very strong ties to the community. The school simply can't afford to alienate them. They have a lease, and more importantly, I gave Dan Cezak my word. It may seem old-fashioned to you, but keeping my word matters a great deal to me. If Dan turned you down, I'm afraid my hands are tied."

"I see." I was trying to quell my irritation, and losing the battle. "Is it their political juice that bothers you, or all that gunfire out in the boondocks?"

"Frankly, both," Van Amstel said. "You've got to understand, when the Thirds first organized, they were like an alternate American Legion for Vietnam era vets. But after the FBI raid at Ruby Ridge, and the fiasco at Waco, everything changed. They became a haven for malcontents and paranoids and began a lot of paramilitary activity. Believe me, if I could honorably undo our lease, I would. Still, I don't intend to turn my back on the daughter of an old friend, either. And there's no reason I should."

"How do you mean?"

"The Kewadin Drift isn't the only abandoned mine in our area. There are several others. The school doesn't own any of them, they're in private hands, but with some friendly persuasion I'm sure we can obtain permission for you to explore them. In fact, I'm hoping we can obtain a state grant to fund the project. You can explore to your heart's content, do some valuable research, and get paid for it. How does that sound?"

"Very generous," I admitted. "I'm grateful for your help."

"Don't thank me too soon. I'm the guy who tried to find uranium in the Kewadin Drift, remember," he said, rising. "Still, I'm not afraid to wrestle with bureaucrats in a good cause and I believe this is one. Why don't you call me in a few weeks? If anything develops sooner than that, I'll let you know."

"Thank you, that will be fine. Corey?"

Corey gave the keyboard one last tap, then quickly typed in an exit code and turned it off. "Thanks for letting me play the game, sir," Corey said, offering Nick his small hand. "It was cool."

"Maybe we can do it again sometime," Nick said, winking at me over Corey's head. "I really must get back to my guests. You're welcome to stay. I'd be happy to introduce you around and there's plenty of finger food."

"No, I think we'll be going," I said. "We've had a long day."

"Of course. Well, it was a pleasure to meet you both and I'm looking forward to our little project. I only hope our efforts turn out better this time than the last."

"Amen to that," I said.

# Seventeen
## After the Ball

෧෨෯෨

"So," Red said, "how did it go?" We were driving slowly back to Grand Portal in the gusty darkness. A storm was brewing up out on the lake, and I could hear the wind rushing through the treetops over the thrum of the motor.

"We got a very polite no about the Drift," I said. "Van Amstel offered to help with other projects for Auld Lang Syne, but basically he's worried about the militia. He'd rather not rattle their cage."

"You can't blame him for that," Red said.

"I don't. I blame them."

"I suppose he has to get along with the locals if he wants to keep his school afloat. Funny, though, there were quite a few Asians at the party, but none of them were kids."

"Well, do the math," I said. "The Vietnam War ended more than twenty years ago, I suppose any Amerasian kids would all be adults now."

"Maybe," Red acknowledged, "but I'd guess most of these folks were even older than that, a fairly tough looking lot. Plus, judging from their threads, damned few of them were poverty stricken."

"What are you saying?"

"I don't know," she said with a shrug. "I just got the feeling there was a lot of wheeling and dealing going on in that room that had nothing to do with higher education."

"Why do you say that? Did you hear something?"

"That's just it, I didn't. Conversations seemed to die an unnatural death when I wandered past. Don't get me wrong, I'm not saying they're axe murderers or anything, it just struck me as odd."

"Some of the numbers don't compute either," Corey said.

"You mean on the game?"

"No, not the game. I could play that dumb game blindfolded. I mean what Mr. Van Am . . ."

"Amstel," I finished.

"Amstel, right. Anyway, part of what he said didn't work out."

"How do you mean?"

"The years, Mom. And the money. When Mr. Van and your dad checked out the mine, it was before you were born, right? Thirty years ago."

"Roughly."

"And they spent their navy money on buying the mineral rights to the mine. But they didn't find anything and he even had to sell his car afterwards."

"Right again."

"So your dad left and Mr. Van Amstel went back to Vietnam or whatever. Then later he came home and set up the school in 1976."

"Was it '76? I don't recall him mentioning that date."

"It's on the sign when you drive in the gate," Corey said patiently. "Established 1976. And that lawyer said that the school bought the mine twenty years ago. So why would they do that if he already knew the mine wasn't worth anything?"

"Maybe it wasn't the mine they wanted. Maybe it was the land."

"Why? So they could rent it out cheap to a bunch of Looney Tunes? Besides, what did he buy it with? He said he was broke, remember?"

"He was broke when he and Shan were working together," I corrected. "Buying the mine and starting the school happened years later."

"So in between he came up with some money, right? Quite

a pile of it from the looks of his house and the school. So maybe there really was uranium or something in that mine. Maybe he cheated your dad out of his share."

"You've been watching too much TV," I said. "Shan was the one who did the actual exploring. If there was anything of value down there, he would have known and gotten his piece of it. Mr. Van Amstel's probably a bright guy, he's a school president after all, but he's not sharp enough to have conned my dad out of doodley."

"I'll second that," Red put in. "If anybody conned anybody, it would have been the other way around."

"So if the place is so worthless, how come it's being guarded by a low-rent dimbulb army?"

"He said they weren't like that at first, that they turned strange later on. I'm not sure the militia's logic would make sense to us even if they explained it. Assuming they could."

"So now what?" Red asked.

"Well, I suppose we should probably pack up and go home."

"Sounds logical," she agreed. "But I've never found logic particularly useful in dealing with you. What do you want to do?"

"Damn it, we didn't come all the way up here just to get a polite brushoff," I said. "I want to take a look at that mine, just to be sure nobody's blowing smoke at us."

"But if the Thirds are using it as a shooting range, it could be dangerous," Red said.

"I doubt they do much target practicing early on a Sunday morning. If I go in the back way, along that old railroad grade at first light tomorrow, I should be able to get in and out without being spotted."

"Are you sure?" Red asked.

I glanced at her.

"Right," she said, leaning back in the seat. "Sorry I asked."

# Eighteen
## By the Dawn's Early Light

༄ঙ৶৶৶

My tiny travel alarm went off at five-thirty A.M. I grabbed it quickly, trying to muffle it's *meee meee meee,* but I wasn't quick enough. Red groaned in her twin bed and pulled the blankets over her head. A moment later Corey rapped softly on the room divider as I was pulling on my jeans.

" 'Morning," I said quietly, mussing his hair. "Are you ready to see me off on an early A.M. adventure?"

"I don't know," he said in a stage whisper, perching on the corner of my bed. In his pajamas, slippers, and with his hair all atousle, he looked all of eleven years old. Which he was, of course. "I've been thinking about this. What if you're wrong about those guys not shooting on Sunday? It could be dangerous."

"Actually, they said they use the mountain as a backstop, which means if I go in the back way, along that old railroad grade near the shore, the high ground will be between me and any shooting that's going on. Besides, if I hear any gunfire, I promise I'll rabbit out of there like a rocket. Okay?"

"I don't like the idea of you being out there alone with those weirdos, that's all. Are you sure it'll be safe?"

"No," I said, "but I'm sure that if I don't try, I'll never hear the end of it."

"That's not fair!"

"I'm kidding, honest," I said, pulling on my Gore-Tex hiking boots and speed-lacing them up. "Look, I'm not trying to play Miss Indiana Jones here, but we didn't come this far just to walk away. It's unlikely Mr. Van Amstel or anybody else is misleading us, but I want to have a look at that mine myself, just to be sure."

"If it's safe why can't Red and I come along?"

"Because if there is any trouble, we can't help each other if we're all blundering around in the underbrush in the middle of nowhere. I need you here to call the cavalry to bail me out if I have a problem. Doesn't that sound logical?"

"Yeah," he admitted, "that's what scares me."

"Are you saying you don't trust me to function on my own for a few hours?"

"No, you managed okay on your own while I was away at school, I guess."

"Thanks for sharing that. Okay, here's the deal, bub. I'm out of here. You guys hang around and wait for my call. If you don't hear from me or I'm not back by ten o'clock, you dial 911 and yell your heads off. Okay?"

"You sure you want us to yell?" Red said, sitting up and knuckling the sleep from her eyes. "Considering the average age of the guests here, they'll probably all have coronaries at once."

"Good," I said. "We can escape during the confusion. But all kidding aside, one way or another I should be back in a few hours, so don't do anything drastic until ten, okay?"

"Don't worry about us, you just be careful out there, hon. I look lousy in black."

"I'll do my best."

I took the broad staircase down to the entrance. A stooped, elderly lady with a cable knit sweater draped over her shoulders was at the front desk, sound asleep.

I hesitated on the porch a moment, and glanced back. I half expected her to be making a furtive phone call, but she was still zoned out. Maybe paranoia was a trace element in the water up here.

I fired up Red's pickup, and drove west through the deserted streets of Grand Portal. I didn't see another vehicle on the road, not one. I met a few trucks on the main highway west of town, but after I turned south toward the Kewadin tract the deserted two lane road ran like a straight shot into the Twilight Zone. I could have been the Last Human on Earth.

There was no sign of activity on the tract itself as I drove past the Third Coast warning markers, though if they were all hotshot guerilla warriors, I wouldn't have seen them.

At the cutoff we'd passed up the day before that led back to the abandoned railroad grade, I had to cut my speed to near zero. The road was a muddy track, narrowed even more by overhanging branches from the clusters of tag alders and cedars standing sentry along its length. They clutched and clawed at the truck as I crawled past in low gear.

And then I came to the end of the road. The trail, such as it was, entered a small clearing that apparently served as a turnaround. The narrow track continued on but the ground looked so spongy that I didn't want to risk driving on it. I swung the truck around in case I had to split in a hurry, parked and climbed out.

The sun was just creeping over the horizon, glowing gold through the forested hills to the east like a distant fire. The woods were damp and dappled with shadows. A perfect day for skulduggery.

I set off at a brisk pace down the remains of the trail and found the old railroad grade about a hundred yards from the truck. The grade stood about five feet above the surrounding country. Roughly eight feet across and more or less level, it was actually a much better road than the one I'd parked on. The rails were missing, probably ripped up for salvage when the mine closed, but enough of the sand and rock chips of the track bed remained to keep the underbrush to a minimum.

I was tempted to jog for awhile, but decided against it. I wasn't sure how far I had to go, and the footing was uncertain. The grade was overgrown in spots where stunted alders and jack pines had burrowed in and managed to survive in the rocky soil. The underbrush was dripping, and I had to thread my way along the track like a broken-field runner; still, it was a pleasant hike.

The trail arched away to the west on a gentle curve. I had no trouble keeping on it, though my pantlegs were soaked to the thighs from the combination of dew and yesterday's rainfall before I'd covered twenty yards. The grade twisted and snaked through a dense tangle of pines and cedar as I worked my way uphill toward the mine. The musty odor of undergrowth and moist earth was gradually supplanted by the ranker scent of the hydrogen sulfide miasma that emanated from the shattered rock and slag of the mine tailings. It smelled like a wound that had turned necrotic, as though the miners had pierced the mountain with a fatal thrust ages ago, but still the stones lingered on, dying slowly. Perhaps they'd need a second century to expire completely.

There was no sound of gunfire, distant or otherwise, and no signs of recent activity. Footprints might not have left much of a trace on the grade, but there were no tire tracks either. But just as I was congratulating myself on how safe my little jaunt was, I came upon a crushed bush.

It was nothing dramatic, just a young sumac that had been flattened, broken off near its base. I knelt beside it, glancing back down the trail. From ground level, it appeared that something had moved through here, possibly an all-terrain vehicle of some kind. A trike or a four-wheeler. Balloon tires wouldn't mark the track bed, and the underbrush was sparse enough that an ATV driver could thread his way through as I had without doing much damage or leaving signs.

So. Apparently the Thirds used the area for something, or at least they'd been back here. I examined the break more closely. The stem was dry and the plant was nearly dead. It had been some time since it happened. Which was some comfort.

I rose cautiously and pushed on, doubly alert now for signs along the trail. I found a few more marks of disturbance in the next hundred yards or so, but then they petered out. Either the ATV driver grew more cautious, or he'd left the grade to work his way across the southern face of the mountain. Fortunately, I was headed the other way.

As I neared the mountain, I realized it wasn't really a mountain at all, just a glacial hill that had been thrust higher than its surroundings by the irresistible pressure of ancient ice. The rise was so gradual that it wouldn't have been perceptible if I hadn't looked back from time to time and realized that I was now above the level of the treetops at the spot where I'd first climbed onto the track.

And then I hit my first snag. A creek had eroded a passage through the stony track bed as it flowed across the face of the mountain toward its base. The slow moving water was only ten or twelve feet across and appeared to be only a few feet deep, but it was so murky with silt and sulfide I couldn't see the bottom clearly. I wasn't about to risk a ducking by trying to wade it.

I left the grade and worked my way upstream until I found a downed cedar that spanned the flow. I managed to scramble across on the trunk, but as I climbed across a low ridge to get back to the grade, I realized it wasn't necessary. I'd arrived.

# Nineteen
## Queen of the Mountain

෴

THE KEWADIN Drift was spread out below me, what there was of it. At first glance, there was scarcely a sign a mine had ever been there. The detritus of erosion and the bitter Upper Peninsula winters had erased the roads, the footpaths, and any buildings the miners might have left behind.

Only the scars on the face of the mountain remained, an unnatural, savage gash sixty yards high and a hundred wide, dynamite-blasted from the living rock. The granite gleamed nakedly in the early morning sun like a skull with the skin peeled away, tiger-striped by a century of sulfide weeping into a rancid pool at its base.

I worked my way slowly down the gradient toward the water. The milky pond spread out from the base of the cliff face in a crude semicircle roughly seventy yards from side to side. If the entrance to the mine was still open, it was invisible, totally submerged beneath the hazy water. I scanned the area, but there was no sign of human activity, recent or otherwise. Not an axe handle or a broken bucket, nothing man-made remained at all, unless you counted the blood-colored chunks of kidney-shaped hematite, the iron ore that littered the shoreline.

I squatted a moment, staring into the reflected light of the pond, vainly trying to plumb its depths, to search it with my spirit. Could my father have brought the body of Frank d'Hubert to this place to conceal it? And if so, how would I feel about it? Would I put it down to my father's temper, which was considerable? Or to his love for my mother? And where did that leave me? What had he actually felt for me all those years? Because, if not for me, none of it would have happened. If anything had.

And that was the next question. Apparently no one had been here recently, possibly not since the sixties when my father and Van Amstel prospected the site. Maybe my grandfather's Ojibwa forbears could have looked at that murky water and known whether there had been blood in it once, but I had no sense of it. Perhaps I was too civilized. Or more likely, not civilized enough.

I rose stiffly and took stock of the area. One thing was certain, Corey's theory about the mine being in operation was shot. I doubted anyone had so much as turned over a shovelful of dirt here in the past hundred years. Or at least, not on this side of the mountain.

I checked my watch. Barely seven. On a Sunday morning. I'd heard no gunfire or vehicle noise on the hike in and considering the hour, it was damned unlikely that anyone was out here but me. I decided to take a quick scout around the base of the mountain, just to be sure things were as peaceful as they looked.

I circled the pond and worked my way up a stony ridge, using an occasional scrub cedar or tag alder for a handhold. The going was rougher here, uneven ground and loose rock made for poor footing. I picked my way very carefully, while staying alert for any noises coming from the direction of the main road. Like cannonfire. I remembered reading somewhere that you never hear the shot that hits you. An interesting quirk of memory: why is it we only remember stories about falling elevators or rollercoasters when we're riding them?

Once I'd clambered over the ridge, the footing got easier but the visibility deteriorated. I was on the southerly side of the Kewadin now, and except for the piles of slag the miners had dumped over the ridge, the countryside was pretty much overgrown.

The underbrush grew thickly here, and the stunted pines

and alders made it difficult to see for any distance, not that there was anything to see. Still, I'd come this far. If I climbed to the top of one of the slag piles maybe I could spot a shortcut back to the grade, perhaps on the same trail the ATV had used.

I worked my way across the face of the mountain, gradually moving higher as I went. The going was getting more difficult by the step and I was beginning to think I'd have to turn back when I spotted a narrow ledge only a few yards ahead. I clambered up to it and took a breather, leaning against a boulder.

I was roughly a third of the way up the face of Kewadin now, with the lowlands spread out below me like a vast, verdant quilt of swaying treetops, poplar and silver maple and jack pines and cedar. The boughs were moving, their leaves shivering and rustling in the morning breeze like an audience in some wondrous woodland theater, whispering expectantly just before the curtain goes up.

And there'd been a performance here recently. Odd-looking white gouges scarred the bark of some of the trees below. I thought someone might have nicked them to mark a path, but I couldn't see a trail, and some of the marks were too high off the ground to be man-made . . . but they were.

My god, they were bullet holes. Rips and slashes made by high powered rounds that had been fired from the south using this mountain as a backstop. Most of the scars were well below me, but as I glanced around, I could see other marks, gouges in the dirt, a smears of copper or lead on the rocks where rounds had ricocheted off. Damn. Thorp was right. This wasn't a safe place to be. Time to go.

I scanned the terrain below, trying to decide on the best way out. I'd traversed roughly halfway across the face of the mountain but there wasn't a trace of a path ahead and the footing had been getting steadily worse. It would be a shorter hike to the grade if I pressed ahead, but it also looked like a great way to break a leg and wind up as a target dummy for the Third Coast Militia. It would be a safer bet to circle back the way I'd come.

Next question: would I be better off retracing my steps or keeping to the high ground? A slippery-looking slag pile off to my right made up my mind. I doubted a mountain goat with cleats could make it over those rocks.

I began working my way methodically back down the face of the mountain, wary of every step and checking my bearings every few minutes. I was only a few yards above the treetops when something caught my eye: a straight line where there shouldn't have been one. I halted a moment, panting, trying to decide what it was.

About eighty yards below me I could make out the faintest hint of a trail. It wasn't anything substantial, a few broken branches, some scuffmarks on the boles of a trees, but it did seem to be a path of sorts that led from the railroad grade across the foot of the mountain. I couldn't see any way to get down to it from where I was. I'd have to fight my way through the tangled woods below, and if I got turned around in that mess, I'd as likely end up in Canada as find a way back to the grade.

The odd thing about it was, I couldn't see that it went anyplace. It meandered through the trees below, then drifted off to the east. I could only glimpse pieces of it after that, until it faded out altogether in a tangle of ferns. I froze!

Something was moving over there. Something big. I stayed where I was, immobile. There. A shadow, close to the ground. An animal? It seemed to be threading its way around the edge of the ferns. . . .

Sweet Jesus. Those weren't ferns. Or maybe they were, I wasn't exactly up on the proper nomenclature of illegal drugs. It was a pot patch. Marijuana. The trail led to a small field of the plants concealed in the woods. I doubt it was visible at all from the far side and I'd have missed it too if I hadn't spotted that path.

The patch was roughly thirty yards across, what was left of it. Most of the plants had been harvested but there were enough stalks still standing to be certain of what they were. It was a marijuana patch, all right, and not the only one. I spotted a second patch beyond it. Hell, there could be a dozen of them scattered back there for all I knew. It was a perfect spot, sunny, sheltered from the onshore winds by the mountain and shielded from prying eyes by the woods and all that convenient Third Coast target practice, one hell of an incentive for casual trespassers to keep out.

I considered working my way over to the patch to score some evidence, but decided against it. It was too far, there was too much undergrowth in the way, and I had definitely seen something moving over there. Was someone watching? I suddenly felt a strong urge to be as far from this place as I could get. I took a bearing on the patches as best I could using the mountain as a landmark.

And there it was again. Movement. A shadow slipping stealthily through the trees. And then it stopped. And stared back at me, crouched in a tangle of brush. I could barely make it out, but as I stared, it crept forward a bit and a band of sunlight played across its back, defining its shape.

Not a man. A dog. A big one. Probably a Doberman or maybe a Rottweiler from what I could see of its black and tan coloring. It was wearing some kind of spiked collar. And it was eyeing me just as intently as I was watching it.

A guard dog. To keep people and animals away from the marijuana. And suddenly I was sweating, an instant, bone-chilling drench that had nothing to do with the hike I'd made. The dog wasn't restrained, it had covered too much ground since I'd first glimpsed it. I tried to remember the proper thing to do. Maintain eye contact? Back away?

Suddenly it didn't matter any more. The dog plunged forward, hurtling through the brush like a dark thunderbolt. It was coming for me, full tilt.

I had nowhere to go but up. The footing was too broken to try to make it to the grade by crossing the mountain, and if I headed back the way I'd come, he'd intercept me before I'd covered fifty yards. I scrambled up the slag pile, slipping and stumbling on the damp, broken rock, hoping against hope that there'd be help of some kind up there. A cave, a weapon, anything.

The footing was impossible. Stones shifted and kicked out from beneath my boots as I climbed, rattling back down the pile. I risked a quick glance back over my shoulder. Couldn't see him. And then suddenly there he was, bursting out of the brush at the foot of the slag heap, forty yards below.

Sweet Jesus, it was a Rottweiler, a hundred and twenty pounds of slavering hellhound. He didn't hesitate for an instant. He came barreling up the rockpile, his powerful shoulders pumping like pistons. He wasn't growling, but his eyes were ablaze. This was no warning feint, he was dead set on tearing me up, and I knew that my chances of surviving a scuffle with him up here were zero.

I reached the top of the slag heap. The mountain loomed above me for another sixty yards but there was no refuge up there, no cover, no trees, and the mossy footing was worse than the slag I was on. There was nothing I could use for a weapon, even the damned stones were too heavy to throw more than a few feet. All I could do was run.

I scrambled through a notch in the rock to my left but suddenly my feet slipped from beneath me and I was sliding down the slope of the Kewadin toward the pond. I clawed desperately at the rock face trying to slow my fall. Pain set my hand aflame as I tore a nail. My right palm snagged on a rocky projection and I clamped onto it. It jerked me to a halt, damned near tearing my arm from its socket.

I was stranded on the face of the mountain, ten or so feet above the ledge over the mine. The pond stretched out a good forty feet below that. I had no idea how deep it was or what rocks or old machinery might lurk beneath its surface. It didn't matter. The dog boiled over the top of the notch and started down toward me. His massive head was the size of a nail keg. He was having no trouble with his footing and his bared fangs left no doubt about the outcome if he reached me.

No choice. I loosed my hold on the rock and scrambled and skidded down the cliff face, fighting to maintain my balance and to keep my feet beneath me. The Rott kept coming, only a few yards behind me now, his eyes blazing like the windows of hell. I halted momentarily on the rim of the mine face, just long enough to get set and take one quick breath, and then I launched myself into space.

# TWENTY

# DEATH DIVE

I FELL for a year. A lifetime. Tumbling in space, I tried to shift myself into an upright position. Couldn't. I crashed into the water on my side, hard, and plunged beneath the surface. Stunned, my head ringing from the impact of the icy water, I twisted and leveled out under the surface, then fought my way up toward the light.

I exploded into the air, gasping for breath, then cast about frantically, trying to orient myself. I found the shore first, then turned to search the cliff face for my pursuer.

My God, he was still coming, clambering over the cleft with his eyes zeroed in on me like gunsights. At the edge of the drop the Rott hesitated for an instant, gathering himself, then he leapt, hurtling down toward me, a snarling black projectile of fangs and muscle.

I backpedaled desperately, trying to get away from him. He smashed into the water like a boulder, disappeared for an instant, then bobbed to the surface only a few yards away. He whirled, spotted me, and then lunged at me, snarling, his jaws agape.

I sucked in a quick breath, then sank beneath the surface, fumbling blindly for his legs in the milky, stinking murk. One of his paws clawed my wrist. I grabbed for it, slipped off, then felt an explosion of flame in my shoulder as his snapping jaws grazed me. I thrust myself away from him, surged to the surface for a momentary snatch of air, then dove again, deeper this time.

I couldn't see anything but a fury of foam above me from his swimming. I plunged a hand into it, grappling desperately for a hold, clamped onto one of his hind legs, and pulled him down.

Couldn't hold him. He was too powerful and too slippery in the water. I surged up for air again, scissor kicking to try to surface as far from him as I could.

I broke into the light a few yards off his flank. He wasn't snarling now, he was hacking and gagging for air, but the instant he heard me surface, he whirled and surged toward me again, his eyes wild with killing rage. I thrust myself backward, gasping for breath, trying to fend him off. Not a chance. He was too strong and too close.

I rolled quickly and dove deeply again, then twisted and reversed to come up beneath him, groping for him in the seething water. I felt one of his forelegs, grabbed onto it with both hands and pulled hard, dragging him under with me. I had a better grasp this time but he still pulled free in a few seconds.

Damn it! I swam away from him again and surfaced with my hands in front of my face for protection. I broke into the air only a few feet from his rump and immediately backpedaled, trying to put distance between us. But this time he didn't whirl and lunge. He was gagging, trying to clear his lungs, thrashing about, desperately trying to stay afloat. I was winded, keening for air myself, but when the Rott turned away and paddled for shore, I plunged after him. I had to take him now. If he made it to the shore and turned on me, he could trap me in here until I drowned.

But I couldn't catch him. Hampered by my sodden clothing and with barely enough strength to push myself ahead, the Rottweiler simply outswam me to the shore. My feet struck bottom before his did though, and I made a last, despairing lunge after him, roaring and splashing water.

And it worked. When his paws touched solid ground he reeled ashore and staggered away as fast as he could manage, tail down, scrambling for his life. Or so he thought. If he'd turned on me he could have finished me off with one pass. No contest.

# TWENTY-ONE
## AGONY AND AFTERMATH

I CROUCHED in the reeking shallows on my hands and knees, head down, throat ablaze, gasping, utterly spent, only a heartbeat away from blacking out. I'm not sure how long I knelt there. Ten minutes? Perhaps more. Eventually, the chill water began to take its toll and I felt numbness creeping up my thighs. I had to get clear of the water and of this place before the dog came back. Or the Thirds did.

I stumbled to my feet and reeled ashore like a zombie on drugs, barely able to walk upright. My shoulder was a fireball of pain where the Rott had nailed me, and my legs were leaden from cold and exhaustion. Still, they worked after a fashion, and I forced myself into motion, stumbling away from the Kewadin pond toward the old railroad grade, one agonizing step at a time.

The hike back down the grade seemed to take forever, much longer than it should have. I kept looking back to see if I'd taken a wrong turn or lost my way somehow, but it was a railroad grade, forgodsake. No turns, no detours, no crossroads. And after what felt like forty years of wandering in the wilderness, I spotted the truck in the distance and thrashed my way through the underbrush to it.

I fired up the pickup, locked the doors, then took a moment to open my shirt and check my shoulder. It was welted and already purpling where I'd been bitten, but it wasn't bleeding much. His jaws had never gotten a firm hold, thank God, or I'd be floating face down back in that stinking pool. I was going to have one humongous bruise, but beyond that no major damage.

The pickup's heater thawed my bones a bit on the drive back to Grand Portal. I was almost sorry it did. As the numbness wore off, my legs and back became a cacophony of aches and hurts, each clamoring for attention. My hands were the worst. In the scramble up the slag heap I'd scraped them raw and torn a nail on my left index finger. At the time I'd been too panicked to feel much pain, but I felt it now, by God. They burned. And so did I.

The more I thought about it, the more enraged I became. Sweet Jesus, I could have had Corey with me. Or a Girl Scout troop. That damned dog had been left on guard out there like a land mine or a loaded gun set to go off blindly to maim or kill anyone who happened along.

Patriots. Right. Maniacs was more like it. A gang of two-for-a-nickel pot growers hiding their crummy little business behind the American flag, secondhand uniforms, and a smokescreen of right-wing rhetoric. It was incredible that they'd managed to snow the locals as long as they had. . . . Or had they?

As my first blaze of anger cooled a bit and the pain settled down to a dull throb, I began to chew over what had happened and what it actually meant. The Third Coasters controlled a four hundred acre tract out here and the patches I'd seen were in the remotest corner of it. Most people would steer clear of the area because of the signs and the stench of the mountain pool and the dog would run off anyone who was just passing through. The patches were camouflaged by the alders and poplars that grew naturally in the area. They'd be difficult to spot from the air, even if anyone was looking.

Still, pot patches weren't unknown in the north country. The DNR kept an eye out for them, and so did whatever local law there was. But the nearest law was in Anahwey, Sheriff Ernie Feige and his six deputies to cover a three-county area. So the question was, why hadn't the law found them already?

Dumb luck? Or were the Third Coasters wired deeper into the local political scene than Van Amstel realized? Everyone I'd talked to, Hagstrom, Van Amstel, even Thorp, had told me these clowns were not only tolerated, some people in the area considered them folk heroes.

So if I went stomping into the county sheriff's office again, what would happen? Would he charge off to take on the Third Coast militia with his little handful of deputies? Or would he cite me for trespassing and send us off on a long drive home down deserted roads?

By the time I pulled into the Heritage Inn parking lot, I'd thought it through. I waved a quick hello at the elderly lady at the desk who gave me a startled look as I hurried by. I took the stairs two at a time up to our room and rapped twice.

"Who is it?"

"Open up, Corey. It's your lovin' mom."

He swung the door open, and his eyes widened. "What happened?"

"It's a long story," I said. "Where's Red?"

"She's out scrounging us some breakfast. She told me not to open the door for anyone but you."

"Good," I said. "Get packed, we're out of here as soon as she gets back."

"But what happened? And what stinks?"

"Hydrogen sulfide," I said, heading for the bathroom. "Don't worry, it's not contagious. I need a quick shower. Find me a clean sweatshirt and jeans and toss them in here. Cram everything else in our bags and be ready to hit the door in five minutes, okay?"

"But . . . ?"

"No buts; do it. And one other thing," I yelled as I stepped into the shower fully clothed. "Check the phone book and see if there's a listing for Nick Van Amstel." And then I turned on the warm water and began soaping myself down, clothes and all.

# TWENTY-TWO
# FAIR WARNING

"THANKS FOR seeing me on such short notice," I said apologetically as Nick Van Amstel ushered me into his living room. He was dressed casually, a sweater vest and slacks, loafers with no socks. His home was already immaculate, not an empty glass or even a water spot.

"Not at all," he said, waving me through to the den. "Sundays are pretty quiet here, besides, you said it was important and you don't strike me as someone who'd exaggerate. Can we offer you breakfast?"

"Thanks, but this isn't a social call," I said. "I have a confession to make. I did some trespassing this morning. I walked back to the Kewadin Drift to look it over. While I was there, I spotted a couple of marijuana patches, good-sized ones. Someone's cultivating some serious dope on your school's property, Nick."

Van Amstel blinked, as though I'd announced I'd beamed down from a saucer. "You're sure of this?" he managed at last.

"Absolutely. I know what reefer looks like, and if I'd had any doubts, the Rottweiler they've got guarding the patches eliminated them. He nearly eliminated me."

"A guard dog, you mean? My God, are you all right?"

"Barely. And no thanks to your tenants."

He shook his head in disbelief. "Those bastards! How could

they do a thing like this? Have you reported it to the police?"

"Not yet. Since I was technically trespassing I decided to talk to you first."

"I'm glad that you did," he said decisively. "We're already bucking a fair amount of resentment, God only knows what the local rednecks will make of this. Maybe we can put a better face on things if we report it ourselves. It might be better for you as well. When had you planned to head home?"

"We're on our way as soon as we leave here."

"That's probably best. It might also be best to keep your name out of this. I can't imagine that you'd be in any danger from the Thirds, but I can scarcely believe Dan Cezak would be involved in a thing like this either."

"I'm not saying he is," I said. "I'm only telling you what I found."

"For which I'm very grateful. You can leave this to me, Ms. Mitchell, I'll take care of the Thirds. Pete's going to get his wish after all. The board's been damned unhappy about the lease we gave the Thirds. I would never have gone back on my word, but if this is true, it could destroy everything we've worked for. Can you tell me exactly where these patches are?"

"I can do better than that," I said, fishing an envelope out of my pocket. "I drew up a crude map. One patch is roughly a hundred and fifty yards southwest of the old mine adit. The other is another sixty or seventy yards beyond the first."

"Excellent," he said, scanning my sketch. "Even Sheriff Feige should be able to find them with this. As far as the trespassing goes, just to be on the safe side, if anyone asks, you had my permission to check out the site. Clear?"

"Clear," I said. "Thank you.

"I ah, do have one question though. When we talked last night, I told you the school couldn't grant you access to the Kewadin Drift tract, and that trespassing might be dangerous, though frankly, I wasn't thinking of anything like this. Yet you chose to take a look around on your own. Why did you take the risk?"

Red and I had discussed what I'd say if this came up, and I had a glib deflection already prepared, something about walking in my father's flipper prints or a fib to that effect. But I hesitated. I dislike lying, even in a good cause. And perhaps this wasn't a good cause. Van Amstel had been straightforward and helpful. The least I could do was return the favor.

"Let me ask you a question instead," I said. "You knew about the trouble between my father and Frank d'Hubert over my mother. If things had gotten bad enough between them, for instance, if my father thought Frank was responsible for my mother's death, do you think . . ." I swallowed. "Do you think he was capable of killing him?"

Van Amstel looked at me sharply, then his eyes widened with growing understanding. "My God," he said softly. "Is that what you think happened?"

"I don't know. But you were there, what do you think?"

"I'm . . . not sure," he said, mulling over the idea. "They weren't exactly pals even before the trouble over Madeline, but . . . murder? No. I don't believe it."

"My father was a SEAL in Vietnam," I said. "I'm no expert but I've done some reading about those days. They were involved in a lot of rough business. Raids, even assassinations."

"Your father took part in some fairly hairy operations," Van Amstel admitted. "I wasn't involved myself, but I knew about them. But that was war. His trouble with Frank wasn't."

"The only difference I see, is that in Vietnam my father killed strangers who were only guilty of being on the wrong side. With Frank, he had a real motive, as strong and personal as they come. He blamed him for my mother's death."

"Even if that's true," Van Amstel conceded, "I think your father was a better man than that. Granted, he was a bit of a rogue, but I can't believe he could have committed murder, for revenge or any other reason. And if he had, why would you think he'd conceal the body near the mine?"

"For the same reason somebody thinks it's safe to grow pot back there," I said. "It's abandoned, isolated, and the air reeks. It's perfect. Plus, it was the only place in the area he was familiar with."

"That damned mine," Van Amstel said, shaking his head grimly. "It's been nothing but bad luck since we came home. Look, Mitch, I simply can't believe your father could have done such a thing. Perhaps I just don't want to. But I owe you a debt of gratitude for bringing the marijuana patches to my attention. If you're still set on exploring that mine, then I'll arrange it."

"What about the militia?" I asked.

"To hell with them! Once this business comes out, Cezak will be in no position to bargain. I'm going to get them off our land and the sooner the better."

"Not too soon, I hope. I'd like to get my son safely home before anything breaks."

"Of course. I'll ask Sheriff Feige to hold off a few days before he takes action. That way they'll be less likely to connect it to you."

"Thank you," I said. "I know all this business with my father must sound a bit off-the-wall to you, but—"

"Not at all," he said, waving off my apology. "Most of us have a skeleton or two hidden away in our family closet. As your father's friend, and yours as well, the least I can do is help you take a look behind the door. I only hope, for your sake, that there's nothing to find."

"That makes it unanimous," I said.

# Twenty-three
# Ambushed

❧

We took a roundabout route south, down M-95 via Witch Lake, then across to the Lake Michigan shoreline. Despite the stunning scenery, vagrant thoughts kept popping up in the back of my mind. Would anything really be done about the weed patches?

I'm no cynic, but I really didn't know Van Amstel well, and though he apparently remembered my father fondly, he didn't owe me a thing. It occurred to me that he might be more concerned with protecting his school's reputation than about doing a favor for the daughter of an old Navy buddy, especially one he hadn't heard from in thirty years.

Red, Corey, and I kicked the situation around thoroughly on the drive south and decided we'd give him four days. Either I heard something by Thursday or I'd notify the State Police at Marquette about what I'd seen. Right.

Tipping off the law turned out to be the least of my problems.

Wednesday morning I dropped Corey at school, then drove to the Nest, as usual. But nothing was as usual.

As I wheeled into the parking lot I spotted a van wearing the logo of the local Huron Harbor television station, NewsChannel 6. There were other cars with media logos as well, and as I wheeled around the side of the building to park, a blond, blow-dried broadcast mannequin I recognized from the evening news, Kevin McMurtry, piled out of his van and came trotting toward me. A cameraman carrying a TV minicam on his shoulder was only a step behind. The cameraman was already filming as Kevin shoved a microphone in my face.

"Miss Mitchell, do you have any comment on your part in the militia standoff at Grand Portal?"

"My part?" I stammered. "What are you talking about?"

"The standoff between the Third Coast militia and the federal task force that raided the militia headquarters this morning. Major Cezak of the militia has identified you as an undercover operative for the FBI. Would you care to comment?"

"Look, I have no idea what's going on. No comment," I said, trying to move around him. He sidestepped to block my path, so I dumped any hope of dignity and simply bolted past them, sprinting for the door of the Crow's Nest like a spooked doe. Red opened the door as I approached, then slammed it and locked it as soon as I'd made it through.

"Nice you could drop by," Red said dryly. "Those vultures out there have been gathering for over an hour."

"What's happened?" I said following Red through the restaurant area to the bar.

"You didn't catch the news?"

"Not this morning."

"Well, take a look," she said, gesturing at the TV mounted over the end of the bar. "Those backwoods blackshirts are all over it." The doughy face of Major Dan Cezak filled the screen even as she spoke.

"But why? What's going on?"

"It's all still pretty confused. Hang on a minute. . . ." She found the remote and goosed up the volume on the TV as the camera cut away from Cezak to a harassed looking news anchor.

". . . raid was the largest drug bust of the year in the Upper Peninsula, and perhaps the most dangerous. Several blasts, apparently from land mines, have reportedly detonated in the area of the illegal fields. Two Grand Portal men have been arrested and charges are pending against a third man from Wisconsin. All three suspects have been allegedly identified as members of the paramilitary group known as the Third Coast Militia."

They cut to a shot of two men in cuffs being hurried from a police van into a county building of some sort. Neither of them looked familiar.

Red was staring at me, wide-eyed. "Mined?" she said. "Did he say the fields were mined?"

"Irrelevant," I said. "I never really got close to the fields."

Someone pounded on the front door.

"We're closed!" Red yelled.

"It's Sheriff Bauer, Red," Charlie yelled back. "Open up."

Red trotted to the front door and let Charlie in. A TV crewman tried to follow him in, but Charlie firmly closed the door and leaned against it, shutting them out.

"You're collecting quite a crowd," Charlie said. "Maybe you should charge admission."

"Not until I know what's going on, Charlie. What's happened?"

"A damned ugly situation," Charlie said. "I'm just glad it's Ernie Feige's mess and not mine. The Feds grabbed two men at a backwoods pot patch early this morning. At the same time, they tried to raid the Third Coast Militia headquarters in Grand Portal. It was a cock-up from the start. The Thirds were tipped. They barricaded their building and forted up. They've fired a few rounds in the air to prove they're serious and the Feds and the local law have surrounded the place. A standoff."

"But what are the reporters doing here? How did my name come up?"

"After they forted up, this so-called Major Cezak character released a statement claiming the raid is a frame-up and that you were part of it."

"What kind of a frame-up?"

"He claims the militia didn't know about the weed the Feds found out in the boondocks. Says it was in a section of their firing range that they never use. He says the Feds only wanted an excuse to raid Third Coast headquarters so they can plant evidence in the building."

"And where do I fit into this?"

"Cezak claims you're some kind of undercover agent. That the DEA or whoever sent you in to ask permission to check out an abandoned mine so you could claim to have discovered the weed accidentally. When the Thirds turned you down, you went ahead anyway, which makes any evidence you discovered inadmissable. Is any of that true?"

"Not much. I'm obviously not a cop. I did ask permission to scout an abandoned mine. Cezak said no, but his outfit doesn't actually own the land, they only lease it. So I contacted the landowner and got permission from him. I spotted the weed back there, informed the owner about it, and that was it."

"The owner? Not the police?"

"I was hoping to keep my name out of it," I said grimly. "That part of the plan needs some work. What should I do now, Charlie?"

"Well, those media types out there won't go away without getting some kind of a statement so you might as well talk to 'em now. Just tell them the truth, the slower the better."

"Slowly? Why?"

"Because TV people won't use any answer longer than fifteen seconds. Print reporters are a little more thorough, but not much. You're not the story here, the standoff is, so they probably won't push you too hard. Just don't get rattled if they seem to doubt you. They're used to dealing with pols and wackos. Truth isn't something they hear very often."

"Okay," I said, taking a deep breath. "As they say in Texas, if you're gonna kiss a frog, don't look at it too long. Let 'em in, Red. Let's get this over with."

Red popped the front door and a small army of reporters bustled in. Two television types had cameramen in tow who quickly set up floodlights with umbrellas to diffuse the glare. Charlie acted as a ringmaster, herding the circus into a corner of the dining room and announcing that there would only be one session and any questions he deemed improper would end it.

"Hold on," McMurtry said. "That's prior restraint. You can't stage-manage an interview. Even in a town this size you must've heard of freedom of the press."

"Yes sir, I sure have, but this conference is on private property. Miss Mitchell's property. So if she asks me to remove anyone, well, we can debate about the rights issue, but we'll be doing it outside. Any other questions?"

There was some grumbling, but everyone settled down into a rough semicircle. I took a seat facing them.

It wasn't so bad, no worse than waltzing naked through a razor blade factory. The lights were the worst, not the floodlights, the little red dots on the mini-cams that seemed to focus between my eyes like gunsights. It meant the cameras were running, that I was being filmed, and I immediately realized there was a milk spot on my blouse the size of New Jersey, my hair was a mess, and I couldn't remember if I'd put on lipstick before I left the house. Terrific. I was going to look like the mummy's curse, plus I couldn't seem to remember how to speak English.

Somehow I blundered through an opening statement. Just the facts ma'am, in the order things had occurred. I managed not to stutter or drool on myself. I think.

And then the questions began. The worst of it was, because of the lights, I couldn't be sure who was asking what.

"Miss Mitchell, are you now, or have you ever been, a government agent?"

"Never. I'm a businesswoman and a mom and that's all."

"Then it's your statement that Major Cezak's claims about you are false?"

"I don't know what he's claimed, so I can't comment."

"How long and to what extent have you been involved with the Third Coast militia, Miss Mitchell?"

"I'm not involved with them at all. As I explained, I was in their headquarters building once, to ask permission to explore an old mine. Prior to that day, I'd never heard of them."

"What are your feelings on the militia movement in general, and the Third Coast militia in particular?"

I almost literally bit my tongue. I had opinions, all right. "I have no comment." That answer worked so well I used it a few more times. And that seemed to do the trick. The questions slowed and things gradually wound down. Charlie was right, I wasn't the story. It was up in Grand Portal. I just hoped it would stay there.

We wrapped up the whole process in roughly half an hour, and ten minutes later they were gone. The lot of them decamped like a flock of ravens in search of a fresh roadkill.

# Twenty-four
## Out of the Shadows

ᏆᏸᏧᏟ

As the crowd thinned out I spotted a familiar figure at a corner table, sitting alone, nursing a Coke. In his robin's-egg blue cotton sportcoat, Repp necktie, and khaki Dockers, he looked like a yuppie computer salesman. His longish hair was neatly tied back in a ponytail, and he'd shaved. Recently. The last time I'd seen him he'd been wearing camouflage castoffs and a three-day stubble. Jack Thorp.

He rose as I approached. "Hi," he said, a bit uncertainly. "Remember me?"

"You look like somebody I met once. Do you have an evil twin?"

"It seems like it sometimes," he said, with a wan smile. "Can we talk somewhere a little more private?"

"Not a chance," I said. "No offense, but the way things are, I'd rather keep any business we have public. Why aren't you in jail?"

"I was, briefly. The Copper County sheriff picked me up for questioning early this morning but they cut me loose. The FBI's taken over the seige now and their computers coughed up my life story in about three minutes flat. I'm not a member of the Third Coast, I just work for 'em. I've never been part of the core group that runs things."

"So what are you doing here, Mr. Thorp?"

"Hoping to avoid trouble for both of us. Sit down, please, I don't want to attract any reporters. I came to warn you," he said, taking a deep breath. "The word's around that you were the one who fingered Chess and Puck for the police."

"You've lost me completely. Who are Chess and Puck?"

"Greg Chessman and Barry Puckett, the two potheads who were cultivating the homegrown weed at the back corner of the Third Coast tract."

"Never heard of them," I said. "But even if I had, what's the difference? They're in custody."

"They are, but Harlan Pettiford isn't. Remember him? He's the third man the police are looking for."

"Pettiford? The blackshirt I met at your headquarters?"

"He's the one. I don't think Harlan likes women much in general and now that you've blown the whistle on his operation, you're definitely on his list."

"I see. Funny, everybody kept telling me what an all-American bunch your militia buddies are."

"The Militia's not your problem. The weed was strictly Pettiford's deal. The Thirds had nothing to do with those patches. They didn't know about them."

"Really? According to the news, the guys who were arrested were both militia members."

"It's a big outfit," Thorp said with a shrug. "Bigger than people realize. In any organization that size, there are bound to be a few losers."

"Bad apples, you mean? Is that the party line?"

"It may seem hokey," Thorp admitted. "That doesn't mean it's not true. Your problem isn't the Thirds, but you've still got one. See, the thing about dopers, they all know each other, especially up north. And one of 'em apparently knows you. You ever hear of a guy named Boone? A biker type? I think he's from Pontiac but he's been laying low with some buddies in Grand Portal. A crank dealer."

"Sweet Jesus," I said softly.

"The name rings a bell, hunh? How do you know him?"

"It's a long story," I said. "How's he tied into the Thirds?"

"He's not. He's not a member and never has been. But apparently this Boone character knows Harlan Pettiford and his two pals. Maybe they've been doing business together. When the fields got busted, Boone split, but not before passing the word that you're some kind of a nark. A Judas."

"But I didn't—"

"That's not the worst of it," he said, waving off my objections. "The police haven't released any names yet, but Pettiford's not in the compound. He's the guy from Wisconsin they're looking for."

"What?"

"They missed him. He split the night before the raid. That's why I'm here. I thought you should know."

"You're saying I'm in danger?"

"I don't know. I've worked for the Thirds for nearly eight months and I never saw this coming. Growin' weed in the boondocks isn't exactly the crime of the century, but planting mines or anti-personnel booby traps to guard their patches is a whole 'nother thing. After the big blast in Oklahoma City the Feds take any crime with explosives involved damned seriously, whether the blasts are effective or not."

"What do you mean, whether they were effective?"

"If the mines were supposed to keep people away, they went off too soon, and if the dopers were trying to destroy the patches, they didn't use enough. Either way, those guys are looking at hard time for using explosives at all."

"I should hope so," I said, mulling over the information. "You said the blasts went off early? You mean before the raid?"

"That's right. In fact, the blasts triggered the raid. The guys they caught were checking out the damage to the patches, probably intended to burn the rest of it. The Feds had to hit the Third Coast headquarters before they were ready."

"But the reporters said the Thirds knew the raid was coming."

"Sure they knew. You've got to understand, Yoopers not only know one another, a lot of them are kin. There must be a half dozen guys in the Thirds with family connections to the local law."

"That's a comfort. This Pettiford, do you think he's really dangerous?"

"If you'd asked that me last week, I would have said he was all guff. But a few bombs going off will definitely change your viewpoint. Maybe I'm not the best judge of who's dangerous and who isn't. I just thought you should know."

"And why is that?" I said, eyeing him. "Don't get me wrong, I appreciate the warning, I'm just not clear on why you came all this way to deliver it."

He met my eyes for a moment, then smiled. "I'm just doing my civic duty, ma'am. Helping out a damsel in distress."

"I'm not in distress."

"But you could be. You'd better understand, the two guys the cops have in custody were just stiffs. Pettiford was the brains of that bunch, and he's still on the loose and there may have been others involved."

"Like Boone, you mean."

"Him or guys like him. I'm not saying it's an organized gang, it might be simpler for the cops to wrap up if it was. But the riffraff up there all know each other, they all do business with one another, and some of 'em think they've got business with you."

"Sorry to hear that, but you still didn't answer my question. Why are you here? You could have told me all this by phone."

"True, and I wouldn't have had to shave and put on a tie, either. The truth is, I wanted to come. For one thing, I wanted to be sure you took me seriously."

"You thought I'd take you more seriously if you wore a tie?"

"You might, but there's a little more to it," he admitted. "Look, Mitch, we don't know each other very well, but you strike me as someone who's pretty direct. Or direct and pretty, whichever. When you walked into the Third's headquarters a few days ago, you made quite an impression on me. And I've been to Panama and the Ontanogan County Fair and I don't impress all that easily."

He paused a moment, offering me an opening to comment. I didn't.

"You're not going to make this easy, are you?" he said ruefully. "Fair enough, the bottom line is, I wanted to see you again. That's why I followed you to the diner to tell you about Hagstrom and why I'm here now. I want to help, but I also wanted to see you again. Is that too direct?"

"Not at all," I said. "As long as you don't mind if I'm just as direct."

"Why do I have the feeling I'm not going to like this?"

"It's nothing personal. You and your evil twin both seem like nice enough guys in spite of the company you keep. But right now my life's awfully complicated. So if you expect anything more than a polite thank you for your trouble, you shouldn't."

"Are you involved with anyone?"

I hesitated, then shrugged. "In a way, yes. My son and I are going through a rough patch and right now working things out with him is the most important thing in my life. It's all I can handle."

"I can understand that,"—he nodded—"but unless I'm totally misreading the situation, you're not saying no, no, a thousand times no, Thorp, you swine. You're saying, not now, Jack. Maybe some other time. Is that a fair assessment?"

I couldn't help smiling. "I suppose so."

"Then things could be worse," he said, answering my smile. "You're not married or gay or going into a convent. As for the timing, maybe it's for the best. Until things cool off a bit, it might be risky for us to be seen together."

"Risky for whom?"

"For both of us. On the other hand, I could be overreacting. Let's hope there won't be any trouble," he said, rising. He took a napkin out of the dispenser, jotted a number on it and passed it to me. "This is my number. If anything comes up and you need help, call and I'll come running, okay?"

"And if nothing comes up?"

"Call me anyway and I'll still come running. Maybe next time our schedules will line up a little better."

"Or maybe not. Either way, thanks for the . . . courtesy call."

"No charge," he said. "Just don't lose my number, okay?"

"I won't," I said.

# Twenty-five
# A Visiting Professor

THE REPORTERS kept coming. The rest of the morning whenever I turned around, I'd see another one headed my way with a microphone or with a notepad. I couldn't get any work done, and worse, I couldn't think. Finally, I gave it up and went next door to the tackle shop to hide out. I only open the shop on weekends in the fall, so I had the place to myself, surrounded by Scubapro diving masks, snorkels in translucent colors, regulators, weightbelts, the tools of my father's trade, and mine. The rafters are decorated with antique diving gear my father and I collected over the years, coils of tarred rope, a tarnished brass diving helmet, the weathered wooden arc of a sailing ship's rib.

I spent some of the happiest days of my girlhood in this room, dreaming of deep water and life and love. A few of those dreams actually came true. I'm still working on the others.

In the familiarity of my shop, the whole Third Coast business seemed almost unreal, as did Thorp's warning about Pettiford and his friends. I might have discounted it except for the trouble I'd had with Boone. He worried me the most. Whether he was just bone-mean or strung out on crank, his trolley was definitely off the track.

Anahwey was across the straits, in another country in some ways, but thanks to the press, Boone and Pettiford would soon know where to find me. Were they whacked out enough to risk coming after me? Possibly. And I had Corey to consider.

At least I wasn't alone. Charlie Bauer had offered his help and any extra protection I thought I'd need. If the trouble did follow me here, Charlie would—

Someone rapped on the shop door, startling me. Reporter? No, no one but Red knew I was out here. I picked up a shark billy, hefted it, then cautiously unlocked the door. And the tallest Asian woman I've ever seen stepped in. She didn't have to duck to enter but if the velvet tam perched atop her raven hair had been a pillbox, it might've bumped the doorframe. Nick Van Amstel followed her in. Both were dressed for travel in dark raincoats. They looked disheveled. And worried.

"I'm sorry to break in on you like this, Mitch," Van Amstel said. "This is my wife, Mei Lin. I don't believe you met the other evening."

"Hi," she said, offering her hand. "Nick's told me so much about you I feel we've already met."

"Not a chance," I said. "I would have remembered. How are you?"

"In trouble," Van Amstel said bluntly. "And very concerned about you. Are you up to speed on what's happened?"

"I saw the news reports on television," I said. "It didn't look like things worked very well."

"No, the raid was a botch, and now Cezak and his people are forted up like Crockett at the Alamo. I've known these men for years, Mitch. I never dreamed things could get this crazy, or that they could be so vindictive."

"How do you mean?"

"Our home was vandalized last night," Mei said quietly, wincing. "Someone threw cans of yellow paint through our living room windows. They made a terrible mess."

"My God," I said. "Was anyone hurt?"

"They weren't trying to hurt anyone," Nick said grimly, "at least, not yet. But they made their point. The cans could just as easily have been on fire. Well, message received. I'm taking Mei down to Detroit to stay with relatives until this blows over."

"But what about your security force at the school?"

"Rent-a-cops," Nick snorted. "They talked me into installing a state-of-the-art electronic monitoring system last year, but it's only effective on cars driving through the gate, not hoodlums that climb fences."

"I'm sorry for your trouble," I said. "Unfortunately, I've had problems too. When I told you about the patches, you said you'd try to keep me out of it. So how did the militia learn I blew the whistle on them?"

"I haven't the faintest," Van Amstel said positively. "When I talked to Sheriff Feige, I never mentioned your name."

"But the Thirds found out, and quickly. They also had time to try to blow up the evidence."

"And you think I might have warned them?" Van Amstel said, more surprised than offended.

"Let's say it occurred to me that you had a lot at stake. The reputation of your school must seem more important than a backwoods weed patch."

"I see," Van Amstel said coolly. "The only flaw in that theory is that I want the militia off that tract, the sooner the better."

"Do you? You've apparently coexisted with them for quite some time."

"That was when they were a social club, not paranoid drug dealers. Being associated with the militia is a disaster for the school. It could destroy us."

"Why? You only leased the land to them. Surely the police won't hold you responsible for what they've done with it?"

"The land doesn't matter," Van Amstel said grimly. "The problem is that even a cursory investigation could cause difficulty for us."

"Tell her, Nicky," Mel prompted. "She went out on a limb for us and she's in trouble for it. She has a right to know."

"To know what?" I asked.

"To know that some of our students might not have all of the proper paperwork to be in this country legally," Nick admitted. "Sometimes we cut corners to bring people in. I'm not ashamed of it, we're simply trying to right wrongs that were done to these people when our government abandoned them to the Communists all those years ago. I hope you can understand our situation. Your father would have."

"I . . . don't know how he would have felt about it," I said slowly, absorbing what he'd said. "For me, I guess it falls under the heading of things that aren't my business. Frankly, I've got troubles of my own."

"I wish I could help," Nick said, "but I don't know how the Thirds got your name. All I can tell you is, that when I informed Sheriff Feige about the pot patches, I got the impression that he already knew. It was nothing he said, it was—I don't know. He just didn't seem surprised to hear about them."

"Do you think he's on the take?"

"I don't know," Van Amstel said. "Perhaps I'm wrong. As I said, it was only a feeling."

"Don't blame yourself for failing to read the hearts of men, Nicky," Mei said dryly. "Even Kung Fu-Tse couldn't manage that."

"In any case, what's done is done," Van Amstel said, touching his wife's hand. "You tried to do the right thing by telling me about the patches and I did the right thing by informing the authorities. We'll just have to salvage what we can. What will you do?"

"There's not much I can do. I'll just have to ride it out, and I prefer to do it here. I have friends on the police force. We'll be okay."

"Spoken like a Mitchell," he sighed with mock exasperation. "Your dad would have said the same thing. I do have some good news for you, at least. I've spoken to several members of the board about the mine projects we discussed and they're sure we'll be able to raise the money for the work. The Kewadin Drift is out of the question of course, but—"

"Out of the question? Why?"

"Because of the damage the blasts caused to the mine. I thought you knew."

"I knew that there were explosions that partially destroyed the patches, but the marijuana was at least a hundred yards from the mine."

"That's right, but another blast was set off just above the mine entrance. It collapsed a section of the rock face, blocking the opening completely. Here," he said, fumbling in his jacket pocket. "I thought you'd be interested so I brought along copies of the police photographs for you."

He handed me the photos, black and white shots of the mine site. The land was dusted with snow but the effects of the explosions were savagely apparent. Both marijuana patches had been ripped by blasts, plants shredded and scattered. The marks above the mine entrance were less dramatic, but more effective. An ugly scar had been gouged in the face of the cliff, spilling earth and granite into the pond below. The mound of debris was clearly visible above the surface of the water.

"As you can see, the entrance is completely buried," Van Amstel said. "It looks like a quarter of the mountain came down."

"But why? There was no marijuana or anything else on that cliff."

"The police theory is that Pettiford and the other two had something stored in the mine and set off a blast to bury it permanently."

"Pettiford's a diver," I said. "He would have had access to it even under water. It would make a great stash all right. Do they have any idea what was hidden there?"

"Sheriff Feige said he thought they might have stored illegal weapons, machine guns or bazookas. I don't think the police know, and I doubt they ever will. Whatever it was is buried under God knows how many tons of rock and they have no intention of trying to recover it, assuming there's anything left *to* recover. They have enough evidence to convict the men involved. The funny thing is, I'm the one who's really disappointed. I hoped that after all these years I might finally get something useful out of that damned mine, if only a few waterlogged artifacts."

"Yeah," I said, trying to hide my own frustration. "Me too."

"There are other sites and other opportunities. We can still go ahead as planned. . . . Is something wrong?"

I didn't answer for a moment. I'd lost track of what he was saying as I examined the mine site photographs more closely.

"There's snow in these shots," I said slowly, "and the pond is iced over."

"That's right, we had our first hard frost and some light snow Monday."

"How cold did it get?"

"In the high twenties I think," Van Amstel said. "The wind chill was lower, of course. Why?"

"Because the pond is only partly frozen over," I said. "You see here? The ice skin covers the entire pond except for a small ring of open water near the rockfall at the entrance."

"I see what you mean. Does that have some significance?"

"It might. If the pond water was the same temperature, it should have frozen all the way across, especially near the cliff face where the exposed rock would be colder than the water. But it didn't. There's a pool of open water here. Which means the mine entrance may not be completely closed. Warmer water must still be rising from the shaft."

"But, with all that rockfall . . ."

"A mine entrance is a big hole. It may be too small a gap to get through, but if warm water's flowing up, then at least part of the entrance must still be open."

"But wouldn't the explosion have made it unstable?" Mei asked.

"That depends on how much damage it did. Those old miners shored up their diggings pretty solidly. They blasted almost every day when the mine was in operation. I doubt that a single explosion at the mouth of the shaft did much damage farther down. It's worth a look, anyway."

"Well, if you're game, then so am I," Van Amstel said. "We'll put it at the top of the list. We'd better wait a bit, though, until things are sorted out with the Thirds."

"You'll have full-blown winter up there soon anyway. Suppose we table things until spring and make a fresh start then?"

"Fair enough," he said, nodding. "We'll stay in touch over the winter months. I'll keep you informed about the status of the museum's grant request and hopefully by spring we'll have a whole slate of sites to choose from. How does that sound?"

"Better than I deserve," I said. "The truth is, I feel responsible for involving you in this. If not for me, none of it would have happened."

"Nonsense," Mei said, "you mustn't blame yourself. We certainly don't."

"Besides," Nick said, "in a way, I'm reliving my youth."

"Your youth?" I echoed, puzzled.

"Absolutely," he said, grinning. "Your dad had an ingenious knack for getting me into trouble. Apparently, that trait runs in the family."

"You may be right at that," I said. "I'm sorry."

"Don't be. Your dad and I always came through all right in the end and we will also. Until spring, then?" he said, offering his hand.

"Until spring," I agreed.

# TWENTY-SIX
# AN EARLY SPRING

SOMETIMES HAVING a sheriff as a friend can be exasperating. For example, I think I get less than my fair share of the county diving jobs, recovering cars or snowmobiles that end up on the lake bottom, simply because Charlie bends over backward not to give an impression of favoritism. Thanks a lot.

On the other hand, after my run in with the press over the Third Coast standoff at Grand Portal, he kept me posted on the situation there, and gave me regular updates on the hunts for Boone and Harlan Pettiford. He also furnished me with extra protection. He didn't bother to ask if I wanted it, he simply supplied it.

Huron Harbor's a relatively small town, about twelve thousand souls, all told. I'm not sure how big its police force is, but they had to be multiplying like bunnies because I seemed to be seeing cops every time I turned around. They were constantly cruising the Crow's Nest parking lot or noshing in the restaurant. And paying for every bite, I might add.

I also offered Charlie coffee every evening when he personally followed me home from work. He never took me up on it, and I was sorry for that.

I wasn't sure when it happened, but I'd found myself depending on Charlie to be there for me without being asked. It wasn't planned, nor was it entirely welcome. We'd been friends for a while, but that friendship seemed to be evolving into something stronger. The timing was terrible. He honestly isn't my type, assuming I have one. And yet I found myself thinking of him at odd moments. And wondering how much the difference in our ages might matter if . . . things progressed.

I think Charlie sensed it too, but he wasn't anymore comfortable about it than I was. Our relationship seemed to be bobbing uncertainly, dancing in deep water as we worked things out between us. So he didn't come in when I invited him. But he would show up at odd hours, make a U-turn in my driveway, and cruise out again. And once when I made a late-night goodie run to the supermarket, I passed him sitting in a turnout halfway down the road to the cottage. He waved.

At home, Corey and I made a few adjustments. He locked his bedroom door every night and I returned to my father's habit of keeping his old thirty-thirty Winchester by my bedside, with cartridges in the magazine but none in the chamber.

I thought I'd prepared as well as I could. But in the end, it meant less than nothing.

I was in my office at the Nest, wading through some paperwork. Corey had just wandered in from school and was shucking his raincoat. "Tough day?"

"School was okay, but it's pouring out now. Rain and snow. Where's Red?"

"In the kitchen the last time I looked," I said, feeling a minor pang of resentment.

"No she isn't, I checked on the way in."

I hesitated. "She went out half an hour ago for something," I said. "She should be back. . . ." I didn't finish the sentence. Something icy closed around my heart. And suddenly I was afraid. And there was no reason for it at all.

"What?" Corey asked.

"Nothing. Hold the fort here, sport. I'll be back in a minute." I made my way through the dining room to the front door and checked the parking lot. Red usually parked beside the building toward the beach. I thought I could see the corner of her truck, but couldn't be sure. Damn.

I stepped out into the icy autumn drizzle and sidled along the building, trying to keep below the eaves for shelter. There.

Her truck was there, so where . . . ? And then I saw her, crumpled on the pavement beside the driver's side door.

And then I was running to her through the rain. There was blood everywhere, on her face, her chest. She'd been shot. I cradled her head in my lap, trying to shield her from the rain. I heard someone screaming for help, to call 911, to get an ambulance. Me, I think.

# Twenty-seven
# Emergency Room

I FOLLOWED the ambulance as close as I dared, flying low in the Jeep only a car length behind it like a hound on a leash. I drove one-handed, keeping the other on Corey even though he was belted in. It wasn't enough to know he was all right, I needed to *feel* him. Somewhere on the way, Charlie Bauer joined the convoy, a second set of lights and sirens to speed us along.

The emergency room at County General was in a state of controlled chaos. I parked Corey in the waiting room near the admissions desk, told him to stay put, then followed in Charlie's wake into the triage ward, a long room with a dozen beds separated by green curtains.

Red was on a gurney halfway down the ward. A deputy, Bo Unger, was talking with a nurse a few feet to one side. A small army of doctors and nurses surrounded Red. I couldn't see her.

"How bad?" Charlie asked.

"Not as bad as it looked at first," Bo said, keeping his voice low. "Apparently she took two hits, one in the shoulder, one in the breast. Crossways. Hell of a lot of blood loss, but they figure she'll make it all right—"

I didn't hear the rest. The room seemed to fade away for a minute, as though someone had turned up the lights so brightly that everything was washing out.

Charlie had my arm, leading me back toward the admissions area. "I'm all right," I said. My voice was barely more than a squeak. "Really, Charlie," I said, conciously controlling my tone to make it sound normal, "I'm okay. I'd like to see Red."

"She's already gone," he said, glancing over his shoulder. "They're taking her up to surgery. It'll be a few hours before she can talk. What the hell happened, Mitch?"

"I don't know. She went on a goody run from the Nest, and when she was late getting back, I checked and"—I swallowed, hard—"and I—uh—I found her. On the ground in the rain. Her truck looks like a cheeze grater, Charlie. It must have a dozen holes in it. I could understand it if some of those lowlifes were angry at me, but why Red? My god, why Red?"

"Don't ask me to figure the psychology of somebody who could do a thing like this, Mitch. Don't jump the gun. We don't know what happened yet."

"We don't? Red and I get crossways of a damned private army, a week later somebody machine-guns her truck and you think it's a coincidence?"

"I didn't say that," Charlie said. "I just said we don't know what happened yet, and we don't. I'd better get back to the Nest to look at the scene. Do you want to come along?"

"No, I'd rather wait here."

"It may be a while, you know."

"I know. I'll wait. You go ahead."

"If you get a chance to talk to her before I get back, ask if she can remember any details. Anything at all. But don't press, okay?"

"I won't."

Charlie hurried off through the waiting room, parting the crowd of patients and staff like Moses at the Red Sea.

I made my way to the admissions desk, collected Corey, and gave the nurse in charge my name and the situation. She promised to keep me posted on Red's condition. Then I found an empty bench near her desk, and Corey and I sat down. To wait.

I hate hospitals on principal. Except for the birth of my son, nothing good has ever happened to me in one. Some people think the grim bustle of an emergency room is exciting; God knows they've made enough movies and TV shows about them. I was barely aware that I was there at all.

All I could think of was Red. She's one of the few people I've known who's truly larger than life. It's more than her physical presence or even her personality. It's her spirit, her inner strength.

I kept seeing her hands, short nails, blunt fingers, her palms and wrists reddened by soapy water. Strong hands. A working woman's hands. My God. I'd come to depend on her so much. . . . But she would pull through this. I knew she would. I knew it. I wasn't so sure I would.

Corey handled it better than I did. I tried to make conversation with him, but flopped. I kept losing my train of thought and trailing off in mid-sentence. After a few minutes of this, Corey pointedly fetched a copy of *Popular Science* from one of the magazine racks and buried his nose in it. I took the hint and left him alone. I picked up a magazine and leafed through it without seeing a word or picture. I couldn't focus. I kept having flashes of memory, of Red, laughing, loping along beside me on the lake shore. . . .

I needed to move, to pace, jog, to do anything but sit. And think. But there wasn't a spare seat in the place, to say nothing of walking room. So I sat. And waited. And wondered. I considered going out into the hallway to pace, but I didn't want Corey out of my sight or to risk missing any updates on Red's condition.

So I tried to focus on what had happened. Who could have done such a thing? It was fine for Charlie to maintain his objectivity. He was a lawman. It was part of his job. It wasn't mine. Besides, he hadn't been in that Third Coast armory, seen the guns and the flags and the attitudes.

Toy soldiers. I'd dismissed them as cranks, perhaps because I couldn't understand how someone could look at the same country I lived in and see it as oppressive.

And because I couldn't take their politics seriously, I'd written them off as harmless. A mistake, apparently. The people who lived up there certainly took them seriously. And both Thorp and Van Amstel had said they had strong ties to the community and even the local police.

And what about Thorp? He was no crank. He was a damned mercenary, for lack of a better word, a man who sells soldiering for money. So he definitely wasn't harmless. He claimed to be attracted to me, but somehow I didn't buy that. Had he really come to warn me? Or to scope out the ground? To set us up? Or maybe even to take Red down for some reason?

I didn't quite believe that. Not because I didn't think he was capable. . . . There was the word. Capable. That's what was wrong here. Thorp was a professional soldier, and there was nothing professional about the shooting.

Bo said Red had been hit twice, but her truck had taken a dozen more rounds, all misses. Bad shooting by any measure. And anyway, I was the problem, not Red. I was the one who'd poked around and notified the authorities. If the Thirds had a beef with someone, it should be me. But I wasn't the one on the operating table. It didn't make sense. Or maybe I just wasn't bright enough to see it.

Two hours crawled past like two years. I kept tugging at the threads of the problem hoping something would unravel, but nothing did. It kept coming back to Red. Maybe she saw someone or something, maybe, maybe, maybe. . . . I leaned back in the chair and closed my eyes. And it occurred to me that Corey hadn't said anything for awhile.

I checked him out of the corner of my eye. As near as I could tell he'd spent the entire time reading first one magazine, then another, cover to cover. No fidgeting, no complaints, totally absorbed. The room seemed scarcely to exist for him.

When someone new came in he'd glance up for a moment but I got the distinct impression the newcomer only registered as a blip on some peripheral radar screen, that he didn't see them as people at all. Only warm bodies entering his territory.

I envied his self-possession, but at the same time I couldn't help wondering if he saw me in that same dispassionate way sometimes. His radar screen picked up my stare. He looked up. His eyes met mine, held a moment, then blinked. "What?" he asked.

"Ms. Mitchell," the desk nurse called. "Your friend is being moved to post-op now. Everything went as expected."

"Can I see her?"

She punched a button on her phone, spoke quietly into the receiver a minute, then hung up. "You can go up for a minute," she said. "Don't worry about the little fella here, I'll keep an eye on him."

"Thank you," I said, rising hastily. "Will you be okay, Corey?"

"I'll be fine. Tell Red I'm sorry she's hurt."

"I will. You sit tight. I'll be back in a few minutes." I hurried out of the room, then realized I had no idea where I was going. I had to ask a passing nurse for directions.

The elevator seemed impossibly slow. At the nurse's station they directed me to an open bay at the end of the corridor. There were no beds, only gurneys, stretchers on wheels. Bo Unger was standing watch in the hallway only a few feet from Red's gurney. Her eyes were closed, she was utterly ashen, and her cheeks were hollow as a death camp survivor's. I tried to approach as quietly as I could but her eyes blinked open as I drew near.

"Hi," I said stupidly, "how are you feeling?"

She let the question hang in the air a moment, then winced. "Better," she said, swallowing. "I've been better. What the heck happened?"

"You've been shot."

"I know that," she said, her brow furrowing faintly. "I mean what happened here? Am I all . . . together? I can't seem to feel much."

"You came through the surgery fine, all in one piece."

"Honestly?" she said. Her eyes met mine and held.

"Honestly. I wouldn't kid you about a thing like that."

"I know you wouldn't," she said, closing her eyes. "I'm not so sure about the doctors. I'm . . . very tired. I think I'll sleep awhile now, I just didn't want to wake up to any . . . ugly surprises."

"Red, do you know who did this? Did you see anything?"

She didn't answer. I thought she'd fallen asleep, but after a moment she coughed.

"No," she said, her voice barely above a whisper. "I can't remember much. Clara asked me to pick up some spices for the dinner hour. It was raining so I pulled my jacket up and ran to my truck, and um, boy. Something hit me. I got hammered in the shoulder so hard I thought somebody'd nailed me with a baseball bat. My legs went rubber and I fell. Glass was flying all over the place so I. . . ." She swallowed. "I slid partway under the truck. I guess I must have passed out. I came around in the ambulance. Then I talked to Bo Unger for a minute in the emergency room and . . . and here we are. What's going on, Mitch? Who did this?"

"I don't know, but Charlie's on it. We'll find out. You just rest now. If you want me for anything, just tell the nurse. I'll be downstairs."

"No you won't. I'll never get any sleep knowing you're haunting the place. Go home, Mitch. And by the way, I never did get Clara's spices. Sorry."

"Forgodsake, Red, don't worry about—just rest, okay? I'll take care of it."

"Mitch, I didn't hear anything."

"I just said—"

"No, I meant when I was . . . shot. I didn't know for sure what happened until Bo told me. I didn't hear any noise. No gunfire. Is that possible?"

"I don't know," I said, "but don't worry about it now. Get some rest. I'll see you in the morning." I'm not sure she heard me. Her eyes closed and I think she was already asleep.

In the elevator, I willed my mind to blank out. It was just too much. Red is the strongest woman I've ever known and the best friend I've ever had. If anything happened to her because of me . . . I couldn't deal with that. So I closed my eyes and waited for the elevator to stop. And when it did, Charlie Bauer was waiting. And Jack Thorp was with him.

# Twenty-eight
# Deep Cover

ॳ৳ֆ

"Hi, Mitch," Charlie said. "The nurse said you'd gone up. How's Red?"

"What's he doing here?" I asked.

"It's . . . complicated," Charlie said, taking my arm. "Let's find someplace private to talk."

I let them walk me down the hall. I glanced over at Thorp, but either he didn't notice or didn't want to. He looked different. Somber. A lot less cocky.

Charlie led us into the hospital chapel, a small, windowless room with four pews facing an altar with candles burning beside it. Charlie closed the door behind us and leaned against it.

"Could Red tell you anything?" Charlie asked.

"Not much," I said, struggling to keep my voice level. "She, uh, she didn't see anybody. She ran to her truck in the rain, and somebody shot her. She said she didn't hear the shots."

"Neither did anyone else," Charlie said. "Whoever did it used an automatic weapon with a silencer. Red's truck took a dozen hits."

"A .223?" Thorp asked.

"It's likely, from the size of the holes," Charlie said. "We didn't find any brass at the scene though."

"It must be there," Thorp said. "Sounds like somebody emptied a full fifteen-round clip."

"Red's truck was parked to the side of the building," Charlie said. "The shots probably came from the dock area—"

"Hold it," I interrupted. "You still haven't told me what Thorp's doing here."

"Mitch—" Thorp began.

"I didn't ask you," I said, cutting him off. "Charlie?"

"His name's not Thorp," Charlie said. "It's Rooney. Agent John Rooney. He's with BATF, Bureau of Alcohol, Tobacco and Firearms."

Thorp/Rooney started to object, then closed his mouth to a taut, narrow line. He avoided my eyes.

"Are you sure about that?" I asked Charlie. "He laid a very different story on me."

"His identification checked out," Charlie said. "He's who he says he is."

"I see," I said. And I slapped Thorp hard across the mouth, a full swing, open palm, as solidly as I've ever hit anyone in my life. The blow caught him by surprise. He stumbled backward against a pew and dropped to one knee. He stayed down a moment, his face suffusing with blood and anger.

"Look, lady," Thorp said, "I know how you must feel—"

"No you don't, you son of a bitch!" I said. "Or you wouldn't still be in this room. You used us to cover yourself, didn't you?"

"What's this all about?" Charlie asked.

"Your fellow *officer* here has obviously been working undercover in the Third Coast Militia. When I asked about some land they hold, they blew me off. That would've been the end of it except that Thorp followed me to offer some friendly advice that kept us around. So the Thirds would have someone to blame when their patches got busted."

"I never intended for anyone to get hurt."

"I'm sure Red'll find that a great comfort."

"Look, you were from out of town," Thorp said. "I thought you'd be long gone before anything came down. Besides, I never dreamed the Thirds were capable of a thing like this."

"Why not?" Charlie asked.

"Because they're not scary, they're pathetic. The Thirds are mostly middle-aged guys watching the world they grew up in rust away. They're angry and frustrated, but they're not crazy.

The past few months I've been taking heat from the bureau to close this case, to burn the Thirds for illegal arms, anything. But except for the pot patches in the back corner of their tract, they haven't broken any laws. Cezak spouts some lunatic fringe rhetoric, they shoot at silhouette targets and bitch about the government, but that's it. Their military surplus weapons are all street legal. I never heard anything about munitions."

"Until they blew up half a mountain, you mean," I said.

"That's right. Somehow I missed that. But even so, I can't see them shooting down a woman from ambush."

"Not even Pettiford? You were worried enough to warn me about him. Or was that smoke too?"

"No," Thorp admitted. "He's risky business, all right, and so is Dexter Boone. We've had a tip that Boone was holed up in L'Anse a few days ago so we believe he's still in the U.P.—"

"But you're not sure," Charlie finished, cutting him off.

"No, damn it, we're not. Look, I admit the bust was a botch. The Thirds' connections were better than we thought and they knew we were coming, but they're in a box now. They're finished. Pettiford must know that."

"For the sake of argument, let's say it was Pettiford," Charlie said. "Do you have any leads on him at all?"

"Nothing solid," Thorp said. "He's from Wisconsin, so the current working theory is that he's gone to ground with friends in the Madison area."

"But he could be here, in my town," Charlie said carefully. "And mad enough about what happened to his pals to want to do something about it?"

"It's possible," Thorp admitted. "But I know Harlan. He's a loser, all talk, no action. Dealing weed or preaching white supremacy is his speed."

"But he said he had army training," I said. "He's a diver. What about the section of the cliff face he blasted down to block the mine entrance. Any idea what he buried there?"

"Whatever it was is under forty tons of rock now. Even if we could dig through the rockfall, there's probably nothing left but a grease spot."

"So you're not going to try?"

"It's not practical, Mitch. Pettiford will tell us what it was when we run him down."

"What do the two you've got in custody say about it?" Charlie asked.

"Zero," Thorp said. "They've both dummied up. Neither one will cop to a thing, not the pot, the explosives, none of it."

"What about the dog?" I asked.

"What dog?"

"They had a bear-sized Rottweiler guarding their patches. What happened to him?"

"I don't know," Thorp said. "I kept my distance to avoid being spotted. I never saw a dog."

"There was one back there," I said. "And he was definitely guarding the patches."

"There was a kennel at Chessman's place," Thorp said thoughtfully. "A big one. It was empty, though, and nobody mentioned seeing a dog during the raid. Maybe he spooked and ran off."

"No way. This dog would have stood his ground against a buffalo stampede. You're sure no one saw him?"

"There was no mention of it in the reports," Thorp said. "What difference does it make?"

"The point is, they not only had time to set off the explosions before the raid," I said, "they even got their dog out. Your operation didn't leak, Thorp, it was more like Niagara Falls."

"I can't argue that," he admitted. "The FBI's investigating a couple of deputies on the Copper County sheriff's department with relatives in the Thirds."

"Only deputies?" Charlie asked. "That's a convenient assumption, isn't it?"

"Especially since some of the Feds were even closer to the Thirds," I said.

"Look, I may have misread this thing and I empathize with some of the Thirds, but I'm not a rogue cop. I'd never side with them."

"That's nice to know," Charlie said evenly. "But right now I'm more interested in why Red was hit. Mitch was the one named in the press reports. Why would anyone go after Red?"

"It was raining, and Red and I are roughly the same size," I pointed out. "To a guy who was pumped up and ready to shoot, one woman running in the rain might look like another."

"It may not be that simple," Thorp countered. "Red was with you at militia headquarters. If it was one of them, it's possible the shooter wants you both and took Red down first because she was convenient. A target of opportunity."

"And Boone?" I asked. "What about him?"

"Also possible," Thorp admitted. "He's got a bad record, and he may be hard to run down. Dopers and bikers are counterculture icons. Boone'll have no trouble finding people to crash with."

"He might if I bump up the charges against him to attempted murder," Charlie said. "I know a friendly local judge."

"I'm not sure the bureau would go along with that," Thorp said. "Federal guidelines . . ."

Thorp's voice faded out as Charlie eyed him as coldly as I've ever seen one man look at another. "You'd better not give me any speeches about jurisdiction," Charlie said evenly. "The shooting happened in my town, to my friends. You people have a full plate with the mess up at Grand Portal. I'll handle things here. Any questions?"

"No," Thorp said, drawing a deep breath. "Not from me. But I'm only BATF. The FBI's running things up north now. They've got a Critical Incident Response Group in place under an agent named Martingale. He's already bumped me off the investigation, so I can't say how he'll react to what happened here."

"There's nothing Federal about a shooting," Charlie said firmly. "This is my turf. Tell him that."

"I'll pass it along," Thorp said, "but I don't carry much weight. Look, the Thirds can't hole up forever. When they fold, the FBI can squeeze the small fry to give up people higher on the food chain. If a Third was involved in this shooting, we'll know it."

"For a guy who's about to see a big case wrapped you don't sound very enthusiastic," Charlie said.

"Damn it, I told them the raid was a mistake. The way it came down, we didn't get their contacts with the local cops, or where they got the explosives. With a little more time I could've gotten those answers before we rolled them up."

"Or maybe you've been working this case too long," Charlie suggested. "Stockholm syndrome? Sometimes guys working undercover get their loyalties confused."

"I know, which is why I know it isn't happening to me. If I'd done my job better, we wouldn't be here talking. I blew it, but I'll do anything I can to make up for that. I'm truly sorry I involved you, Mitch, and even sorrier about what happened to your friend."

"No offense, but right now your apology doesn't count for much, Thorp."

"No, I suppose not," Thorp said, glancing at his watch. "I'd better get back. I'll keep you both posted if I hear anything. Good luck." He started for the door, but hesitated. "This dog you mentioned. How big was it?"

"It was a Rottweiler," I said. "Probably a hundred and twenty pounds."

"Really? How much would you guess I weigh?"

"One eighty-five," I said.

"One eighty-one, actually," he said, nodding in approval. "Very good. Witnesses often overestimate the size of dogs, especially big ones."

"I grew up around dogs," I said. "This was a full grown male Rott I met up close and personal. I might be off a little, but not more than a few pounds."

"I believe you," Thorp said, showing his quizzical smile for the first time. "Thanks. See you both around."

He closed the door quietly behind him, leaving us alone in the chapel.

# Twenty-nine
# Dinosaurs

"A COP," I said quietly. "I should have guessed."

"Why? People who considered him a friend didn't," Charlie said.

"He came to warn me a few days ago." I eased stiffly down on one of the pews. "Pretended that he had a thing for me."

"So? Was that so hard to believe?"

"Actually, it was," I said dryly. "When people have a thing for each other, chemistry or whatever, you usually have a sense of it on one level or another. We like each other, you and I, and we both know it. Neither of us has actually said anything about it because . . . I don't know, because it hasn't been necessary."

"I guess that's true," Charlie admitted. "What's that got to do with Thorp?"

"Because when he told me about this great unrequited love of his, I didn't feel anything. Zero. He's not unattractive, you know, but I had no sense of chemistry in the air at all. None."

"Maybe he isn't your type. Or maybe your woman's intuition was on the blink."

"God, Bauer, don't be such a dinosaur. Men lie to women all the time, usually when they're trying to melt our little hearts. And because we're used to seeing performances, we're usually fairly adept at spotting them. That doesn't mean we won't play along if we choose to, or that we can't be conned. The point is, we usually know when someone's running a game. I had a definite sense that Thorp wasn't being straight about his feelings, but not for the usual reasons."

"And it bothered you?"

"I didn't give it much thought at the time. A lot of guys play the love game out of habit, I swear. They're like puppies chasing cars whether they want to catch one or not."

"Maybe some men do," Bauer said.

"Come on, Charlie, haven't you ever pretended to care about someone a tad more than you really did just to advance your cause?"

"No," he said simply. "I don't believe I ever have. But then, some people think I'm a dinosaur. Look, Mitch, we've got more to worry about than whether Thorp was straight with you. He's definitely right about one thing. Nobody's got a handle on the situation yet. Not the FBI or the State Police and God knows I haven't."

"How do you mean?"

"It's my understanding there are nearly thirty hard core members in that militia, and a lot more sympathizers. For all this talk about manhunts and busts, we don't have a clue where the wild card suspects are, and maybe not even who they are."

"But Boone and Pettiford—"

"Both of them look likely for it," Charlie conceded. "And my bet is that one of them did it. But right now that doesn't matter. They're both on the loose and even if they aren't working together, that doesn't mean they're working alone. There may be links in this case we aren't aware of or players in the game we don't know about yet. Let's say Thorp's right and the Third Coasters are just backwoods malcontents who like to play soldier. If he's only ninety-nine percent right we could still have a wacko on the loose who isn't on any wanted sheets. He could still be looking for you, and somebody already found Red."

"Yeah," I said, leaning back in the pew. "Somebody sure did. Okay, what should we do?"

"Take a vacation," he said bluntly. "You're mixed up in a Federal case and the Feds have access to safe houses and other resources I can't match. You can—Jesus, Mitch, quit shaking your head. At least let me finish."

"That thought is finished. I can't just go away, Charlie. I've got a business to run, bills coming due. Even if I wanted to scram, I can't afford to."

"And you don't want to, do you?"

"No," I said evenly. "I don't. If I throw away everything I have because I let them drive me off, then they've won. They'll have nailed me without paying any dues for it."

"All right, I half expected you'd feel this way. But what about Corey? He doesn't owe any dues."

"No, he certainly doesn't," I said, slumping back in the seat, rubbing my eyes. "God, Charlie, I don't know what to do. Help me out here, please."

He eyed me a moment, then nodded slowly. "How's this? Bo Unger's brother-in-law, Chet, is home from the Marines. He's crashing at Bo's place, helping out on the farm. Plans to go to Michigan State in the spring."

"So?"

"So Bo and Lila have five kids. One of the boys, Tommy, is Corey's age, same grade at school, I think. Why don't you let Corey stay out at Bo's for a few weeks? Bo and Chet are good men, and Lila's a country girl, no slouch with a gun herself. Plus they've got stone redneck neighbors. It's farm country, everybody knows everybody's business. Corey'll be safe as houses there."

"Are you sure?"

"Personally, I'd rather tangle with an FBI SWAT team than mess with Bo Unger's family on their own ground. Corey'll be fine. I'm not so sure about you."

"Why me?"

"You'll have to stay away from him, Mitch. One reason Corey will be safe is that no one will know he's there. It's not him they're after, it's you. And if somebody is stalking you, you can't risk leading them to your son."

"No," I said slowly. "Of course not. All right. Let's go talk to Bo."

"I already have," Charlie said. "It's fine by him, he's as angry about all this as any of us. He goes off duty in half an hour. He'll take Corey home with him."

"But his clothes—"

"Corey can borrow something from Tommy to wear tomorrow, and we'll make arrangements to send his things along. Tommy's a little bigger than Corey but even millionaire's kids dress like slobs nowadays."

"Not Corey," I said. "He dresses like an apprentice undertaker."

"Then maybe it's time he loosened up a little. Which brings us to you. What are you going to do?"

"I don't know. Go home, I guess, try to catch a few hours sleep—"

"Not at your home," he said firmly. "The Point is just too isolated, Mitch. I can't spare the people to keep it under surveillance. Why don't you crash at my place until this is over. I've got a spare bedroom."

"Really, Charlie I—"

"The question isn't open for debate," he said flatly. "Look, if you want to put yourself at risk for your own reasons, I can't stop you. But at least let me work with it. It's a twelve mile run out to your place at the Point. This guy could lay for you anywhere along the way and I couldn't prevent it. If you stay with me, he'll have to make his play in my town. Maybe even at my house."

I eyed him a moment, then nodded. "Bait," I said. "That's what we're talking about isn't it? You're asking me to be bait."

"You're the one who's choosing to stay in the open. I'll protect you either way but it'll definitely be easier to do at my place."

"All right," I said, rising. "It'll be your place. I'd better go down and tell Corey."

"Good, I'll tell Bo he's gonna have company. Oh, and Mitch, you don't have to worry about . . . well, staying with me. I'm not a sleepwalker."

I tried to stifle a smile, but couldn't quite manage it. "Thanks for the assurance, Charlie, but I wasn't really worried about it."

"I'm not sure if that's a compliment or not. I may be a dinosaur, but I'm not quite extinct."

"I didn't mean it that way, I just . . . trust you, that's all. Maybe you're old fashioned in some ways, but they're good ways, or at least I think so. Maybe I'm part dinosaur myself."

"There are worse things to be," Charlie said, opening the chapel door for me. "As long as you remember what happened to 'em when they got careless."

"Careless? Did I miss that class? I thought evolution did them in."

"Evolution's a neat theory, but it's not very useful, to us, I mean. It's no help to think that a race of creatures that big got killed off by a nasty run of luck because we can't do much about luck. I'd rather think they got careless. Careless, I can fix."

"I hope so," I said, shivering. He offered me his arm as we walked to the elevator. It was a very old-fashioned gesture. Something a dinosaur might do.

# THIRTY
## CHARLIE'S SURPRISE

IN THE past ten years I've bunked on oil platforms and in motels and crashed at co-workers homes so often that living out of an overnight case is second nature for me. Charlie's home took me by surprise, though. It was a suburban tri-level ranch in the rolling hills west of Huron Harbor. I expected a rough-and-tumble interior, wagon wheels on the walls, football trophies on the mantel, maybe a moose head in the bath. *Au contraire.*

His home was modern, spare, and very, very artsy. The floors were carpeted in a thick bone berber that seemed to flow into the walls. The furniture was only slightly darker, all Swedish simplicity, bleached muslin stretched on ash frames. An open hearth was formed of individually fired, hand-painted ceramic tiles. The walls were covered with original oils in barnboard frames, an eclectic mix of surreal still lifes and sharply executed traditional landscapes.

One particularly stark waterscape looked startlingly familiar to me, not the style, the subject. The waves had been captured so perfectly I could almost hear them hiss. I've spent most of my life in or around deep water, and though I couldn't remember the place, I was certain I'd seen the lake from that exact vantage point. It was odd seeing it recreated in oils, as though someone had painted one of my memories. I checked the corner for a signature, but there wasn't any. Charlie came in

just then, carrying my duffel bag and caught me scanning the
painting.

"What do you think?"

"It's wonderful," I said, stepping back and glancing around.
"They all are, even . . ." One of the modernist still lifes caught
my eye, and suddenly its jangled lines, and the flow of its colors came together in perfect harmony. I'd just seen that same
movement in the painted waves. Charlie parked my duffel bag
on the bed, pointedly ignoring me. I've known him half my life.
Not very well, apparently.

"These are yours, aren't they?" I said. "I mean, you painted
them."

He nodded, as wary as I'd ever seen him.

"Charlie, they're magnificent. The waterscapes are absolutely
breathtaking. Why didn't you sign them?"

"It's only a hobby," he said gruffly. "I started it the year after
my wife died. It . . . took my mind off things. I'm glad you like
them."

"I do. Very much. But why haven't I heard about this before?
You've never mentioned it."

"Maybe it's one of those old-fashioned things we were talking about. I wasn't brought up to tell everybody everything. People who did were considered . . . I don't know. Braggarts, I
guess."

"Some people are entitled to brag. Do you have any other
surprises in store for me?"

"Not just now. It's late. One thing though, I noticed you
brought your thirty-thirty Winchester along. Do you plan on
keeping it handy?"

"I've been keeping it handy, either beside my bed or in my
Jeep for the past few days. Do you mind?"

"Not at all. It's just the two of us here. As I recall your dad
had an Army .45 automatic, too."

"I still have it," I acknowledged. "I keep it locked in my office at the Crow's Nest."

"Do you know how to use it?"

"Shan started teaching me about guns when I was ten. I'm
no Annie Oakley, but I know which end to hold."

"Good, then you'll know how to use this," he said, taking a

pistol from under his coat at the small of his back. "It's a Taurus nine-millimeter automatic. This is the safety, this is the slide release. You can fire the first round double-action, just by pulling the trigger. I want you to carry this."

"You mean all the time?"

"Exactly, Mitch. You've got to understand, we're dancing in deep water here. We've got bombs going off, Red's been wounded. It's only dumb luck that no one's been killed so far. I don't want it to be you. Okay?"

"All right," I said, accepting the gun. "You're the pro here. If you want me to carry it, I will."

"Good. If nothing else, the weight of it'll remind you to be careful." He glanced around a moment, eyeing the room critically as though seeing it for the first time. "Well, I guess that's it. Make yourself at home. You can take over the bath at this end of the house, I don't use it. If you need anything at all, just holler. Would you like something to eat?"

"I'm too whipped, Charlie, but thanks. For everything."

"No charge," he said. "It's . . . nice to have you here, Mitch. I mean that. It brightens the place up. Goodnight."

"Goodnight."

After he'd gone, I sat on the edge of the bed, looking over my surroundings. Nice. And I wondered for the fortieth time how Corey was making out. Probably just fine. Aye, there was the rub. Corey.

When I'd explained the situation, he'd mulled it over for a minute, then nodded.

"Okay," he said. "It sounds like a plan."

"You're sure," I said. "I mean, if you'd rather do something else . . ."

"Mom, I'll be fine. You guys, you and Red, are the ones you have to take care of. Don't worry about me. It's not like I haven't done this before."

"No," I said, stung slightly by his casual acceptance of a separation. "I know you have, but I'd hoped we wouldn't . . . never mind. I guess we'll do what we have to. Now, I won't be able to see you out there, it's too risky, but you can call me anytime. Day or night, anytime. You understand?"

"Sure," Corey said impatiently. "Jeez, Mom, I'm going to

Tommy Unger's house, not the Foreign Legion. It's not that big a deal."

Maybe it wasn't for him. It was for me. As I slid between the clean sheets of a strange bed, separated from my son for the first time in a month, it was a very big deal for me. I was sad and angry and so frustrated it was all I could do to keep from crying. For my friend, and my son, and myself.

# THIRTY-ONE
# THE DAWN

∾∾∾

I SNAPPED awake at first light, jangled, as though I'd barely slept, and disoriented by my surroundings. Charlie's house. No, his home. This place had too much soul and style to be just a house. A man of many surprises, Charlie. I wondered what else I'd been overlooking about him . . . coffee. I blinked, coming fully awake now. I definitely smelled coffee brewing. And not generic coffee either. Unless my nose was fibbing, I detected a definite hint of cinnamon in the air.

That did it. I rolled out of bed, stepped into the bath long enough to splash cold water in my face and glower at the witch in the mirror, wishing I had time to set my hair. I settled for combing it with my fingertips. I think the tousled look is "in" somewhere. Then I pulled on jeans and a sweatshirt and padded out to the kitchen.

Charlie was already busy. He was wearing his uniform slacks and a white tee shirt and socks. He was setting the table in the glow of morning light through the kitchen windows. He glanced up, our eyes met. And everything changed.

I could feel the electricity between us like a dark current, unspoken. We've known each other a long time, and I've often suspected he had feelings for me. But not like this. This wasn't some vague attraction, it was the real thing, physical, mental, and basic. The differences in our ages and outlooks were suddenly irrelevant. We were down to one on one. And I wasn't quite sure how to handle it.

"Good morning," I said, trying to mask my confusion. "Do I smell coffee?"

"Ground fresh," he said, neatly arranging the silverware beside the two plates on the table. "My own blend. I have tea or juice if you prefer."

"Coffee's fine," I said, "but you needn't lay out a plate for me. I don't eat breakfast."

"You sure? I think you may need it."

"Why? Has something happened?"

"Not here," he said. "But up in Grand Portal, somebody delivered a videotape to the local paper. It's a short speech by a militia-type named Harlan Pettiford, or at least that *was* his name. He's calling himself Commander Three Zero now, head of the Third Coast Underground. He claims it's a hundred members strong, and that Red was the first traitor to fall. But there will be more."

"Traitor?"

"That's what he called her," Charlie said evenly. "It's not true, of course, Red didn't betray anyone. I doubt that much of the rest of it's true either."

"Which part?"

"Any of it. The underground army, for instance. I've already talked to Brian Martingale, the Feebie in charge of the force at the standoff—"

"Feebie?"

"Sorry. FBI agent. Anyway, Martingale says they have no indication whatever that this underground group exists, or that Pettiford would head it up if it did. He's just a Hitler wannabe with delusions of grandeur."

"Who's the source of that information? Thorp? They haven't gotten anything else right, why would they know about this?"

"The FBI might not, but I'm betting Ernie Feige would. Maybe it's just an old dinosaur's instinct, but I'm not buying the idea that there are a hundred yoopers willing to take up arms against their neighbors no matter what this wacko Pettiford says. The only part I might go for is that he shot Red. From what Thorp said about him, that'd be his speed."

"I've met him," I said. "He's definitely mental, at least by my standards. Do they know where he is?"

"Not a clue. The tape was dropped off around midnight. They don't know whether Pettiford left it or someone else."

"But he's probably in the U.P., right?"

"More likely than not," Charlie conceded. "But I wouldn't bet your life on it."

"I won't," I said, sitting down across from him. "Do you have a plan for the day?"

"Just go about your business," he said, carefully pouring a fresh cup of coffee. And avoiding my eyes. "All I ask is that you be extra alert and stay within a holler of me or one of my men at all times."

"I can live with that," I said. He placed a mug of steaming dark mocha in front of me. The aroma alone would have revived King Tut. "This is wonderful," I said, taking a sip.

"I've always thought the smell of coffee was one of life's great unkept promises. Coffee, tobacco, and revolutions always promise more than they deliver."

"My, aren't we philosophical for six A.M."

"Sorry," he said. "I don't have company here very often. In fact, you're my first overnight lady guest since . . . well, ever."

"I'm honored," I said.

"No need to be," he said. "That's what friends are for."

"If you don't mind," I said, touching the back of his hand with my fingertips, "I'd rather feel honored." His eyes met mine and held a moment. They were gray, flecked with gold. Like a cat's eyes. And equally difficult to read.

# THIRTY-TWO
# MARTINGALE

FOR THE next few days, I saw Harlan Pettiford's weasel face every other minute on a TV screen, a newspaper front page, or in my mind's eye. He stuck in my memory like a shred of melody from a cracked record, the shifty lines around his eyes, the immaculate black uniform, even the sour stench of his breath. Commander Three Zero. Right. Commander Certifiable Mental Case.

It enraged me that a psycho whose sole accomplishment was gunning down a woman he'd met only once could corner the market on media coverage. Fortunately, I was too busy to spend much time worrying about it. I thought business at the Nest might be affected by the shooting. It was. It was up by nearly fifty percent.

If anyone was frightened by the idea of an underground army lurking about, they certainly didn't show it. Our regulars considered it a badge of honor to show up as usual. In addition, we garnered a substantial tourist/curiosity seeker trade, plus the press people, radio, TV, and otherwise.

I couldn't totally avoid reporters, but I kept them at bay by following Charlie's suggestion of telling the little I knew straight-forwardly and very slowly. The only problem with that was, when I saw snippets of myself on the tube, I looked brain dead. And the camera doesn't lie.

With Pettiford on the loose, the interviews I did were difficult. I wanted to call him the cowardly psychopath I knew he
was, yet I didn't want to endanger Red or my son any further.
So mostly I ducked the press and stayed busy in the kitchen or
my office, incommunicado.

I visited Red for an hour each morning and again in the afternoon during lulls at the Nest. She was coming around, but
slowly, so slowly. She was walking on the second day, but she
looked so vulnerable and weak that it was all I could do to keep
from bawling as I watched.

On the other hand, she was soon griping about the food,
reading materials, wimpy painkillers, and daytime TV. There
was hope. But her left arm had no feeling in it. The neurologist
said it would return, but I wasn't sure she believed him. As a
lone-wolf woman who's survived on her own in this world, Red
isn't much in the blind faith department.

The State Police evidence team turned up the cartridge cases
near the scene on the superstructure of a tugboat moored in
the harbor. The shooter must have fired from the flying bridge
on the pilot house, so most of the cartridge cases ended up in
the harbor.

I volunteered to dive to try to recover them from the muck
of the harbor bottom, but Charlie declined. The four cartridge
casings they had would be enough to identify the weapon when
they recovered it. If they recovered it.

By themselves, the casings were a dead end. The brass was
.223, common as dirt in surplus military-style rifles. Hundreds
of thousands of the weapons had been sold, so without the actual gun in hand, there was no way the police could tie the
brass to Pettiford or anyone else.

Charlie'd explained all this on his lunch hour break in my
office at the Nest. I was sitting at my desk, he was staring out my
office window at the harbor, sipping coffee, eyeing the gulls
wheeling over the harbor.

"Hundreds of thousands of these guns?" I said. "I thought
they banned assault rifles."

"The ban's a joke," Charlie grumbled. "It only affected a
few models, and model is the proper word. It was all cosmetic.
The law only banned guns that looked dangerous to Washing-

ton types who don't know doodley about weapons. They banned guns with bayonet studs and drum magazines. Meanwhile, a million surplus weapons from Red China and Soviet bloc countries were being imported legally. AKMs, AK-47s, SKSs. Honest-to-god combat weapons. Red was lucky the shooter didn't use a piece that fires 7.62s. She'd have lost that arm for sure."

"She may have lost the use of it anyway," I said, massaging my eyes tiredly. "She has no feeling in it yet."

"It's too soon," he said. "Don't worry."

"Don't tell me not to worry," I snapped. "Just tell me what a million military weapons are doing loose in this country."

"This is America," he said simply. "We're free to make choices. To be honest, I've got mixed feelings about it. I like guns. We both grew up around 'em and I've worked with one most of my life."

"That's different. This is hunting country and you're a cop."

"A lot of guys I knew as a kid hunted with military surplus weapons, Springfields, Mausers, even old Krags. But these new guns aren't hunting weapons. They're clumsy and crude, they throw a lot of lead in a hurry and none too accurately. Unfortunately, nobody's figured out a way to ban 'em without outlawing half the hunting weapons in the country. So, for now, I'm just hoping they're a fad that'll pass, like the hula hoop or Milli Vanilli."

"I don't recall hula hoops being available with bayonets," I said grimly.

"Might've been less painful if they had," Charlie said. He glanced at his watch. "I've gotta get back to the office. See you this evening?"

"Sure," I said. I didn't really see him leave. I was still lost in the image of Pettiford and his goon friends. And a million surplus weapons.

"Are you Michelle Mitchell?" A blond, dapper type, five-six or -seven, stepped into my office and closed the door. His blue suit was a perfect fit and his hair was razor trimmed.

"Do I know you?" I rested my hand on the cool steel of my father's army .45 automatic, just out of sight in my partially open desk drawer.

"Brian Martingale, FBI," he said, reaching inside his jacket. He froze in mid motion as I drew the automatic out of the drawer. It wasn't aimed directly at him, but I wasn't far off. His eyes widened.

"Ma'am, you'd best put that away. You're already in a lot of trouble."

"Not as much as you'll be if I don't like what you take out of your pocket. What did you say your name was?"

"Martingale. Brian." He slowly lifted an identification folder out with his fingertips and opened it to show me a badge and picture ID "I'm with the FBI Critical Incident Response Group at Grand Portal."

He didn't offer to shake hands, nor did I. But I did put the .45 back in the desk drawer. "What can I do for you, Mr. Martingale?"

"For openers, you'd better show me a permit for that weapon. Or tell me why I shouldn't cite you for a firearms violation."

I tried counting to ten to keep my temper under control. Only made it to six. "Mr. Martingale, in this state you don't need a permit to have a weapon on private property. Which leaves you roughly three seconds to tell me what you want or hit the door, sport. I've had a rough week. I'm not in the mood to take any guff, from you or anyone else."

"Sheriff Feige said you were a hardhead," Martingale said, unimpressed. "All I want are the answers to a few questions, Miss Mitchell." He sat in the chair opposite my desk without being invited. "How long have you known John Thorp?"

"Too long. I met him a few weeks ago at Third Coast Headquarters. I'm not sure of the date."

"And that was the first time? Perhaps I should rephrase the question. How long have you known John Rooney?"

"I thought they were same person," I said.

"Of course they are, but if we're going to play games, I want to be sure I stay within the boundaries."

"What game are you talking about?"

"That's what I'm here to find out," Martingale said. "How much did Jack tell you about his work?"

"Not much," I said, puzzled. "I gather he's a government agent, BATF, I think, and that he was working undercover in the Third Coast militia. That's about it."

"He must have said more than that. Did he tell you he considered most of the Thirds harmless cranks?"

"He said something like it," I said, "but since nearly everything he told me from day one was a lie, I wasn't paying much attention at that point."

"Then let's cut to the bottom line," Martingale said, leaning forward intently. "You claim you only met Jack a few weeks ago, yet he brought you into an investigation that had been ongoing for nearly a year?"

"I don't *claim* anything," I said angrily. "It certainly wasn't my choice to get involved. Thorp used my friend and me as some sort of cover. Deniability, is that the word? He didn't do us any favors. And unless you start making some sense, we're through talking. What do you want, Mr. Martingale?"

"A straight answer to a simple question," he snapped. "When did you see Jack Thorp last?"

"About . . . three days ago. At the hospital. In the chapel."

"The chapel?"

"It was a private place to talk."

"I'll bet it was. And do you know where he is now?"

"I have no idea. Why should I?"

"He didn't tell you he was pulling out because he'd been yanked from the investigation?"

"He said he'd been bumped, but he didn't say anything about quitting that I recall. He apologized for involving me and my friend with the Third Coast, and to be honest, I was so upset at the time, I don't remember the conversation all that clearly. Look, what's this about? Why would you think I'd know where Thorp is if you don't?"

"Are you trying to tell me you're not involved with him?"

"Involved?" I echoed stupidly, as though he'd shifted into Swahili.

"To put it more directly, are you and Jack Thorp having an affair?"

I must have looked as amazed as I felt. Martingale eyed me

a moment, then slumped back in his chair. "Damn," he said, looking away.

"My God," I said, flushing. "Where on earth did you get that idea?"

"Please, don't tee off on me," he said, waving away my protests. "I guess I was just hoping it was true. Jack said a few things about you that, well, implied that he found you attractive. Nowadays, these things can happen very quickly."

"Not to me they don't," I said. "But I don't understand, why did you say you hoped it was true?"

"Because if the two of you'd gotten involved and Jack decided to stay here to protect you, I could understand it and maybe even cover for him. As it is, I can't imagine what he thinks he's doing."

"You're saying you don't know where he is? He's missing?"

"He's cleared out, lock, stock, and suitcase," he sighed. "It looks like he's jumped ship."

"Why would he do that?"

"He's had misgivings about this investigation for months. He warned us a raid on their headquarters would backfire, but if we just busted the dopers, it would prove to the others that we weren't the bad guys. After the mines went off, I removed him from the case. Since he hadn't known about the explosives, he was either incompetent or too close to the Thirds. I thought he needed a break, a chance to get his attitude straight. Apparently, he took it badly and took off. Did he give you any indication at all of where he was going?"

"No. My impression was that he was heading north to go back to work. He admitted he'd underestimated how dangerous the Thirds were and apologized for involving my friend and me with them, and that was it. This was before Pettiford's tape came out, though. Maybe that changed things."

"We won't know until we ask him. Did you recall talking about anything else?"

"As he was leaving, he asked me about the dog."

"What dog?"

"There was a Rottweiler guarding the pot patches when I found them. It chased me into the pond. Jack didn't know about the dog and asked me how big it was, things like that."

"A dog," he sighed. "Terrific. Rotts are pretty bright but I can't picture one cranking off a dozen rounds with an AK-47, can you?"

"It makes as much sense as anything else about this. I keep hearing how strong the militia's ties are to the local police. Maybe somebody tipped them off about Jack."

"Or maybe he blew his cover by coming down to see you. The Thirds may have had you under surveillance."

"No, I'm fairly sure no one's been following me since Red's shooting. I've been staying with Sheriff Bauer and we've been very careful. And if he was spotted on his first trip down, why did they shoot Red? We may have ticked them off, but Jack was a real threat. He actually was betraying them."

"Betraying them?"

"That's what Pettiford claimed Red's crime was and he tried to kill her," I said. "If that was their beef, Jack would be a more logical target."

"Maybe he was," Martingale said, massaging his eyes. "Damn it, a few weeks ago I would have sworn he had this case nailed. He had the Thirds charted and diagrammed, knew who was related to whom, their politics, even their weapons of choice. Thorp could recite chapter and verse on everyone involved. Then you stumbled over those patches and derailed a year's worth of work. God, what a mess."

"I'm sorry we complicated your investigation," I said evenly. "But I've got a friend in the hospital now wondering whether she's going to be crippled. He had no right to involve us."

"It was a misjudgment made in the heat of the moment," Martingale conceded grudgingly. "I'm sorry."

"Red'll be very comforted to hear that. Was there anything else you wanted, Martingale?"

"I understand that you're angry," he said, holding his palms up in defense. "Even so, we're on the same side. If you hear from Jack, or anything develops that we should know about, will you call me at this number, please?" He handed me a business card. "And for the record, if I seemed rude, I apologize. It was nothing personal."

"Right now, injured feelings are the least of my problems, Mr. Martingale. I just want to get me and mine out of this in one piece."

"Yes, ma'am. Believe me, I know that feeling very well."

# THIRTY-THREE
## PATIENTS AND PATIENCE

RED'S BED was empty and there was no guard on her door when I stopped by the hospital that afternoon. In a panic, I raced to the nurses' station only to see Red and the deputy at the far end of the hall, trudging slowly toward me.

I hurried to her and gave her a peck on the cheek. Marvin Needham, the pencil-thin, carrot-topped deputy on duty was walking three paces behind Red, carrying her IV bag like a puppy on a leash.

"Hi," I said. "How are you doing?"

"Never better," she said grimly, concentrating on putting one slipper in front of the other, a single pace at a time.

"My God, you almost gave me heart failure," I said, falling into slow step beside her. "Next time, leave a note on your pillow."

Red glanced at me. "You look edgier than usual. What's up?"

"I had a visitor today. Our friend Mr. Thorp's dropped out of sight, so his boss stopped by my office to ask me about my love life."

"Love life? You mean with Thorp?"

"Hey, we've spoken several times and we're the appropriate genders. We must be getting it on, right?"

"Sounds like masculine logic to me," she said, wincing.

"Bubba back there would understand it perfectly. He thinks he's in love."

"With you?"

"Well *excuuuse* me," she groaned. "I may not be in mint condition, but I'm not quite ready to have my organs harvested for spare parts."

"Of course you're not, you look terrific. For a woman of a certain age. But you and Bubba—"

"Call him Marvin, please. He's very sensitive." She turned and smiled at him and he waved back hopefully. "Marvelous Marv. And yes, I did explain to him that we're not the proper gender for a match. He wasn't discouraged. He thinks he can rescue me. What do you mean Thorp's dropped out of sight?"

"He's missing. He cleared his gear out of his apartment and split without so much as a lipstick note on the mirror. His boss doesn't know what to make of it."

"And he thought you would?"

"Apparently I was the last one who saw him."

"Lucky you," she said, frowning. "Do they, um, think something might have happened to him? Like what happened to me, for instance?"

"I think if they had any ideas they wouldn't have wasted time asking me about it. Thorp and I didn't exactly part friends. I thought he was headed north to hang out with his pals, the misunderstood patriots."

"Then maybe he's disappeared permanently," Red said, wincing. "Those guys play for keeps. If you don't think so, I'll show you my stitches."

"Maybe, but I got the feeling that Martingale had his doubts about that. I mean, the Thirds are the logical suspects, right? With the contacts they have with the local cops, it's amazing Thorp kept them snowed as long as he did. But most of the Thirds are forted up in their headquarters. They couldn't have done Thorp any damage."

Red mulled it over a few painful paces, then nodded. "You're right. And with Thorp on the inside all this time, he must know how often the Third Coasters change underwear, which I'd guess is seldom. So if this Martingale came down here to talk to you, then he must have taken the Thirds out of the picture."

"But what about Pettiford? He's still on the loose, and you can vouch for the fact that he's dangerous."

"We don't actually know he did this to me."

"Are you kidding? He's admitted it."

"And a half dozen nutcases claim credit every time a firecracker goes off in Ireland," Red countered. "He's the likeliest candidate, but he's not the only one."

"You mean Boone, or one of his friends? They have no beef with you."

"No, but they might have with Thorp. If they knew about him. And they seem to know a lot."

"That they do," I conceded. "Which leaves us where?"

"It leaves me shuffling back to bed, girlfriend. I'm not quite ready for prime time, and talking is using up energy I can't spare."

"Sorry, but this thing is making me crazy. Corey's staying with strangers again, you're limping along like the Bride of Frankenstein—"

"Thanks ever so much."

"You know what I mean. This whole mess is my fault. If I'd looked the other way—"

"And not reported the fields?" Red interrupted, flaring. "So some thug could peddle weed to Corey or some other schoolkid because we left him in business? Bull! It pains me too say it, literally, but dammit, we did the right thing, Mitch. Stop beating yourself up. That's what your friends are for."

"But I do have the feeling that I'm to blame somehow. Martingale said the case was all but closed when we stumbled into it."

"Right. So it's my fault I got shot?"

"Maybe it is, in a way. We must have raised the stakes somehow, or things wouldn't have suddenly gotten so violent."

"Look, all we did was ask about the damned mine and fall over some pot patches, neither of which are capital offenses the last I heard. Did I miss anything?"

"No," I conceded. "And the only other thing Thorp asked me about was that damned dog, the Rottweiler that was guarding the patches."

"What about it?"

"That's just it, he didn't know about it. It wasn't around when they raided the patches."

"What difference does that make?" Red asked.

"I don't know, and Thorp didn't either. He just asked about how big it was, how much it weighed. I don't think he believed it was as big as I said it was."

"Like it was really a schnauzer that pumped himself into a Rott in your girlish imagination?"

"Something like that."

"It must be a guy thing," Red said, sighing. "Guessing a dog's size is just too much for our little heads."

"Probably. I just wish they'd nail Boone and shut Pettiford and the militia down so we can get our lives back on track."

"Assuming we can. I've been doing some thinking the past few days. When this is over, I think I'm going to make some changes in my life."

"What changes?"

"I don't know, I just know some things will be different. What about you? How are things working out at Charlie's place?"

I shook my head without replying.

"Whoa," she said, grinning. "That bad, hunh? Has he been rap, rap, rapping on the bedroom door in the wee hours to see if you need a hot water bottle?"

"Nothing like that. I might feel better if he did. His home is really beautiful. It's a side of Charlie I never even guessed might exist."

"He's a special guy," Red said thoughtfully. "And a bat could see he's got a thing for you. So how do you feel about it?"

"Mixed up. I like him a lot, as a friend. I'm not sure I want to change that."

"Then don't. Or at least, not now. Your life's complicated enough. And the thing is, Charlie's . . . older than we are. Not just in years, it's more of a generational thing, you know? Guys like him take affairs of the heart seriously. Which isn't all bad. But he's not someone you'd want to light up and then blow out."

"I'd never do that."

"I know you wouldn't. That's why I'm saying walk soft, girlfriend. Don't open that particular door unless you want to waltz through it."

"That's terrific advice," I said, "especially coming from a fainthearted maidenly type like yourself."

"Hey, giving good advice doesn't mean I have to take it. Plumber's toilets never flush and mechanic's cars always need a tune. And right now I could use a tune-up myself. Or maybe a good flush."

"Or maybe just a nap," I said. "I'd help you to bed but Marvelous looks so eager I'd hate to disappoint him."

"Thanks so much," Red groaned. "It's nice to have friends you can count on."

"True," I said. "So true."

# THIRTY-FOUR
# A WEIGHTY MATTER

CHARLIE AND I ate dinner at his place that night, grilled salmon in white wine. The aroma alone was worth five stars, but I couldn't seem to focus on food. I kept falling silent in mid-sentence, thinking about Martingale's visit and Thorp's disappearance. I tried to talk to Charlie about it, but he seemed oddly reluctant. Maybe he'd made the same leap that Martingale had, that Thorp and I were involved somehow.

Well, in a way, we were. Thorp had gotten me mixed up in this mess and his disappearance seemed to tie me to it even tighter. I just didn't understand why. I was lousy company, and for the first time, Charlie and I seemed uncomfortable with each other. I excused myself and went to my room.

I called Corey at the Ungers, and we talked for a few precious minutes. He said that he and Tommy were getting along great, and that Mr. Unger had been planning to buy a computer, so Corey was helping him translate brochures. He seemed cheerful enough about being there. I know I should have been grateful for that. I wasn't.

I'd already spent too much time away from him and I resented every damned minute this business was costing us now. Because I was losing them forever. He was growing so fast, changing so fast. I was afraid we might turn into strangers again if we stayed apart too long.

I told him I loved him before I hung up. He didn't reply. Maybe there were other kids within earshot. Or maybe not.

I lay back on the bed on top of the quilt, my fingers laced behind my head, thinking. Martingale. An officious little bureaucrat. It was hard to think of him as a policeman. But he was. And he assumed Thorp and I were involved. Why?

Because Thorp said something complimentary about me. Maybe to a guy like Martingale, that's all it took to assume we had something going. Too bad he hadn't seen me slap Thorp. I could still feel the sting of it on my palm. I didn't regret it.

But it wasn't much comfort either. It must have hurt. Thorp was angry, but probably more about being bumped off the case than the slap. And he'd seemed truly sorry about what happened to Red.

But at the end, when he was leaving and asked me about the dog. . . . His attitude changed. He was more upbeat. As though he'd thought of a way to make up for what happened.

Why? Because of the dog? What could the dog have to do with anything? The breed? Rottweilers are guard dogs, big, bold, but even tempered. The one I'd tangled with was obviously well trained, because he was running loose in the patches. Whoever'd left him there trusted him not to run off. Yet he was gone when the police raided the place.

Was that it? That someone got the dog out of there before the raid? Thorp said that one of the dopers, Chessman, had a kennel at his house. An empty kennel. But Chessman was in custody. If the dog was his, then where was it? With Pettiford? Did it matter? I couldn't see how.

What else had Thorp said about it? He'd asked me how big it was. And when I guessed the dog weighed at least one-twenty he thought I'd overestimated it. So he asked me to guess at his weight, and I came fairly close. But even then, he hadn't seemed particularly impressed until I mentioned that I'd grown up around dogs, and was pretty good at guessing their weights. . . .

That was it. When I said that, his attitude changed. Not because the dog was big, but that it was heavier than I was. But what difference could that make?

I was getting nowhere, so I closed my eyes and tried to visualize the dog. I took myself back to the mine site. I was clambering around the cliff face when I first glimpsed it. I wasn't sure what it was at first, because it was half concealed by the plants in the marijuana patch. . . .

Exactly! When I first saw it, the damned dog was running loose in the marijuana patch. And the dog weighed as much as I did. A hundred and twenty pounds, maybe more. Which meant the patches couldn't have been mined then. Any mine that would be triggered by a man's weight would have been set off by the dog. That's why his weight was important. It meant the explosives couldn't have been mines.

What were they then? There were three explosions. Two had torn up the patches, but the blasts had been too small to do much damage so the police guessed they were land mines designed to maim anyone who happened along. But they couldn't have been.

The third blast had closed the shaft entrance. But suppose it was the one that mattered and the other two were only supposed to deflect attention away from the Drift. That third blast was probably meant to bury whatever Pettiford had hidden there.

That worked. At last, something about the Third Coast tract began to make sense. What could be hidden there? The heavy weapons Thorp and Martingale were after? Maybe marijuana that had been harvested earlier? Pettiford was a diver, so he could have had access to it easily enough.

But if they had gone to the trouble to store something important there, why bury it with the blast? Why not just take it away? Too big to move? Or maybe it was stored a little farther back in the mine. And the blast was never intended to bury it, only to make people think it had been. It could still be there. Waiting for Pettiford to come back for it.

Or waiting for me. I'm not sure when I conciously made the decision. It was more like I already had begun to plan, and then realized what I'd decided to do. This mess had begun with my questions about my father and that mine. And it had escalated into explosions and attempted murder and a siege. Well, maybe I could end it. Maybe I was the only one who could.

Should I tell Charlie? I trusted him implicitly, he'd always been straight up with me. But things were changing between us.

If I told him, he'd insist on going by the book. He'd contact Sheriff Feige or Martingale or whoever was in charge at Grand Portal, and that might blow any chance of finding the truth. I simply didn't trust the police in Third Coast country. In the few days it took them to organize their raid after Van Amstel tipped them off, someone had beaten them to it. There was a leak in their operations the size of the Soo Locks.

Yet I was sure Charlie would tell them what I wanted to do. Not because he was a stickler for protocol, he wasn't. He'd do it because he cared about me. He wouldn't want to put me at risk.

But I was already at risk. I was in hiding, so was my son and Red was wounded. Our best chance to be free was to rip this thing open, to put Pettiford and the Third Coast out of business, and whatever was down that mine might just do it.

But I'd have to go after it alone. If the Thirds learned I was going to take a crack at the mine, they'd simply blow it closed for good this time. Maybe with me inside.

The dive itself wouldn't be all that risky for a pro. If the entrance was blocked or looked unsafe, I'd simply back off. If not, all I'd need was a quick look around.

The Drift had stood empty for a hundred years, off limits to all but a few since the water table had claimed it. But that water was no threat to me. Deep water is my office. My element.

And if there was something down there in the dark, I would bring it out.

# THIRTY-FIVE
# NORTH

ᘯᐎᓍᓎᓅ

THE NEXT morning I collected the gear I'd need and stowed it covertly in my Jeep. Evading Charlie proved to be easy, if dishonorable. I simply lied. I told him I needed to work late at the Nest. Since he had his people checking on us regularly, he wouldn't have to worry about me. I told the cook to cover any calls for me then left an envelope in the top drawer of my desk explaining where I was going and why.

Ordinarily I would have taken a diving partner along for safety, but there was nothing ordinary about this situation. One friend had already been injured because of me and I simply couldn't put anyone else at risk. Diving alone can be chancy business, but it's my business and my chance to take, no one else's.

I slipped away just before lunch, timing my departure to miss the prowl car that had been keeping an eye on the Nest. It was a rough day for a drive, at least in a Jeep. I took US 23 north along the coast, and a chill wind with a promise of snow buffeted my little Cherokee all the way to the Straits of Mackinac.

The drive across the Big Mac bridge in a rising gale was a heart-stopper. A few years ago a stiff gust lifted a Yugo off its wheels and blew it clear over the railing, a five-hundred foot drop to the waves, plus another five hundred to the lakebed.

They close the bridge to traffic now when the wind reaches dangerous levels, but I wondered about their margin for error every time a gust thumped the side of the Jeep.

A dusting of early snow transformed the drive up to the Drift into a crystaline magical mystery tour. The time fairly flew past, partly because I knew the route now, but also because I wasn't sure what I'd find.

Would the mine be under some sort of police guard? Unlikely. The Drift was in the middle of nowhere. Why should the cops keep an eye on it while Cezak and the Third Coast were hunkered down in their headquarters? I only hoped the same would hold true for militia sympathizers.

I arrived at the turnoff a little after three o'clock, and followed the same route back to the Drift that I'd taken in Red's truck. The Jeep had a much easier time of it. In low range four-wheel drive, the little Cherokee tackled the trail back to the old railroad grade with no trouble, so I gunned it up onto the grade itself and continued on.

The only problem was the noise. In the hush of the snow dusted forest, the whine of the engine seemed deafening.

The stream that I'd forded on foot before barely slowed me at all. I barreled the Jeep straight into it, counting on momentum to carry me through. The water surged up to the doors and the Jeep sideslipped a little, but then the wheels caught and it lunged out of the water like a Labrador retriever.

The road was rougher on the far side, with more undergrowth due to the wet soil. I slowed down to a few miles per hour, being very careful to keep to the center of the grade. The shadows were beginning to lengthen in the woods but I didn't want to use the Jeep's headlights unless I had to.

I was able to drive almost to the edge of the pond at the mouth of the Kewadin Drift. I shut the Jeep off, climbed out, stretched, and took stock. After the whine of the Jeep, the silence of the forest seemed absolute. It wasn't, of course. As my ears adjusted, I could hear the wind blowing in from the lake, rushing through the treetops like a distant train, branches creaking and cracking, swaying in an eternal ballet with the north wind.

The stench of the wounded land had been rising so gradually that I'd barely noticed, but I could taste it now, on the breeze and in my mouth. I knew it would fade. In ten minutes I'd cease to be aware of it. But I'd notice again later, when I cleaned my gear. The pressure would force it into the pores of the suit and it would reek for weeks.

The light dusting of snow changed the look of the mine site completely. I could see much farther into the surrounding forest than before, to the ripped up marijuana patches and beyond. If my friend the Rottweiler had been there I would have seen him a mile away. But he wasn't. There were no tracks of any kind in the new fallen snow, canine or human. I was very much alone. Good.

The pond looked much as it had in the pictures Nick Van Amstel showed me. A skin of ice covered it completely except for a five or six foot ring of open water near the cliff face directly above the adit. Warmer water was definitely flowing up from below. And if it could get out, maybe I could get in.

Seeing the water galvanized me into action. I'd waited a long time for this moment—maybe half my life, in a way. And now it was here, in front of me. A ring of darkness. And suddenly I couldn't wait to plunge into it, to plumb its depths and learn its secrets. If it had any.

I popped open the Jeep's tailgate, then stripped off my jacket and jeans and began donning my diving gear, preparing for a descent into icy blackness: Inuit hell, the land of neverending December.

I climbed into my wooly-bears first, a full body suit of long underwear. Then a Farmer-John-style foam-neoprene wet suit, high-top pants topped by a hooded vest, boots, weight belt, and an inflatable life vest. The vest was strictly to give me neutral buoyancy. Once I entered the mine itself, assuming I could get in, blowing the vest wouldn't save my life. It would only pin me to the ceiling like a bug on a windshield.

I double-checked my equipment, two regulators attached to twin 80 air tanks, two flashlights and a larger helmet light powered by a belt-mount battery pack, a capillary depth gauge, and a dive timer. So far, all systems go. I slipped my crepe-soled diving boots into my Hyperthane fins, eased into my tank pack, strapped it on, then waded cautiously down the snowy bank to the dark pool.

# THIRTY-SIX
## INTO THE DARK

᠊ᡅᡄᡅᡅ

THE FIRST bite of the water was as sharp as a shower of ice cubes, but I knew it would fade as my body heat warmed the water trapped in the suit. I waded slowly out to waist deep water, then chest deep, and then I slipped beneath the surface into a pearl-gray universe.

I rolled slowly without breathing, looking upward for a telltale stream of bubbles that would indicate an O-ring leak in my equipment. Nothing. I checked both regulators, then leveled out, switched on my helmet lamp and looked around.

Beneath the glistening ceiling of the ice sheet, the ground beneath the pond looked almost pristine. There were only small clumps of algae, no weeds or underbrush at all. The sulfide smothered any organism that lived by extracting oxygen from the water, but that same merciless function preserved whatever it covered as well.

I moved slowly through a world of eternal twilight, hazy water turbid with silt and sulfide suspension—and suspended time.

Above the waterline, only the scars in the rock face remained to mark the miners' efforts, but down here everything was preserved, protected by the chill, subterranean current from the elements that scoured the surface. Empty dynamite boxes littered the mine entrance, rimed with silvery silt as though they'd been dipped in pewter. Shattered pick handles and barrel staves lay where they'd been tossed aside more than a century before. Here a crushed bucket, there a broken pike.

As I approached the mine entrance, the light faded as I lost the reflection of the overhead ice. And then I came to the blast. The adit entrance was largely blocked by a rockfall. The explosion had brought down a huge chunk of earth that filled most of the mine's shadowy maw. It was soft fill, dirt and gravel bulwarked by chunks of stone piled to the top of the opening and beyond. From the look of it, it might have been possible to tunnel in along the roof, but I didn't think it would be necessary.

On the left side of the adit there was a narrow opening, three or four feet by six. Some loose boulders had collected at the bottom, partially blocking it, but it was large enough to admit me. More important, the rockfall beside it looked stable, neatly sloped as though it had been landscaped. Still, if something let go while I was inside. . . . I forced back the thought.

I took a deep breath and swam warily through the opening. The water immediately brightened as the walls reflected my helmet lamp. Rusted steel cart rails leapt up a few inches from the floor of the shaft, outlined in bold relief. Once past the rockfall, the entrance opened up again. I saw a large carton near the tracks ahead. A weapons crate? Willing myself to remain calm, I swam toward it.

It grew larger as I approached. Too big to be a crate. For a crazy moment I thought it might be an outhouse, but as I looked it over closely, I realized it was the original timekeeper's shack. A small stool stood in the corner. The last man who sat on it probably would have died long before my father was born.

I swam past the shack to scope out the rockfall from the inside. Except for a stray boulder or two that had rolled down off the pile, I could see nothing that hadn't been here a century or more. No sign of recent activity at all. If Pettiford or his friends had hidden anything down here, it was either buried under the rockfall, or it was farther back.

I swam back to the timekeeper's shack to check in with the shades who guarded this place, and attached my lifeline to the rusty doorlatch. Then I turned and swam deeper into the mine, following the cart track into the tunnel, keeping my movements minimal to avoid roiling the silt, feeling the comforting umbilical tug of the lifeline playing out of the reel on my belt.

Gray-green silt slicked the walls and clumped like leech colonies on the corroded remnants of a four-inch iron pipe that snaked along the ceiling. When the Kewadin Drift was active, this corridor would have echoed with the thunder of blasting, the ring of picks, and the ceaseless, cardial thumping of the steam pumps doing battle with the water. There was no noise now. Except for the metallic burble of my breathing, it was deathly silent. Nothing lived down here but moss, not fish, nor snakes nor even insects could survive in the poisonous sulfide stew.

The corridor sloped gradually downward for seventy meters, ending at a rough wooden platform with a two-meter square hole in its center. The elevator shaft. The miners would have ridden a rattletrap steel cage down to the next level, jammed together like lemmings. Many of them were youths of fourteen or fifteen who'd never known childhood, and yet they sang their way below, caroling hymns from Finland and Wales and Germany as they clattered down into the hammering din to work fourteen-hour shifts in a dusty, twilit purgatory where death and laceration lurked in the shadows, waiting for little men to make little mistakes.

Too many died young. Of maiming injuries or black lung or tuberculosis. But in the many group photographs I've seen displayed in area museums, the young men are almost always smiling. Did they know something about life that we've forgotten? Or were they just happy to be on the surface again, away from the toil and dust and thunder?

I paused on the elevator platform and took stock of the situation. I'd seen no indication of anything being dragged or floated along the corridor, nor any sign that anything had been stored down here, not weapons, weed or anything else. It didn't look as if anyone had been back here since my father had explored it all those years ago.

Still, I'd come too far to settle for half a look. And I had questions of my own to answer. Had my father's last visit been during the time he and Van Amstel had worked together? Or had he come back a year or so later on his own? To bury a crime? If nothing else, perhaps I could settle my family business once and for all.

I still had plenty of air and the mine seemed solid as . . . rock. There were no signs of recent damage, no fallen timbers or boulders or even stone chips, which was surprising, considering that someone had blown one hell of a substantial chunk of mountain down a week before.

I decided to explore the elevator shaft and make a quick check of the various levels. Whether I would go farther would depend on what I found.

I knelt on the platform and screwed a safety ring into the waterlogged timber that framed the opening, then snapped my lifeline into the ring. Then I picked up a kidney-shaped piece of loose ore for extra weight, and stepped off into the elevator shaft.

Free fall. Drifting slowly down into the dark, monitoring my depth gauge, I sank silently into the center of the mountain, enveloped in the pale lunar halo of my helmet lamp. Forty, fifty, sixty-five feet. I touched down on the rude plank floor of the next level at just under seventy feet.

Five tunnels radiated away from this platform like rays from a dark star. And there was something odd here. Rocks and stone chips were scattered around on the platform. They'd dimpled the rime of silt when they'd fallen, so they'd come down recently. Shaken from the wall of the shaft by the blasts? That seemed unlikely. The blast was over the entrance and I'd traveled quite a distance from there. Besides, I'd seen no fallen rocks along the way. Only here.

Was the mine less stable than it looked? I didn't care for that thought much. But except for the fallen stones, everything looked solid. Damn it, I definitely didn't want to come back here again, so I'd better check it out as thoroughly as possible.

A glance at my pressure gauge told me I had time to look over several of the tunnels if I hustled. I tried to screw a safety ring into the planking for my lifeline, but the wood had gone spongy from the greater pressure at this depth, and the ring's threads wouldn't hold.

I scanned the littered platform for something to anchor the

line. A hurricane lamp with a shattered lens, chunks of rock. A cinderblock on a pile of rags.

The cinderblock would have to do. At least it was square. I swam over to it and unhooked the reel from my belt. I tried to slip it through the hole in the block, but it was tangled in the rotted cloth. I yanked the block free—and a corpse jerked bolt upright out of the filthy sacking!

Bloodless, shreds of flesh sloughing away from its bones like melting suet, clotted eyesockets glaring up at me, its mouth opening to speak, then the face dissolving as the jaw unhinged and tumbled into the roiling whirlwind of silt!

"Noooooo!!!" I arched backward as though I'd been jolted by a thousand volt shock, instinctively thrusting away from *It*, and slammed into the shaft wall with a thunderous clang that shook me to my soul. The corpse began shrieking and I rolled and fled into the nearest tunnel, thighs pumping, heart hammering in my chest, thundering in my temples, breath keening through the regulator. I swam for my life, faster than I ever have. And still the screaming continued, drawing closer and closer. So I swam harder still, flying down the tunnel like a manic torpedo.

# THIRTY-SEVEN
# LOST IN THE UNDERWORLD

I swam furiously on, my throat on fire, gasping for air faster than my regulator could supply it . . . until suddenly the tunnel walls dissolved and I plunged into a fathomless pearl mist. And welcomed it. Invisibility. Refuge.

I coasted ahead, but more slowly now, chest heaving, perspiration fogging my mask. And I gradually slowed my progress, and my breathing. And began to reassemble the shreds of my self control. The howling continued behind me, but it was quieting now. And I recognized it for what it was. The shriek of escaping air. I'd smashed one of the tank valves on the shaft wall when I'd jerked away from . . . it.

*Sweet, sweet Jesus. That face . . .* My hands were trembling, and I couldn't stop gulping air, hyperventilating. *My God! Her jaw had fallen open as if she were trying to speak . . .*

"Stop it!" I yelled aloud, at the corpse, and at my own terror. My voice sounded strangled and inhuman in my mask. I bit down hard on my mouthpiece, grimly forcing myself to calm.

Okay. It was a corpse. A dead body. That's what it was. That's all it was. And I've seen bodies before. Even underwater. *But her face, falling to pieces—* I blinked, and harried the image of the corpse back into a shadowy corner of my mind. Later. I'd deal with it later. If there was going to be a later for me.

The audible alarm was rattling a warning, and the regulator was beginning to choke off which meant the tank was nearly empty. I fumbled over my shoulder for the backup regulator, said a silent prayer, sucked in a final gasp, and switched mouthpieces. If I'd damaged the backup tank too, I'd be as dead as that thing back on the platform in a minute. But the backup tank was still intact. Nothing in this life tastes as sweet as a breath that might have been your last. Reprieved, then. But for how long?

I wheeled slowly around, scanning the turbid water in the halo of my helmet lamp. There was nothing to see. Nothing. I was adrift in a shapeless vapor, a vast, subterranean cloud. Only the slow rise of my exhaust bubbles allowed me any sense of direction at all.

Evidently I was in a stope, one of the caverns left by the removal of the ore. I had no idea how big it was, or how I'd gotten in here, or how to get out of it. I closed my eyes and concentrated, trying to recall how long I'd swum after I left the tunnel, but it was hopeless. Thirty meters? Fifty? Too far to risk trying to blindly make my way back. I was on my last tank, twenty-two minutes, no more. There could be dozens of tunnels connected to this place, and if I took the wrong one, I'd die. I would barely have enough air to make it out as it was. I had to do something, and fast.

First things first. Up was the only direction I could be certain of, and there might be air or even some kind of an exit above. So I kicked off gently, following the rising bubbles, tracking my own silvery spoor up and up for what seemed an eternity. A minute. A minute and a half. And then I saw tiny explosions overhead, and slowed my pace. And very gently broke the surface.

My God. The stope was immense. I was only a few feet below the ceiling of a gigantic underground cavern that rolled away from me into the darkness like an inverted moonscape. I removed my mouthpiece and risked a shallow breath. And gagged. The foul sulfide stench was horrible, barely breathable. This wasn't air from the outside. It was a gigantic bubble, trapped against the granite by the rising water, concentrated, flat and stale. Which meant there was almost certainly no exit from this place above the waterline.

I switched off my helmet lamp, waited for my eyes to adjust to the blackness, but black it remained. Total darkness. No hint of light, no exit. Somehow I'd have to get out of here the same way I got in. And soon. I was beginning to shiver and my hands and ankles were beginning to go numb. Hypothermia. It wasn't bad yet, I could keep warm by moving. But not for long. And the real danger was that my judgment would be affected. That I'd make a mistake. And any mistake now would certainly be fatal. Hell, I could do everything exactly right and still die in here.

The trapped air meant I wouldn't suffocate immediately, at least, though considering the fetid stench, that wasn't much comfort. I unclipped one of the Scubapro halogen flashlights from my belt, touched the recessed switch, then narrowed its light beam and played it along the silvery surface of the pool.

Even using the water as a reflector, the beam could only reach one wall of the cavern, roughly forty meters away. That must be the one, then. I couldn't be sure how far I'd swum after leaving the mouth of the tunnel from the elevator platform, but the stope was so huge I didn't think I could have crossed it, ergo, my tunnel should be somewhere in that wall. I'd bet my life on it.

Staying on the surface to conserve air, I swam cautiously to the wall, slipped my diving knife out of its ankle sheath and scraped a patch in the silt to serve as a marker, hoping to God I wouldn't need it. Then I inserted my mouthpiece, jackknifed, and swam for the bottom.

I decided arbitrarily to work to my left. If I couldn't find the entrance tunnel, I could surface, find my mark again and work the other direction. For as long as my air held out. And I also decided that if I couldn't find the tunnel, I'd accept the consequences here in the depths, rather than prolong things up above in the reeking dark.

I found a tunnel almost immediately, but knew at a glance it was the wrong one. And then I found a second only a few yards over. The damned stope was honeycombed with tunnels, but at least they all seemed to be on the same level. The fourth tunnel I examined contained the jewels I sought, an indescribably exquisite chain of silvered pearls trapped against its roof;

the trail of air bubbles my leaking tank had left behind like breadcrumbs in the forest, to mark the way back. All I had to do was follow them out. And to retrieve my lifeline from the thing on the platform.

But I wasn't quite ready to do that. Perhaps it was fear, an atavistic revulsion at the thought of facing that corpse again. But it might be more than that, and I needed to be sure. I had no margin for error now, so I needed to think my next moves through very carefully and I couldn't waste any more air doing it. Reluctantly, I backed out of the tunnel and rose again to the surface of the underground pool.

I spat out my mouthpiece and used my dive knife to scrape another mark on the wall, then I checked my pressure gauge and tried to recall my route. How much time had I spent breathing the air in the stope? Five minutes? About that, I thought. But I'd spent another six minutes locating the tunnel. I had 2200 pounds of pressure remaining, which at this depth would give me roughly sixteen minutes of air. And that simply wasn't enough.

Damn it! It wouldn't compute. No matter how I figured it, it would take me at least twenty minutes to make my way back to the entrance. I'd raced down the tunnel to get here, but I couldn't go out that way. I'd have to follow the bubbles very carefully. I'd already destroyed one tank by banging into a tunnel wall. If I wrecked another, or if I took a wrong turn, I'd die. And even if I gambled and swam as hard as I could, hyperventilation would use the air that much faster and I'd still run out about halfway up the damned elevator shaft, a good five minutes from the entrance.

And yet . . . I wasn't panicking. Why not? Because I had the nagging sense that I wasn't beaten yet. That I was missing something obvious. Maybe it was just exhaustion. God knows I was tired enough that the idea of eternal rest had some appeal. But not here, in this stinking hole. Not like this. Not like she . . .

She. And there it was. Or part of it. In the split second before I'd recoiled from the corpse and fled, I'd gotten the impression it was a woman. Why? I couldn't be sure. For one thing, I couldn't seem to focus on the image. It was too horrible, too. . . . Damn it! I switched off my headlamp. I didn't need to save the batteries; they'd outlast my air by hours, but I needed to think clearly. The total darkness was disorienting, but it was a wonderful goad to concentrate. As soon as I decided what to do, I could have light again.

The corpse. A woman? Yes. There was some hair on her skull, long and dark. But it was more than that. Clothing? As the corpse had fallen to pieces before my eyes, I'd glimpsed a collar. One with a rounded corner. Okay, I might be wrong, but my best guess was that the corpse was female.

So what? Well, for one thing, it exonerated my father. The corpse wasn't Frank d'Hubert. A pity. If I was going to die down here, I would have preferred the company of a relative. But something else about the corpse was bothering me, too.

The concrete block had been tied to it as an anchor, twenty or thirty pounds' worth. But blocks like that one didn't exist a hundred years ago, so the miners hadn't left it here. More likely, whoever put the corpse down here brought the block with them.

Pettiford? I couldn't be sure. It didn't seem likely, though. Thorp said he'd recently moved up here from Wisconsin, and the corpse had been here a long time. At least ten years, probably much longer. Besides, Pettiford was a diver. If he'd brought the corpse down, he wouldn't have bothered to bring the block along. It was simply too heavy to haul that far. The corpse would have been trouble enough.

Unless it had gotten down here some other way.

And that was it. If the block and the corpse had come down together, then they hadn't followed the same route I had. Besides, the corpse was on the platform. Why? My best guess was that the platform was barely halfway down the shaft. The mine was much deeper. So if a diver brought the body that far, why not just push it over the side and let the block drag her all the way to the bottom? Unless . . . she'd been dropped from above somehow and simply came to rest here.

From where? Another tunnel? Possibly. Or maybe a shaft for the pumps that kept the mine free of water. An operation this size working so far below the water table would need enormous pumps to keep the water at bay, but I'd seen no sign of them on my way in. There should be another shaft, then. Someone had dropped the body down from it, and it had landed on the platform. Which meant there had to be another exit somewhere above that platform. Or at least, there'd been one when the body had been dropped down here.

No, it was still there. It just had to be. Because if it wasn't, I was dead.

I took a last deep breath of fetid air, then reinserted my mouthpiece, switched on my helmet lamp, and followed the rock face down to the tunnel entrance. I entered it slowly. The tunnel was fair sized, tall enough for a man to walk upright, but I had to stay close to the ceiling to keep the trapped, silvery pearls of air in view. Fortunately, the structure itself seemed solid, the timbers and braces all in place. And as I tracked the air bubbles along the corridor roof, for a moment I wondered again about the loose rocks I'd seen scattered on the elevator platform.

And suddenly I was there. The tunnel ceiling ended and I swam into the open elevator shaft directly across from the platform. It took every ounce of willpower I had left to turn to face the . . . thing on the platform. But when I did, she was gone.

# Thirty-eight
# A Dance in Deep Water

꙰

THE PLATFORM was empty. No corpse. My heart froze and I stopped breathing. She couldn't be gone. Could I have taken a wrong turn? No, I'd followed my own bubbles back to this place. This was the right platform, its silt cratered by fallen rocks, and a disturbed area where the corpse. . . . Damn it, she'd been there! And she was dead and the dead don't move. Not without help. Could someone else be down here? Pettiford?

I glanced around frantically, but there was no sign of anyone else. No bubbles, no noises. I switched off my helmet lamp a moment and the shaft was swallowed by utter blackness. No other light was in view. I switched it back on and pulled myself together.

All right then. I was seventy feet down in a mine abandoned a century ago, which is about as alone as a human being can be.

I swam cautiously to the platform. I could see the scuffed area where the corpse had been and the water around it was still roiled. The cement block was gone. That must be it. I was fumbling with the block when . . . she'd surged up out of the silt. When I panicked the block must have tumbled over the edge of the platform and dragged her down with it.

I unsnapped my flashlight and pointed it down into the darkness. I didn't really expect to see anything. But I did. A shadow, a movement far below. I couldn't make it out, but something was definitely moving down there. In the dark.

Another diver? No. His exhaust bubbles would have to rise past me. Not a diver then. A fish? Damn it, nothing could live in this swill, fish or anything else. The lost lady, then? But how could she be moving?

I checked my dive timer. Fourteen minutes. If there was an opening above me, I should have three or four minutes to spare. If not, it wouldn't matter. Damn it, I had to get out of here. I was telling myself that even as I dove over the edge of the elevator platform and kicked hard for the bottom of the shaft.

It was probably another sixty feet to the floor of the shaft, but I didn't have to go nearly that far. I played the beam of my halogen flashlight ahead of me as I swam, and after twenty feet or so, I began to see the shadows of the debris that had collected on the floor over the past century.

And then I saw the missing lady, a crumpled tangle of bones and rotted cloth lying beside the cement block in a cloud of roiled silt. But she wasn't alone. There was another body near her, in similar condition. And yet another.

My God. I slowed unconsciously as my mind struggled to grasp what I was seeing. The floor of the elevator shaft was littered with bodies. Corpses and skeletons jumbled together in an obscene tangle, with the silt from the fallen one coiling above them like a whirlwind in hell. Were there a dozen? More? I couldn't tell. The bodies were too tangled to know where one ended and another began.

And then I saw the movement again, against the far wall of the shaft. I swam nearer, playing the light on it, and for a moment I seemed to blank out. It was another body. A fresh one. Floating, suspended by the gases of its own decomposition.

Tethered to something on the floor of the shaft, it was swinging slowly in a circle, apparently driven by the current of the icy underground stream that fed this place.

I had to know. I swam toward it, but the disturbance of my approach turned it away from me. I tried to swim around it, but it pirouetted away, and I followed, twisting and shifting, desperately trying to glimpse its face without having to touch it as we joined in a macabre ballet, a dance in deep water.

At last it swiveled toward me. Dead eyes, mottled skin, a gray, bloated face. A face I knew. Jack Thorp. No question. I unconsciously reached out for him, but the movement turned him away again. As if he was leaving me. And wished to rejoin his friends on the charnel house floor.

And suddenly I seemed to shatter. The horror of this place crashed in on me and I couldn't bear it another moment. I thrust myself upward, upward, following my own bubbles higher. I soared past the second elevator platform without slowing, and then the first. And still the shaft continued upward, twenty feet, thirty.

I wanted to check my depth gauge, but I didn't dare waste the moment it would take. And it didn't matter. If I didn't break the surface soon I'd . . .

But I did. I burst out of the water into open air like a Poseidon missile, with a suddenness that took me by complete surprise. I fell back to the water, floundered about a moment trying to right myself, then gathered my wits enough to raise my mask, unclip my flashlight and play it around.

It looked like a stone antechamber, but it wasn't. It was only the high-water line of an abandoned shaft. The vertical tunnel continued above me for another twenty-five feet or so, then ended in what appeared to be solid rock on all sides. I could see no opening to the outside.

There was a steady stream of water trickling down one wall and a jagged crater near it about ten feet over my head. The gouge in the stone looked fresh, as though a blast had gone off in here recently, which would explain the fallen rocks on the platform below. I turned again, scanning my prison, and my light picked up a huge dark shape floating near me.

It was the Rottweiler. The body of the dog had bloated to half again its normal size and its fur had sloughed away from its grayish skin in scrofulous patches. It had likely been dead for a week. I couldn't tell what had killed it, and I didn't dare examine it more closely. The stench in the shaft took on a new and repulsive tang. God, I had to get away from here.

I swam to the far side of the shaft and felt the stone walls. Could I climb up? I'd have to. There had to be an entrance up there somewhere. The bodies of Thorp and the dog were the proof of that.

I eased out of my shoulder pack, looking around for a ledge or cleft to stash them. There was nothing. The water streaming down the far wall made it slick with silt and algae, and the others were much too smooth to hook anything to.

I knew I should drop the damned tanks. I was already shivering from exposure to the chill air, and my limbs were going numb. I was definitely in the first stages of hypothermia. Still, I couldn't bear the thought of letting my tanks tumble down to the horror below.

I unsnapped my lifebelt and jerked the tab that inflated it, then I lashed my tank pack to it at let it float off. I slipped my flippers off and dropped them. They floated on their own, so they'd remain here. As I would if I didn't get out of the cold soon.

A steady flow of water streaming down the wall to my left from above made the going impossible on that side. I thrust away from it to the opposite side of the shaft, then hauled myself out of the water, found a few handholds and began to work my way up the rock face.

I'm no mountaineer, and the granite walls were cold and slimy; but fortunately the blast, or whatever had happened down here, had roughed up the surface enough to furnish some purchase. I crawled up the stone foot by painful foot. My felt-soled diving boots gave little traction. Twice, I slipped and skidded down a few feet, but managed to scrabble myself to a halt. Then I was back at it, clawing my way upward. Ten feet. Twelve.

But there was no exit. The top of the shaft was a shambles of rock and debris and I couldn't see any way out. Some kind of structure had stood here once, perhaps the housing for the pumps or the engines that ran the elevator. But it had long since collapsed into the shaft and had been buried by rocks and dirt that washed down the mountainside. There was nothing that looked like an opening at all. Yet there had to be one. Because the dog was below. And Thorp was farther down. They must have been brought in this way. And since they'd been dead when they were put here, then someone must have dragged them. So there should be tracks or scrapes of some kind.

But I couldn't see any marks on the rock at all. The water, then? Where did it come from? The stream seemed to enter the shaft through the opposite wall, slightly below my perch on the rocks. I played my light around the stream and spotted them at last.

There were white patches where the silt had been scuffed off, and dirt smudges on the rock face near the water. It looked like something had been dragged in from the outside and pushed over. But how? There was no opening.

I inched my way around the shaft to the water flow, and managed to wedge one hip on a narrow rock shelf just below the marks. The water trickled and spilled through the cracks and crevices of what seemed to be a rockfall. I couldn't see a passage to the outside, but it had to be there. There was nowhere else.

Desperately, I began clawing at the rocks, pulling them in on myself, sending them splashing down into the blackness below. I don't know how long I dug. Ten minutes? A year? My legs were rapidly going numb, chilled by my stone perch and the water splashing on me, but I couldn't shift position without risking a fall. I could only keep scrabbling away at the rocks with my failing strength. I was freezing slowly, feeling my consciousness ebb. I knew there was no way out now. I'd lost, but I was too dullwitted to quit or even to care very much. . . .

Something icy brushed my cheek. I flinched away, nearly tumbling back into the pool below. I clung to the wall, dazed and terrified. And then I felt the touch again on my numbed cheek. And this time I recognized it. A fingerling breeze. An icy kiss of the nightwind.

My God! I could see it, an opening in the rocks no bigger than my fist. But there was no light—of course there wasn't! I'd been down here so long that darkness had fallen. But it hadn't fallen on me. Not yet. I still had a chance to live.

I tore into the rocky soil with renewed fury, ripping at the stones until suddenly the wall collapsed and a small avalanche of soil and stones and water rolled over me. The mud and gravel swept me off my perch and I slid down the rock face a good six feet, catching a handhold only a second before I would have plunged the rest of the way down into the freezing dark.

The breeze was whistling into the cavern now, calling me, and I responded, scrambling up the dripping rockface like a drunken monkey. The opening was the bed of a small stream. I crawled through the hole on my belly in the icy water, out of the mineshaft into the night air.

Snow was wafting down out of a dirty gray overcast. It was the grungiest, most glorious sky I've ever seen. I tried to stand. Couldn't. So I crawled on my knees to the stream bank. It was rimed with ice, slick as greased glass. It was all I could do to roll myself out of the water. But I made it. I knelt on the bank, head down, panting like a dog for what seemed like hours.

I wanted to lie down for awhile, to rest. But I had to move, to get out of the wind, to make it back to the Jeep and its warmth, or I would surely die here.

I forced myself to straighten up, then stumbled to one knee, and then to my feet. I stood there a moment, swaying unsteadily. And it was only then that I realized I wasn't alone.

# THIRTY-NINE
## OUT OF THE DARKNESS

ᛰᛒᚖᛢᚖ

NICK VAN Amstel was working his way down from a notch in the rocks above. He'd been sitting up there like a vulture, watching both entrances, waiting to see if I'd make it out alive. He was dressed like an ad for Eddie Bauer's foul weather gear, in an olive drab parka, corduroy pants, and Vibram-soled hiking boots. He was even wearing an English tweed shooting cap. Which was appropriate, since he was holding a rifle; a carbine, actually, a Ruger, Mini-14, with a fifteen-round clip. He stopped on the far bank of the stream a few yards from me.

"Are you all right?" Nick asked.

I didn't answer for a moment. Hadn't the strength. "I'll live," I managed at last. "Or will I?"

"Of course," he said, looking away. "My God, I never meant you any harm. I just . . . need to think. To decide what to do. I'm out of my depth here. If your father were here he'd know what to do."

"How did you know I was here?" I asked.

"I didn't, I only knew that someone was. I had one of my security people reconfigure one of the college's infra-red sentry lights and set it to trigger when anyone used the railroad grade. It's quite marvelous, solar powered, with a broadcast range of. . . . Well, it doesn't matter. But, I half expected it would be you.

You're very much like your father, you know. Tenacious. A bull-dog. But when I saw the Jeep, I wasn't sure."

"Because the night we met at the school, I was driving a red pickup truck," I said. "It wasn't mine, it was Red's."

"I see," he said, nodding. "I didn't know. I realize that any apology is inadequate, but I'm terribly sorry about what happened to your friend. I was desperate, half-out of my mind at the time. I didn't know what else to do."

"But why?" I asked. "To protect this mine? What the hell for? What's so special about it?"

He eyed me for a moment, then shook his head slowly. "If this were an oral exam for Mendacity 101, I'd have to give you a 'D.' Don't try to lie to me, Mitch. You haven't the talent for it."

"Sorry. I guess I cut that class."

"Then it's time for a crash course," he said. "You're going to have to help me, Mitch, because we're in this together. I don't want to harm you, truly. I don't want to hurt anyone. But everything I've worked for, devoted my life to, is at stake here. I can't be brought down by a twenty year old mistake. The work is too important."

"What work?"

He hesitated. "People," he said, with a shrug. "I told you back at Huron Harbor. I'm in the people business, Mitch."

"I don't understand. All this is over a few undocumented students?"

"Oh, far more than a few. Over the years I've helped a great many people, Vietnamese, Nationalist Chinese, even Thais and Cambodians, enter this country from Canada. The school is a perfect front for it. We have tour buses, exchange programs. It's grown into a very complex operation."

"You're saying you're some kind of a high tech coyote?" I asked, trying to understand.

"Coyote is the term the Immigration Service would probably use," he admitted. "But it's not accurate. The people we bring in aren't migrant peasants looking for the nearest beanfield, they're people of substance and education."

"And money?"

"That too," he acknowledged. "Running an organization of this size is expensive, but it's not about the money. These people were allies. Many of them fought for us in Vietnam, or their families did. When we pulled out of Southeast Asia, we abandoned them and disgraced ourselves. We owe them a debt of honor."

"And the people at the bottom of the mine? What did you owe them?"

"More than I could ever repay," he said, looking away. "Not long after I married Mei and came back to the U.S. again, I was approached by a Vietnamese from Montreal, a man named An. He asked for my help in smuggling a group of refugees into this country. I was the wrong man to ask. I mean, I truly wanted to help, but I was never really a soldier, I was a supply officer. I'm not a very . . . practical man. Still, I came up with a way to manage it. It was simple, really. We could cross Lake superior on the ice. A snowmobile can make the run from Ontario in an hour, even towing a sled. We could come ashore near the mine, completely isolated and . . . anyway, it all went wrong."

"How?"

"An accident," he said, wincing at the memory. "I'd ridden snowmobiles, but I wasn't an expert driver. I hit some sort of an . . . air pocket in the ice, and cracked up the machine. The sledge I was towing overturned and some of the refugees were injured. It was horrible. We still had nearly ten miles to trek across the Lake Superior ice in the dark, and the wind was rising. None of us were dressed for that kind of cold. Even now I can barely comprehend how bitter it was. But it affected the Asians sooner. They simply couldn't take it. And they began to die. And there was nothing I could do. None of them made it off the ice alive. Not one."

"But you did."

"Barely," he acknowledged. "I stumbled ashore half-frozen. Mei was waiting with a van. She helped me to it and saved my life. And, ah," he swallowed, blinking back tears. "And the next day we went back for the bodies. And brought them here."

"And you just . . . dropped them down the mine?"

"There was nothing to be gained by going to the authorities. I would have been jailed, possibly for homicide. And my wife as well. But even if we hadn't been, there would have been reprisals from the families of the refugees. Even now, there would be."

"You didn't tell their families what happened?"

"No, I wouldn't have lived a week if they'd found out. Fortunately, it was An who'd organized the group. When relatives
came around asking, I said I'd talked to him, but had warned
against trying to make the crossing in winter. I said that they
must have been lost on the ice. Which wasn't far from the truth.
And since An was here with the others, he was in no position to
debate the point."

"And the families believed you?"

"Many of them knew me. I don't think they considered me
capable of mass murder. And so many had died in that damned
war and were still dying. Yes, they accepted it. And over the
years I've tried to atone for it by helping as many as I could."

"For a fee?"

"This is America," he said with a shrug. "There's no law
against doing well by doing good. Many of the families I've
helped are wealthy. They expect to pay, and we need the money
to continue the work."

"And Thorp? What did he pay?"

"He called my office and asked if I had a diagram of the
mine. Somehow he'd guessed the blasts in the fields were only
meant to camouflage the blast that closed the entrance, or was
supposed to. He guessed there was something important about
the mine and also that there might be a second entrance. So I
told him I had no map, but offered to meet him here to show
him the entrance to the airshaft. And I did what I had to. I had
no choice. You must see that."

"Sounds logical," I said. But it didn't. Nothing he was saying made much sense to me. I was too cold, too exhausted. I
could barely feel my arms and legs. I needed to rest, to lie down
for a only minute. "Look, I've got to . . . move." I said. My
tongue felt swollen, sluggish. I scarcely had the energy to speak.

"We'll go in a few minutes," Van Amstel said. "But first we
need to reason our way through this. I need some assurance
from you that you won't destroy what we're trying to accom-
plish. I want your word."

"My . . . word?" I managed.

"That you'll keep silent about what you've seen. And what

I've told you. You're the daughter of an old friend. I'm willing to accept your word."

God, it was such a ridiculous lie. Van Amstel couldn't have passed Mendacity 101 either. He was no better at lying than he'd been at hauling a sledge full of refugees across the ice. He was such a close friend of my father's that I'd never heard of him. And on the strength of that, he was asking for my word that I'd conceal mass murder? To say nothing of Thorp's death and his attempt on Red. On me, actually. I almost smiled. But I couldn't. My face was nearly immobile. If I could just rest. . . .

My legs began to wobble so I stumbled to an upright boulder a few feet away and leaned against it. The stone felt oddly warm. Like Red's shoulder. And then it was her shoulder. It truly was. And it felt so soothing, so comforting, that I rested my head on it and drifted off. . . .

"Michelle?"

I wanted to see who was calling me, but I couldn't quite manage to open my eyes. The voice was familiar. A man's voice. Dad? No. Van Amstel. His old friend. That was it. Answer him? No. Too tired. He didn't call again.

"Is he gone?" I asked Red. I think I spoke aloud, but I wasn't sure. She didn't answer me, which ticked me off. If he was gone, Red and I could walk to the Jeep and get warm. Though I wasn't nearly as cold as I had been. Red might be, though.

I managed to open an eye a little. He was still there. He was sitting on a rock, the rifle in his lap. Watching me. I wanted to ask Red why he hadn't gone. But as I turned to her, she changed. Into a boulder. The metamorphosis was so startling it struck me like a slap in the face.

He's not gone. He's waiting. He only talked to you to keep you here. While you froze. He doesn't want to shoot you. He wants you to die of exposure. With no marks. So he can move you somewhere else. To draw attention away from this mountain. This . . . tomb.

The people below were dead because of him. And so was Thorp. And Red might be crippled. And he'd made her cry. And somehow this last seemed more heinous than the others. Perhaps it was all I could truly understand. But it was enough. It lit a spark of rage in my breast that seemed to warm me a little. A very little. I staggered upright.

"Where are you going?"

"I . . . need to walk," I mumbled. "I'm cold."

"Sit down, rest awhile. You must be exhausted. You'll feel better after a rest, then we can go."

I didn't reply. Hadn't the strength. I took a step, then another. And then I slipped on the icy bank and stumbled into the creek. I fell to my hands and knees in the water. I hardly felt it. It was less than a foot deep here, and sluggish, barely moving. I knelt in the water a moment, my head down, then slowly, ever so slowly, I staggered to my feet again.

I tried to walk but the mix of ice and silt in the creek made it as slick as a greased skillet. I lost my balance and nearly went down again. Somehow I managed to stay upright. I slogged across the stream toward the other bank. And Van Amstel.

He moved to meet me, blocking my path.

"Mitch, I can't let you leave here. Surely, you must see that."

I didn't answer. I couldn't. Instead, I placed a foot on the bank and tried to climb out. Van Amstel's pretense of concern vanished. He shoved the rifle crossways against my chest, pushing me off the bank. I reeled back and went down on my seat in the water. Almost stayed there. But not quite. I rolled over, got my knees under me and forced myself to rise, one last time.

I turned to face him. I fumbled for the dive knife in the sheath on my calf, but it might as well have been on Mars. I couldn't pull it free. My hand wouldn't close on the hilt. I was all but done. But I made my legs move and floundered through the water, angling for the bank a few yards upstream from him.

He sidestepped to cut me off, thrusting me back with the rifle butt. I clawed at it, pulling myself toward him, rocking him off balance. I grappled clumsily, clutching at his waist, but only managed to tangle one of my arms up with the rifle. He tried to push me away, but I hung on.

"You little bitch! Let go!" He jerked the gun free and swung the butt savagely at my head. It was the moment I'd waited for, my last chance. As he struck at me, I slid down his trunk, wrapped both arms around his thighs and toppled backward, dragging him headlong off the bank, plunging us both into the stream!

I tried to twist to get him beneath me, but I was too slow, too numb. We splashed into the shallow water in a sidelong tangle. He went rigid as the icy water struck him, then frantically tried to writhe free of me. I clung to his thighs with the dregs of my strength. My hands had no feeling now, so I thrust desperately with my legs, keeping him off balance and in the water, sliding us both along the icy stream bed.

Nick jerked the rifle free and tried to slam the butt into my temple but I was too close to him. My face was buried in his chest, pressed as tightly to him as a lover.

He hammered the gun down across my shoulders and back. I could feel the stunning force of the blows, but the pain seemed oddly dull. I was detached from it, numbed beyond feeling or sense. I clung to him like a slug, mindlessly thrusting him forward.

"Damn it, Mitch! Let me go!" He was trying to push me off, to twist free of me. He sounded more annoyed than angry. He knew I was nearly spent. I was an inconvenience, nothing more. He'd be free of me in a matter of seconds.

He tossed the rifle aside and clawed at my arms, but could find no purchase on my wet suit. I don't think he realized what I intended until it actually happened, when I thrust us both through the opening into the mineshaft!

He screamed as the earth fell away beneath him and he skidded down the rockface into the dark, and plunged twenty-five feet to the black pool below. I nearly fell with him, but at the last second I swung my hips sideways to let him drop away from me.

Scrabbling desperately at the rocks, I fought for a hand-hold, as the stream tried to carry me down after Van Amstel. I managed to slow my skid, then halted as my knee caught on a rotted timber.

Nick was gone. I heard him shout once, and then again. I couldn't make out any words, it was more of a . . . howl. An awful wail of fear and pure horror. For a moment I envisioned him thrashing around below in the blackness of the icy water, with his clothing turning leaden. And the corpse of the dog. . . .

I pushed the thought away. I was crossways in the stream

bed with the water playing over my legs and waist. I had to move now, or I would die here.

I managed to roll over and got my knees beneath me. I couldn't feel my legs, couldn't get up, so I lurched upstream on my hands and knees. I knew I had to get out of the icy water. I knew it. I just couldn't seem to comprehend the mechanics of the process. Should I put my hands on the bank for support, or try to stand first? It was too complicated. Couldn't deal with it. So I kept crawling in the water. To the rifle.

My hands wouldn't close around the stock, but somehow I pawed it up and got the butt under my arm. Using it as a crutch, I levered myself upright and staggered to my feet.

I stood there, swaying like a willow in a windstorm, trying to understand where I was. The stream flowed down from the higher ground to the . . . west. It was a rivulet from the creek I'd crossed in the Jeep. The Jeep. I had to get to it. No one knew exactly where I was. There would be no help. And if Pettiford or one of the Third Coasters found me here . . .

The Jeep was on the far side of the mountain, near the pool. The footing would be easier to the east, but it would be a longer trek. No choice. A few minutes might be the difference. I'd have to climb the shoulder of the mountain. In the dark. My flashlight was still clipped to my belt but it was rimed with ice and useless to me. My numbed fingers couldn't free it. Still, with starlight refecting from the snow, I could see well enough. I'd have to.

In one way, the cold was a blessing. Snow froze to the felt soles of my diving boots, providing some crude traction. I can't remember making the climb. At some point, halfway up to the crest, I must have blacked out. And yet somehow my body labored numbly on, until I felt the bitter sting of the night wind in my face and found myself on the ridge. I could see the shape of the Jeep across the pond. I couldn't remember why I wanted to reach it anymore. I only knew I had to.

But there was no way I could clamber down the steep grade to my left, and I certainly couldn't jump to the open pool near the mine opening. I solved the problem by collapsing. I lurched to one knee, then toppled over, and began to slide down the frozen face of the mountain.

I couldn't control my fall, could have skidded over the ledge and dropped thirty feet to the pond at any point, but I didn't. Maybe an angel kept me from the edge. Or the ghosts of the Vietnamese dead below. Or perhaps my grandfather, if he was truly in this place. Or maybe it was just dumb luck.

I was too battered to rise when I tumbled to a halt at the base of the hill. And so I crawled to the Jeep. Getting the door open was almost more than I could manage with my numbed hands. My arms felt like fenceposts and were no more adept.

But somehow I worked the latch, and levered myself inside. And started the engine. And switched on the heater. And passed out.

I awoke sometime in the night. In agony. My arms and legs were ablaze with returning circulation. I was barely aware of my surroundings, but as I came out of the haze, I knew I had to leave this place. Before Van Amstel found me. Or the Thirds, or . . . I didn't know.

I forced myself to sit upright. My hands were on fire. I couldn't grip the wheel, couldn't make them close. I'd have to steer with my wrists draped over the crossbar. I dropped the Jeep into low gear, and began a long, slow U-turn in the snow.

# FORTY
## AFTER THE FALL

$\mathcal{Qbdl}$

"I DON'T think you should leave yet," Martingale said. Bud.
He'd told me to call him Bud. But he wasn't a Bud. Buds have
calluses on their hands, and bib overalls. Brian Martingale
would never be a Bud to me.

"The doctor says if I can walk out, I can leave," I said. "End
of discussion." We were sitting in a small waiting room at the
end of the hospital corridor. St. Joseph's Hospital, in Marquette.
I'd been here four days.

"In all fairness, I have to warn you. You may not be safe if
you leave. I expect Cezak and his pals in the Third Coast militia to surrender soon now that they know we can't tie them to
the explosives at the mine, but we won't be able to hold them
for long. All we've got on them now is a loose tie to the marijuana patches. Both of the men we have in custody are willing
to testify that Cezak knew about the patches."

"And is it the truth?" I asked. "Or just what they're willing
to testify to?"

"It will be . . . sworn testimony," Martingale hedged, looking away. "But I'm not at all sure a local jury will buy it. We
could charge them with resisting arrest, but I doubt we could
make that fly either."

"What does that have to do with me?"

"It's just that we don't have anything else. We haven't

turned up any heavy weapons, nothing illegal. We thought they must have explosives in their headquarters, but apparently the Thirds had nothing to do with the blasts on the tract. It was Van Amstel trying to cover his tracks."

"He nearly did."

"Actually, he didn't come as close as you might think. The blast he set off in the airshaft didn't do much damage. If he'd set the same blast higher up, he might have collapsed the whole mine."

"Why didn't he?"

"Ignorance," Martingale said. "He was a supply officer, not a combat soldier. He simply didn't know enough about ordinance to place the charges properly. If he'd been competent with explosives or a better shot, the mountain would be gone and you or your friend might be dead now."

"He came close enough. For both of us."

"But that's what I'm trying to tell you. You're not out of the woods yet. If we go to trial against the Thirds with the evidence we have now, they may well get off. And some of them still blame you for what happened."

"Sorry, but I can't help that. I have a home and a life. I'm not going to run off or hide out on the chance that some backwoods losers may be ticked off at me. I won't live that way. Besides, it wasn't the Thirds who followed me south, it was Van Amstel. And now that he's gone . . ." I hesitated. "You did find him, didn't you?"

"Of course." Martingale nodded. "I told you that, the second day."

"I'm sorry," I said. "I seem to be having a little trouble remembering what we talked about then. I was pretty groggy, and I've had some . . . bad dreams about what happened. Sometimes I'm not sure which is which."

"You're entitled," Martingale said. "Yeah, he was there. He'd gotten all tangled up with the body of the dog, or at least that's how we found him."

"And the others? Have the dive teams finished bringing them up?"

"We expect them to wrap it up today. The State cop in charge told me his team's going to make one last pass this afternoon, but he was fairly sure they got all of the bodies out yesterday."

I looked away, swallowing. Suddenly my eyes were stinging. I wasn't sure why. "How many?" I asked at last. "How many were down there?"

"Twelve, total," Martingale said, looking away. "Van Amstel, Jack, and ten more."

"And they were all in one place? At the foot of the shaft?"

"That's right. But the divers searched the rest of the mine thoroughly on the chance that some of the bodies might have drifted before they decomposed. They photographed every inch of the site, but they didn't find any more bodies."

"I see." I nodded slowly, thinking. "Have they identified them yet?"

"From what the coroner says, they may never identify some of them," Martingale sighed. "It's been twenty years, and most of them had entered Canada with phony papers. All we have is a list of names Mei Van Amstel furnished. And frankly, I'm not sure how credible she is. She has interests of her own to protect."

"But you're sure that . . . the ten you found, were the ones Van Amstel dumped there?"

"I'm not sure what you mean," Martingale said, frowning. "The forensic evidence indicates they were all Asians and that they'd been down there roughly the same length of time. Why? Did he indicate he might have put another body there?"

"No. I just . . . wanted to be sure. Look, I'm a little tired. I'd like to rest now."

"Of course," he said, rising. "You've had a hell of an ordeal. I still wish you'd reconsider about leaving, though. Wait a week, Mitch."

"Not another day," I said. "If I don't see you again, Mr. Martingale, thanks for everything."

"You've got to be kidding," he said, hesitating in the doorway. "I'm the one who owes you. The bureau owes you. Not for Van Amstel, actually, he wasn't our problem. But for Jack Rooney. He was one hardcase, crazy sonofabitch, you know? You have to be a little nuts to do the kind of work he did. But he was right about the Thirds and I shouldn't have bumped him from the case. If I'd believed him maybe he wouldn't have gone to Van Amstel trying to solve it alone and . . . well. If it hadn't been for you, we might never have known what happened to him. Hell, I'd half convinced myself he'd gotten fed up and packed it in. I should have known better."

"I'm not sure how well anyone ever really knows anyone," I said. "Maybe the point is to keep learning. About each other, and ourselves."

"Maybe." He nodded. "In any case, I owe you one, Mitch. Personally. If there's anything I can ever do, just ask. This is my pager number at the bureau. Call me. Anytime."

He handed me a business card. I eyed it a moment, as though I'd never seen one before. Couldn't seem to make sense of the numbers. I put it in the pocket of my robe.

"You rest now," he said. "I'll drop by tomorrow."

"Don't come on my account." I said. "I'll be gone, God willing. But um, hey, Martingale? If you're serious about that favor, there may be one thing you can do for me."

"Name it," he said.

And so I did.

# FORTY-ONE
## HOME FROM THE HILLS

I CHECKED out of the hospital at noon the next day. I felt like I'd been eaten by a bear and shat over the side of a cliff. As my father used to say.

There were no cameras waiting when I walked out, nor any reporters. The deal I'd made with Martingale gave the FBI total credit for finding the bodies in the mine. At his last TV press conference, Martingale said that Van Amstel's death would be listed as a probable suicide. Overcome by guilt, he apparently threw himself down the shaft to join his victims.

The explanation seemed so rational I almost believed it myself. I'd been so numb and exhausted in the struggle that my memories of it were blurry, surreal shapes recalled from a fever dream. Perhaps they'd fade even more with time, but I doubted I'd ever be free of them. Why is it the memories that cling most fiercely are the ones you truly want to forget?

Red knew the truth of course, and she'd told Corey, but as far as the public was concerned I'd suffered a minor injury while helping the Bureau recover the bodies. Boone had been arrested in Pontiac and most of the Thirds were in jail. It was over and I was a nobody again, which was exactly as I wanted it.

I took it easy on the drive south, pacing myself. I took US 43 to avoid Grand Portal, but I swung easterly on a back road to pass through Anahwey. I gassed up there, then headed south again. Until I saw a small curio stand by the side of the road with a sign that said Indian Artifacts. I pulled in.

The shop was as dim as before, aromatic with the scent of woodsmoke and cedar chips. Bitch From Hell was curled in a foetal tuck beside the glowing cast iron stove. She deigned to glare at me, but didn't bother to raise her head. Dolph Fereau was at the far end of the room, chipping away at a tree stump. He rose as I entered, laid his chisel aside, and came to meet me.

"How good to see you," he said, but his smile faded as I drew near and he saw my face. "You look terrible. You've had trouble. Come in, sit down. We'll have coffee."

"Thank you, no. I can't stay, I've been gone from home too long. But I did want to see you. To say goodbye."

"I'm glad you came, here, let me show you something." He led me to the rear of the shop. The floor was littered with cedar shavings and the aroma in the air was delicious. "What do you think?" Dolph said, gesturing at the stump.

I peered at it more closely but it still looked like . . . a stump. "I'm not sure. What are you making?"

"Making?" he said, surprised. "I'm not making anything. I found this a mile from here, part of an old split rail fence. Maybe the light was just right or maybe his spirit spoke to me, but for just a moment, I caught sight of him. A standing bear, trapped in the wood. I'm letting him out now, a chip at a time. A good project for the snowy months. I'll drop you a note when it's ready."

"I'd love to see it."

"Not to see it, to accept it. My gift, to the granddaughter of an old friend."

"No." I shook my head. "I'm sorry. But I couldn't accept anything as . . . Frank's granddaughter."

"Then accept it as Madeline's daughter," he said, smiling. "She was my friend too. If she had stayed here I would have given her a wedding gift, and christening gifts for you, and later for your son. Let this make up for some of the things I would have done for your mother, and for her child."

"All right," I said, smiling for the first time in days. "As Madeline's daughter, I will gratefully accept. Thank you."

"Don't thank me yet. Maybe he'll stay hidden from me.

Maybe I won't be able to find him in the wood. And you? Did you find what you were looking for?"

"No," I said, swallowing. "All I found was . . . a lot of trouble. For myself, and others. You told me once that truth was overvalued. I think you were right."

"That's funny," he said wryly. "I've been thinking about the talk we had, and wondering if maybe I told you wrong. For me, not knowing a thing is no problem. The world is full of mysteries. TV, phones, I don't know what they do, but it don't bother me. But the truth you asked me about is maybe more important than that. Maybe you shouldn't let it go. I don't think Frank would have. And you are his granddaughter."

"From what I've heard, that's nothing much to be proud of."

"He could be difficult," Fereau admitted. "Sometimes he had a bad temper. But I'm not always sunny. Are you?"

"No," I conceded, "I'm not."

"Then maybe that's your legacy from him. Or maybe it's something else. Maybe some weakness of his is strong in you. It's hard to know what comes down to us through blood. It's hidden sometimes, like the bear in this stump. Still, for one like you, I think you don't let go of things, even when you should. You have to know you tried. Even if that's all you know when it's done."

I thought about what he said on the long drive south, across the Big Mac then down along the sunrise shore. But other images kept intruding. Ugly flashes. The body on the platform. The feral snarl of the dog floating in the elevator shaft. Each time, I managed to push it away, to blink it off the screen of my memory. I was all right. I was. Still, I noticed that the Jeep kept increasing its speed when I wasn't watching, as if it wanted to be home. And eventually I gave it its head, and we raced south through the hills as though all the demons of hell were after us.

# Forty-two
# Almost Home

~~~~~~

Dusk was settling in as I rolled into Huron Harbor. The long shadows gave my home town a surreal look, as though every-thing had changed in the few days I was away. Emotionally, it felt more like years. I drove to the Crow's Nest first. I hadn't called ahead, afraid Charlie would try to talk me out of driving myself home. Considering how exhausted I felt, it would have been sound advice. All I could think of was getting to my office to call Bo Unger to check on Corey.

When I stepped through the front door, everything looked so normal that it took a moment to realize what was wrong. The dining room was about a third full, mostly with locals, and Red was behind the bar serving . . . .

Red was behind the bar! Her left arm was in a sling, and she looked a little haggard, but she was there. And her welcoming grin could have lit up the dark side of the moon.

"My God, Mitchell," Red said. "Are you back from the dead or do you just look like it?"

I was too surprised to answer, and as I glanced around, I realized the customers weren't just locals, they were all friends. Charlie Bauer was at our usual table in the corner, but better yet, Bo Unger, his wife and kids were seated around one of the banquet tables amid the carnage of a meal. The smaller kids started clapping a smattering of applause that ricocheted around the room and swelled into a modest ovation.

I looked for Corey, didn't see him, and then my eyes were swimming and my throat seized up. And it was all I could do to totter toward the bar. Red came around to meet me, gave me a one-armed embrace, and eased me down on a stool.

"What . . . are you doing here?" I managed at last.

"Taking care of business, what's it look like?" Red said. "The hospital notified Charlie that you'd checked out, so . . . we figured you'd be back as soon as you finished saving the world for democracy or whatever the hell you've been doing."

"But should you be working so soon?"

"Damned straight I should. Another day in that hospital and I'd have been bunking in the psycho ward. In fact, I wish I'd come back sooner, now. You can't believe the tips a one-armed waitress earns, especially if I wince at the right moment. I may just make this little fashion accessory permanent," she said, tapping her sling. "But what about you? You look like hell, like an inflatable date who's lost half her air."

"Thanks so much, it's just what I needed to hear."

"Ugly truths are what girlfriends do best. Compliments we leave to the lesser genders. Seriously, are you all right?"

"I'm better than I look. I got banged up a little and had a brush with frostbite. My face and limbs are swollen but they promised me the worst of it'll be gone by the end of the week. Is Corey here?"

"He's out running around on the docks with his new best buddy Tommy. He was so impatient I was afraid he'd fidget off ten pounds while he was waiting for you and undo all Lila Unger's good work. You want me to call him?"

"No, let him play," I said. "I need a minute to collect myself."

"Is this girl talk?" Charlie Bauer asked, joining us. "Or can an old dinosaur join in?"

"I don't know," I said, meeting his eyes. "Are we still speaking?"

"I thought we were," he said, "until you fed me that line about working late and then dropped out of sight."

"Excuse me," Red said, backing away. "I've got customers to take care of. I'll leave you to it."

"If I'd told you where I was going," I said carefully, "you would have tried to keep me from doing it."

"And I would have been right," Charlie said. He looked away from me, chewing his lower lip. "I talked to Martingale and he said they'd likely never have turned up Thorp or the other bodies without you. Hell, they weren't even lookin' for 'em. He also said you came pretty damned close to buying the farm."

"I went up there looking for the wrong thing for the wrong reasons," I admitted. "I was trying to settle things. It didn't work out very well."

"Some of it did. I got a buzz from the Staties an hour or so ago. They picked up Pettiford early this morning in the basement of his mother's house in Madison. He's apparently been there all along. He's already made a deal to roll on his two buddies, but he claims the militia had nothing to do with the marijuana. Looks like they're going to walk."

"God," I said. "I was hoping life could get back to normal around here."

"I'm not sure I want it to," Charlie said, taking a deep breath. "Not if it means going back to the way things were between us before you . . . stayed with me. Unless that's the way you want it."

Our eyes met, and held. And I felt lightheaded, as though all the oxygen was going out of the room. I looked down at my hands. A mistake. They were swollen and raw. Like the rest of me. "Charlie," I said, swallowing. "I don't think we can have this conversation now. I'm just not up to it."

"I'm sorry," he said. "You're right, I'm out of line. I shouldn't have brought it up."

"No, I'm glad you did. I do want to talk about . . . things between us. I'd just rather wait until I look a little better and have my head screwed on straight. I've made so many mistakes the past week that I'm afraid I'm on a roll. I don't want to make any more with you."

"Whenever you say," he said, doubtfully. "I didn't mean to put you on the spot—"

"Hey, little stud-muffin," Red called. "Guess who finally showed up?"

I turned. Corey and Tommy Unger had stormed in from the

dock, laughing, brushing a light dusting of snow from their jackets. "Hey!" Corey yelled when he spotted me. He sprinted across the room toward me, grinning. A grin that faded, then disappeared as he got closer. He stopped a few feet away, ashen as a ghost, swallowing, fighting back tears. And rage.

"In my office," I said, offering him my hand. "We can talk there."

He ignored my hand and marched beside me to the office as though we were on our way to the guillotine. I closed the door behind us and leaned against it.

"You look good," I said. "Has Mrs. Unger—?"

"I feel stupid," he gulped. "Crying in front of those people."

"You didn't exactly break down and bawl," I said dryly. "I doubt anyone noticed."

"I was just so . . . mad." He turned to face me. "You look terrible. You're hurt, aren't you?"

"I'm a little banged up," I admitted. "It's nothing serious."

"Nothing's ever serious with you. You're so *tough!*" He spat the word. "It's not such a big deal to be brave, you know. Shrews are brave. Hyenas are brave. Even rats will attack dogs if—"

"Hold it," I said, waving off his tirade. "I may be a shrew sometimes, and I might even buy the hyena part if you don't like my laugh, but let's leave the rats out of this, okay?"

"I'm not calling you those things. I'm just saying you're like them because they're brave, and sometimes they're stupid."

"I'm stupid?" I echoed, feeling a surge of anger in spite of my best intentions.

"Sometimes. I mean, if a rat's brave and gets killed, who cares? There are millions of 'em. But if you do something stupid, I end up in an orphanage or something, right?"

"Sometimes I think you'd prefer that."

"Now that *is* stupid. Of course I wouldn't. I'm just saying you make me crazy sometimes."

"Well, the feeling's mutual. Okay, so maybe we're not real good at this mother-son stuff yet. On the other hand, maybe we just need some practice. Do you think you could spare me a hug? I've had kind of a rough week."

He eyed me for a moment, then shook his head. "You really do look awful, you know. Are you sure you're okay?"

"I've been better," I admitted. "What about that hug?"

He came to me, a bit reluctantly. And gave me a tentative hug. It hurt, a lot. His skinny little arms seemed to zero in on the sorest part of my torso. But I bit my lip. And enjoyed the moment. I nuzzled his hair, but then the telephone rang and he pulled away.

I sighed and picked up the receiver. "Crow's Nest."

"Michelle Mitchell, please." The voice was unfamiliar.

"Speaking."

"Ms. Mitchell, my name is George Linebaugh. You don't know me. I'm with INS, the Immigration and Naturalization Service? Brian Martingale asked me to run a check on a . . . Francis Dee Hubert."

"Du-bear," I said, correcting his pronunciation.

"d'Hubert," he said, a little closer. "Sorry, I have trouble with French names. Anyway, it took some major digging, and I mean major, but we did find something. Francis d'Hubert left the lower forty-eight nearly thirty years ago. We have no record of his re-entry."

"I don't understand," I said slowly. "Left for where?"

"Canada," he said. "Ontario. According to our records, he's never been back."

"I see. You mean you have no record of his coming back. But you don't know whether he's . . . living or not?"

"Oh, he's living all right, or at least he was last month. Martingale told me it was important so I traded a few favors. Mr. d'Hubert receives a small stipend from the Canadian government. Unfortunately, I couldn't come up with a home address, but the check goes to a post office box in Priscilla, Ontario. It's a small town near the Cree Tribal Reserve. Would you like his mailing address? Miss Mitchell? Are you there?"

"Yes," I said. "Give me the address, please." I jotted it down. I was in a daze, scarcely comprehending what I wrote. "Thank you, Mr . . . ?"

"Linebaugh. Glad to help. And you tell Martingale he owes me big for this one. Dinner. Maybe two dinners. With champagne."

"I'll tell him," I said. "Thanks." I replaced the receiver carefully, as though it might shatter. Or I would.

"What is it?" Corey asked. "What's wrong?"

"It's your . . . great-grandfather," I said slowly. "Frank. He's um, he's alive. My God, so many good people in this world have died in the past thirty years, but not him. He's been living in Canada."

"You don't seem very happy about it."

"I . . . don't know what I feel right now. I was so certain he was dead I guess I'd gotten used to the idea."

"But he's not. So when are you going to see him? Can I come along?"

"I don't know. I need to think about it awhile. Maybe a long while."

"Think about what?" Corey pressed. "Why wouldn't you want to see him?"

"Because of what happened to my mother. Are you sure you want to meet this man? Because I'm not sure I want to. Or what will happen if I do."

"I don't know about that," Corey admitted. "From what we've heard about him, maybe he's not somebody I'll want to hang with. But you'd better do the math before you decide not to go, Mom."

"What math?"

"Crunch the numbers. The guy's gotta be in his mid-seventies at least. So if you decide not to see him now, you'd better figure that decision's gonna be . . . well, kinda final. You know?"

I stared at him a moment, then nodded slowly. "Yes. I see what you mean."

# FORTY-THREE
# PRISCILLA

ᘁᑲᑋᕈᑊ

THERE WAS no regularly scheduled flight to Priscilla, Ontario. The nearest town with a landing field was Nipigon, and I had to charter a flight to get there. The light plane was a six-seat Beechcraft, but Corey and I were the only passengers. He went a bit chartreuse shortly after we took off, and was very quiet the whole flight. I didn't feel much like talking either, so we traveled in thoughtful silence, staring out our respective windows.

The rolling forest stretched out beneath us to the horizon without a trace of humanity on it, not a road or a powerline, no artificial structures at all. I've never seen country so empty, or so achingly beautiful.

We rented a battered station wagon at the field at Nipigon, and made arrangements to meet the pilot for our flight back the next morning. Then we drove south.

Priscilla, Ontario, pop. 100 more or less, the red maple-leaf sign said. A Christmas card of a town. A half dozen white clapboard houses lightly dusted with snow, a general store, and a small hospital.

The post office was in a private home, a white clapboard saltbox complete with a picket fence. A sign in the yard was the only indication of its function. Inside, the living room was divided by a painted plywood counter. Rows of brass post office boxes with glass windows lined one wall, floor to ceiling.

A cheerful, heavyset woman with orange-tinted hair and weathered, ruddy cheeks was sorting mail at the counter. She was wearing a flowered bathrobe, humming along with a song on the radio. Her living quarters were in plain view beyond the counter, a comfortable room with a hand-carved rocker, rustic furniture, rag rugs that looked hand made on a hardwood floor.

"Newcomers, eh?" the lady said brightly. "I'm Marge McKenzie. Welcome to Priscilla. Can I help you?"

"I hope so," I said. "My grandfather has a post office box here. I'm hoping to locate him. His name's d'Hubert. Frank d'Hubert."

Her smile waned just a trace. "d'Hubert," she nodded. "Aye, he's registered here. Not much correspondence, though. I don't recall any personal letters at all. You've not been in touch with him then?"

"No, we've never met him, actually. I only recently learned he was in the area."

"I see," she said. "Well, he's um, he's here in Priscilla all right, miss. At hospital. That's where his mail is forwarded."

"The hospital?" I echoed.

"Aye, it's the brick building just past the general store. You can't miss it." She resumed sorting the mail, avoiding my eyes, I thought. I noticed she wasn't singing when we left.

The hospital was a single story white brick and cinder block building, the only modern structure in the town. St. Denis Samaritan. The girl at the front counter was a willowy Native American in a pink smock that contrasted wonderfully with her dark skin and eyes. Even Corey noticed, and I'd never seen him give a girl more than a passing glance.

"Frank d'Hubert?" she nodded. "Yes, he's a resident here. And you are?"

"Michelle Mitchell, and this is my son Corey. Mr. d'Hubert is my grandfather."

"I see," the girl said. "Well, you can see him now, if you like. He's in the day room, but . . . I should warn you, he may not say much, miss. He never says much."

"Is he sick?" Corey asked. "Why is he here?"

"He's a long-term patient. He's incapacitated, I'm afraid. He had a stroke a few years ago that paralyzed his left side. His condition has stabilized but he probably won't be leaving here. Unless you choose to take him home. St. Denis is the only facility within three hundred miles. We're a hospice as well as a hospital."

"I see," I said slowly. "I didn't know."

"Perhaps you'd better go in alone, first," she suggested. "I don't know how he'll react to strangers. He can be difficult sometimes, even with us. Sometimes he, um, he strikes out at people."

"Then he hasn't changed much," I said with a taut smile. "Where is he?"

"The day room's at the end of that hall. Don't worry about Corey, here. We'll get along fine."

I glanced at my son, and he nodded. But for once he didn't find a magazine and bury his nose in it. Instead, he asked the girl something about her computer. He even smiled. Will wonders never cease?

I left them to it and walked slowly down the tiled hall. I passed a half dozen hospital rooms. Some occupants glanced up at me curiously. Most didn't.

There were three patients in the day room, and one other visitor, a fifty-ish woman in a flowered housedress chatting quietly in the corner to a much older woman in a hospital gown . . . and then I saw Frank. And the rest of the room seemed to fade away.

He was sitting in a wheelchair, bathed in a pool of sunlight that streamed through a pair of french doors. The doors were closed, of course. Snow devils whirled and glistened on the veranda beyond, but I don't think he saw them. His eyes were vacant. Nobody home.

His hair was pure white, and very thick. The rest of him seemed . . . small. From the photographs, I'd pictured him as a much larger man. Perhaps he had been, once. He was shrunken now, his shoulders slumped, his thin wrists on his lap. The left side of his face sagged like a waxen mask melted in a fire.

I circled his chair and faced him. He was hollow-cheeked, but had a strong Roman nose. Or Ojibwa, perhaps. His eyes were darker than mine, and glittered fiercely; a hawk eyeing prey from a great height.

"Hello, Frank," I said quietly. He didn't look up. The woman in the flowered dress smiled and started to rise, but something in my look must have warned her off. She sat down again and turned away from us.

I eased down on the corner of a white vinyl sofa near Frank's chair.

"You look pretty good, all things considered," I said. There was a faint scent about him, of rubbing alcohol and talcum powder. A sterile scent, without humanity. He cocked his head to regard me a moment. Then looked away.

"That's not very polite, Frank. I've come all this way, after all this time. But you've already gone, haven't you?" I released a long, ragged breath. "God, the things I wanted to say to you. What a bastard I think you are, and . . . but what's the difference now? I can't hate you, not even for my mother's sake. I wouldn't wish this on anyone. Not even you."

He looked at me again, with slightly more interest, but his eyes were clouded, with no glint of spirit in them.

"Are you in there?" I asked. "Do you understand me at all?"

He didn't reply. And I realized he had no idea who I was. Or even who he was. Or why either of us were here. I rose slowly, looking down at him. "Goodbye, Frank," I said quietly, patting his shoulder. "I'm sorry I bothered you."

He grabbed my wrist! His right hand clamped onto me like a steel trap and held. I tried to pull free. His chair swiveled to face me, but his grip didn't budge.

"Let go of me," I said quietly. He didn't. He wasn't looking at me. He was still staring off into some unimaginable distance. And then he slowly turned his head and raised his eyes to mine. And they were ablaze. With passion or rage, I couldn't tell.

"Madeline?" His voice grated like a rusty hinge.

I didn't know what to say. I couldn't move.

"Madeline?" he repeated, more forcefully this time. He swallowed, and his eyes were swimming. "Madeline, I'm sorry. Please. I'm sorry."

I knelt beside his chair, and reached out for this man who had cursed a part of my life. And created it. I cupped his cheek with my free hand. "I know," I said softly. "I know. It's all right."

We huddled together like that for a moment, then his grip eased, and he released me. I rose again, and his eyes stayed fixed on mine, watching me. "Wait here a moment," I said. "There's someone who wants to meet you."